THE ALTERED CASE

THE ALTERED CASE

A Hennessey and Yellich Mystery

Peter Turnbull

This first world edition published 2012
in Great Britain and in the USA by
SEVERN HOUSE PUBLISHERS LTD of
9–15 High Street, Sutton, Surrey, England, SM1 1DF.
Trade paperback edition first published
in Great Britain and the USA 2012 by
SEVERN HOUSE PUBLISHERS LTD.

British Library Cataloguing in Publication Data

Turnbull, Peter, 1950–
  The altered case.
  1. Hennessey, George (Fictitious character) – Fiction.
  2. Yellich, Somerled (Fictitious character) – Fiction.
  3. Police – England –Yorkshire – Fiction. 4. Detective and
  mystery stories.
  I. Title
  823.9'2-dc23

ISBN-13: 978-0-7278-8154-0 (cased)
ISBN-13: 978-1-84751-419-6 (trade paper)

All Severn House titles are printed on acid-free paper.

Severn House Publishers support The Forest Stewardship Council [FSC],
the leading international forest certification organisation. All our titles that
are printed on Greenpeace-approved FSC-certified paper carry the FSC logo.

MIX
Paper from
responsible sources
FSC
www.fsc.org   FSC® C018575

Typeset by Palimpsest Book Production Ltd.,
Falkirk, Stirlingshire, Scotland.
Printed and bound in Great Britain by
MPG Books Ltd., Bodmin, Cornwall.

ONE

Friday, 15th September, 17.30 hours – Sunday, 17th September, 15.37 hours.

in which two men in their middle years return, with the police, to a scene of their youth.

Cyrus Henry Middleton had first realized that he had entered adulthood when, one afternoon during an early spring day, he and three friends had sat at a wooden dining table, which stood by the rear window of a small terraced house, and they had partaken of tea and Dundee cake. Their conduct and their table manners had been impeccable, and their conversation had been polite, restrained and sensible. At the conclusion of the afternoon tea Cyrus Middleton had quietly made the observation that that was the first time in his life he had conducted himself with such faultless propriety without at least one of his parents' generation being present, and then, following his observation, a very profound silence had fallen on the group as each of the three others realized that they too could say the same thing. The youngest member of the small group was but twenty years of age and the eldest was a venerable twenty-two years old. They had, they had realized, just entered adulthood.

It was in much the same way that Cyrus Middleton realized he had entered his middle years of adulthood when he and a childhood friend agreed to meet each other in central York for the first time in many years. In keeping with the arrangement, he and his friend, Tony Allerton, had rendezvoused early one evening at the Starre Inne on Stonegate (which, dating from the mid-seventeenth century, laid claim to be the city of York's oldest licensed premises). On that first meeting their conversation had been about their children's progress at school and university, their daughters' apparent absence of taste and also absence of downright common sense when it had come to choosing their boyfriends. 'He spends all day playing computer games now that he has lost his job and every evening he's out with his mates drinking in the pub, so what on earth she sees in him confounds me,' and then the conversation would turn to the purchase of their first Volvos and the merits of Volvos over Audis, and then of their pension plans. It was the talk of two men in their middle years. They had then settled into a routine of meeting once a month, on a Friday, at the Starre Inne.

At the conclusion of one such rendezvous, Middleton had turned to his friend and had said, 'Well, Midland bound for Cricklewood?' and Tony Allerton had smiled and replied, 'Hartly Dells and Sale and Co.,' to which Middleton had responded, 'One more, then I'll go.' He had then levered himself with no little difficulty from the corner seat he and Allerton had occupied. The pub was beginning to swell with loud youth who were most eager to kick-start their weekend and he weaved his way to the bar to order two final pints of real ale. He paid for the beers and negotiated his way through the heavy press of youngsters, carrying the glasses back to the small round table at which Allerton sat, glancing at the framed prints of Old York. He placed the glasses gently down on the polished surface of the table.

'That day,' he said, when once again he was settled in the tight corner seat, and found he had to raise his voice somewhat so that it could still carry to Tony Allerton, 'that long, long day.'

'Yes, when we found a ruin covered with ivy, a green stump of a thing.'

'Has anyone rescued it, do you know? Seems unlikely.'

Tony Allerton raised his glass in a gesture of thanks.

'Yes, I doubt it too; it really was too far gone, wasn't it? Just low walls remaining.'

Middleton raised his glass in response and then turned and glanced in annoyance at a young man who was standing close to where he and Tony Allerton were sitting and who was talking loudly on his mobile phone, apparently to a friend, and telling said friend about the problems he was having with the conveyancing of the house he was evidently hoping to buy.

'Doubt it,' Middleton replied, glancing with annoyance at the loud-mouthed youth and his mobile phone. 'Even then, you could only just make out the lines of a building, all over-grown and covered in moss and ivy. I remember that there was an old stone gatepost there as well, in the middle of the wood. There must have been a road there, or a driveway or something, though it was all overgrown back then and it will be more so now. But . . .'

'But?' Allerton sipped his beer.

'Well . . . you know, Tony, of late I have found myself thinking about it more and more frequently.'

'Thinking of that day? There was nothing that was particu-larly special about it.'

'Wasn't there?' Middleton held eye contact with Allerton. 'I mean, I suppose you are right.'

Allerton put his glass of beer down on the table, just as the youth with the mobile phone terminated his call, and he said in a softer voice, 'You know, I have thought about it too, probably not as often as you seem to have been thinking about it . . . but yes . . . supposing I was right?'

'I now think it was a grave after all, probably still is.'

'So do I.' Allerton spoke softly, looking at his beer rather than at Cyrus Middleton. 'We laughed at it and then ran away.'

'It was a grave at the edge of the field, just beyond the wood.'

'Yes.' Allerton's eye was caught by a slender blonde-haired girl who weaved gracefully and confidently through the patrons, and who held a drink in one hand whilst pressing a mobile phone to her ear with the other. She left a distinct yet delicate scent of perfume in her wake as she passed by their table. 'Yes,' he said again, 'a grave . . . right size . . . just the right sort of place for one.'

'Yes, you couldn't dig a grave within the wood; you couldn't get past the root system.'

'Plate,' Allerton replied softly, 'it's called the root plate.'

Cyrus Middleton glanced at Allerton and did so with an anger, which he found difficult to control. Middleton had once described concrete as 'setting' during a very sensitive conver-sation about some home improvement work his recently deceased father had undertaken, to which Tony Allerton had indelicately responded, 'Concrete doesn't "set", concrete "cures". That's the correct term.' It was similarly not the right time or place to correct someone on a wholly unimportant turn of phrase, but Middleton chose restraint and diplomacy and remained silent as Allerton continued. 'You couldn't get past the root plate, but a spade is all you would need to dig a hole in a field, especially an arable field, regularly ploughed and irrigated . . . and it was just this time of the year. The harvest had been gathered, only the stubble remained.'

'Yes . . . yes . . . I remember. Stubble was being burned in the neighbouring fields because smoke wafted over towards us and for a brief period we couldn't see or breathe.' Middleton tapped his fingers on the tabletop. 'I remember that because you commented that that had once caused a major car crash in which a relative of yours had been injured.'

'My Uncle James.' Allerton nodded. 'He sustained head injuries. He recovered, others were not so lucky. Three fatalities in that pile-up due to smoke from burning stubble in a field at the side of the road wafting over the road causing sudden zero visibility. The wind had veered, apparently; but, yes, I remember telling you that as we coughed and floundered about in the dense smoke, then it cleared and that encouraged us to move away from the field.'

'That's right, that's why we left the scene, we didn't want to get another lungful of smoke.' Middleton sipped his beer. 'But in all honesty you'd think the farmer or one of the farmhands would have noticed an area of disturbed soil. I mean to say, if we noticed it, two fifteen-year-old town boys, then surely the blokes who worked those fields would have noticed it . . . certainly so.'

'You'd think so, but perhaps they had no reason to return to that field.' Allerton shrugged. 'I mean, when all was safely gathered in, the stubble could then have been set on fire at the far side of the field and left to burn across the ground to where the disturbed soil was. There would be no need to pay any more attention to it until it was time to plough before sowing the winter wheat and by which time the area of dug up soil wouldn't be so obvious . . . not so obvious at all.'

'Yes,' Middleton murmured, 'that would explain it; it would explain it quite neatly.' He paused and held eye contact with Allerton. 'So what do we do, Tony? Something or nothing?'

Allerton briefly looked to his left and then to his right, and then he looked back at Cyrus Middleton. 'There's only one thing we can do, one solitary and sole thing, and I think we both know that.'

'How old were we?' Middleton asked.

'Fifteen . . . you just said so.'

'So I did. Yes, it was the last few days of the summer holiday in the year we went to Scotland with the school.' Middleton nodded with a smile.

'Aviemore . . . tenting . . . yes, it was that summer, it was a very good holiday. We went with the advance party, two members of staff and the older boys, to put the tents up and prepare the field kitchens . . .'

'And dig the latrines,' Middleton added, 'and we had to fill them in at the end, sloshed paraffin all over the stuff and then set it on fire . . . talking about fire and holes in fields . . . then filled them up again.'

'Yes, that was the year all right. We returned; we had two or three weeks before the start of the final academic year at Hoytown.'

'So.' Middleton refocussed the conversation. 'So, we go now? To the police, I mean?'

'No . . . no.' Allerton spoke softly but firmly. 'If we go there now we'll be with them all night. How about tomorrow? Are you free tomorrow in the forenoon?'

'I can be.' Middleton's eye was caught by two svelte girls in ankle length skirts who swayed elegantly by on their way to the bar. 'Susan and I go out shopping together on Saturday mornings, rain or shine . . . it's become our routine, and she hates her routine, any routine, being derailed or interrupted in the slightest, but I reckon I could get a pass out . . . especially for this reason.'

'I'm pretty much in the same boat with Adele; her routines lead to an efficient house, so I can't complain, but I can also get out of it, especially for this, as you say, especially for this,' Allerton replied. 'So we'll do that, agreed?'

'Agreed.' Middleton pursed his lips and nodded slightly. 'Agreed.'

That particular Saturday, so Cyrus Middleton would later recall, dawned bright and sunny over the ancient city and its flat, green environs. A little rain had fallen at eight a.m. and it had continued to rain steadily for about an hour and a half, so that when Middleton and Allerton met shortly after ten a.m. in the narrow alley leading from Stonegate to the Starre Inne, as arranged, the sun was shining down from a clear blue sky with sufficient strength to cause the moisture on the pavement following the rainfall to evaporate in a light, misty haze.

'So.' Allerton raised his eyebrows. 'Can we . . . shall we have a coffee first? I freely confess I very much feel the need of caffeine. I need something else in me other than the slice of toast I had for breakfast in order to go through with this.'

'Likewise,' Middleton replied softly, 'even though it will probably turn out that a farm worker had buried his beloved Labrador. It will psyche us up; help us muster the courage to go through with this.'

'It was too large an area for a dog,' Allerton muttered. 'Come on. Coffee.'

The two men wound their way in and out of the other foot passengers who were, as predicted, of plentiful number, until they reached the Paragon Hotel on Lendal, close to the post office and opposite the imposing Judge's Residence Hotel where, upon Allerton's recommendation, they both ordered a large latte. They sat in silence as they betook of the beverage, both admiring the slender form of the waitress who had, they both thought, the mannerisms of a university undergraduate who was working to help her pay her way to a good degree, and the doors that would then open for her.

'Damn lucky, we were,' Middleton commented drily. 'We had grants.'

'I know –' Allerton glanced out of the window assessing the weather – 'tuition fees paid and a grant to live on, money intended to pay rent and to buy food which all seemed to be spent on beer, strangely enough.'

The two men lapsed into a further silence which lasted until both had finished their coffee, upon which Allerton said, 'All right. Let's do it.'

Allerton and Middleton then stood and put on their identical green waterproof coats with tartan patterned lining and walked out of the coffee lounge of the hotel, and, dear reader, after, it may and must be said, leaving a more than generous tip for the young and most fey waitress, walked in single file out of the hotel entrance and on to Lendal. They turned and faced each other.

'Well.' Tony Allerton smiled and, affecting a comic rustic accent, said, 'Well, boy, by Lendal Bridge be quicker it be but by Ouse Bridge be prettier . . .'

'The quicker.' Middleton smiled. 'Let's just get it done; let's just get it over with.'

Cyrus Middleton and Tony Allerton walked side by side on to Museum Street and crossed Lendal Bridge with the wide, smooth, cold-looking water of the River Ouse sliding silently beneath it. Both being native to the city of York, and both having lived in the ancient city all their lives, they knew, as all locals knew, that by far the speediest way to cross the city is to walk the walls, which after years of neglect and dereliction, had been lovingly reconstituted by the City Fathers in Victorian times and so they thusly, without speaking, stepped on to said walls. They then followed the walls from Station Road to Micklegate Bar.

Middleton and Allerton stepped gingerly down the stone steps as they left the walls at Micklegate Bar, being acutely aware that the morning's rain had left the walkway of the walls in a greasy condition in the areas where the stone lay in the shade. Once upon the pavement they turned right and obediently waited at the crossroads until the 'green man' traffic light glowed, thus giving priority to foot passengers. As they crossed the road Cyrus Middleton found himself suddenly pondering the folly of his youth, particularly the time when he and a number of his friends had attempted the 'Micklegate crawl', the challenge being to have a small glass of beer, just one half pint, in each pub on the street and still remain standing. No one had, or still has, so far as he knew, ever succeeded in the venture and it was, he thought, so very, very foolish of them to even have attempted it. But he, like those who attempt it today, was just eighteen years old and so very, very immature and so very, very foolish. Without any further words being exchanged, Middleton and Allerton, upon crossing Nunnery Lane, walked solemnly up the steps and through the narrow stone entrance of Micklegate Bar Police Station.

Reginald Webster was the duty CID officer on that Saturday morning. When the phone on his desk rang he let it warble three times before he slowly picked up the handset in a controlled and very leisurely manner. 'CID,' he answered, 'DC Webster speaking.'

'There are two gentlemen here at the enquiry desk, sir.' The voice of the desk constable on the other end of the phone was equally calm and assured, and yet also clearly very deferential. 'They say that they wish to report a possible murder.'

Webster smiled and glanced up from his August statistical returns. 'You know, I thought it was too quiet to last.'

'Yes, sir,' the constable replied with a soft chuckle.

'All right . . . all right.' Webster reached for his notebook. 'I'll be there directly.' He stood, uncomplaining, because in all honesty he would rather receive a report of a possible murder than spend his time placing figures in columns, and then submit the forms on time for onward conveyance to the Home Office where, he doubted, not much notice would be taken of them anyway.

'Very good, sir,' the desk officer replied and then added, 'the two gentlemen say that there is no hurry. If there was a murder it happened a long time ago.'

'Less than seventy though?' Webster clarified.

'Oh, yes, sir,' the desk officer answered with evident good humour, 'going by the appearance of these two gentlemen, well within seventy years.'

'For a brief moment I knew hope,' Webster continued, smiling, 'but yes . . . right-oh . . . I'll be down there directly.' He replaced the handset of the phone.

'Business?' Thomson Ventnor glanced up curiously from his own August returns.

'It does seem so.' Webster reached out and picked up a

ballpoint pen which lay at the far corner of his desk and put on his loud chequered sports jacket with a flourish. He grinned at Ventnor. 'Murder no less. It happened a few years ago . . . if it happened at all, but murder is murder. Code Four-One takes priority over pretty much all else.' He glanced out of the office window at the view of the skyline, being in that part of York a harsh blend of old and new buildings. 'It is brightening up nicely,' he commented. 'So . . . let's see what we see.'

Some twenty-five minutes later Webster reclined in the slightly upholstered low-slung chair in the interview suite and glanced over the notes he had taken when talking to Cyrus Middleton and Tony Allerton, both of whom now similarly reclined in identical chairs. 'So this was thirty years ago, you say?'

'Yes, sir,' Middleton replied. 'We are both forty-five years old now and the summer in question that we came across the disturbed soil made us fifteen years of age at the time. We can pin down the year in question with complete . . . total . . . one hundred per cent certainty.'

'Fair enough.' Webster spoke quietly.

'We can be certain of which summer it was,' Allerton insisted, 'because we had, just a few weeks earlier, returned from a school holiday in Scotland and we had by then just a week or so left before we returned to school for the autumn term. So it was early September. Autumn term commenced in the second week of September; it still does, in fact.'

'Fair enough,' Webster repeated, 'as I said that can, and in fact it probably will, be very useful.' Webster looked at the notes he had taken. 'Very useful indeed.'

Cyrus Middleton glanced quickly around the room in which he and Tony Allerton and DC Webster sat. He had been pleasantly surprised to find that, instead of the harsh, hard, uncomfortable, unnerving interrogation room he had expected, the interview suite where non-suspects were escorted to was gently decorated with varying shades of orange, a dark, hard-wearing carpet, lighter-coloured orange chairs and walls painted with a pastel shade of the same colour. A highly polished coffee table with black metal legs and a brown surface stood on the floor between the four chairs in the room. The room had no source of natural light but was illuminated by a single light bulb within an orange-coloured shade. Middleton detected the scent of air freshener which hung delicately in the room. It was, he thought, quite sensitive and clever of the police to bring witnesses or victims of crime into a room like this, so as to put them at ease; some very distressing information often had to be coaxed from such persons.

'But we emphasize . . . again . . . we emphasize,' Allerton continued, 'that we saw nothing which in itself was untoward, we saw only the small area of disturbed soil, close to the corner of a field which had recently been harvested of its crop. It must have been a very hot summer come to think of it . . . last week in August or first in the September . . . that's quite an early harvest. It was only in hindsight that it became to seem suspicious, but we both very clearly remember it. Definitely remember it.'

'That I can fully understand,' Webster reassured Allerton. 'It is quite often just the way of it, sometimes it is only in hindsight that things become significant or events are remembered years after they have happened. You know, quite a few people have sat in this room because they have recovered a memory of some violent incident which their consciousness has kept buried. They often report that for a while, a short while – as in a few days – they wonder if they are remembering a dream then realize and come to accept that it is a memory of something that did actually happen, and then they do what you two gentlemen have done. They present at the enquiry desk and give information. It happens quite a lot, quite often. It is, as I said, just the way of it.'

Middleton sighed. 'Well, I confess that makes me feel a little better. I was feeling guilty about the time lapse . . . thirty years . . . but I feel better in myself now.'

'Me too.' Allerton smiled gently. 'Thank you for saying that, sir.'

'Pleasure,' Webster offered. 'As I said, at least you came forward. It might yet be a dead dog down there but at least you came forward.'

'I think we both did that,' Cyrus Middleton continued, glancing to his left at Allerton who nodded in agreement. 'I think we both buried it and moved on with our lives. It's only recently that we have begun to meet up again for a beer. We were good friends at school but drifted apart and it was in February of this year as I was walking through York that I bumped into Tony here . . . after all these years . . . and we went into a pub and agreed to meet up on Friday evenings for a drink once a month.'

'We each get a pass out,' Tony Allerton joked. 'We found out that we both had a lot in common in respect of the way our lives have evolved. For one thing, we both married strong-willed women and so the phrase "Getting a pass out" has a ring of truth to it. We're allowed out one Friday evening a month, but that is all we need really.'

'If we met more often we'd run out of conversation,' Middleton explained.

'I see.' Webster was content to let the conversation wander, seeing it as an opportunity to further take the measure of Cyrus Middleton and Tony Allerton. He thought them probably genuine, but still only probably.

'We both have daughters who have made a poor choice of boyfriend, in our opinion, and we both have sons who are doing well in life.'

'Yes,' Middleton said, 'my daughter turned down a place at Cambridge University to go and live in a new town in Scotland with a man who once worked in a shoe shop and is now unemployed.' He sighed and glanced up at the ceiling. 'I mean, what can you do? What can you say? She's an adult, and so all you can do is worry.'

'And my daughter gave up her place reading medicine at Manchester University to keep house for a male nurse, nice boy in himself, but with limited prospects compared to my daughter's prospects had she continued her studies.'

'We both entered the world of finance,' Middleton explained. 'I am in insurance . . . a claims investigator, and Tony is an accountant.'

'Very good.' Webster inclined his head; both were professional men with much to lose should they prove to be trifling with the police. Their credibility increased in his perception of them.

'Quite modest really,' Allerton explained. 'I am only a certified accountant, not a chartered accountant . . . that would be
something to be impressed with. It's akin to a small town
solicitor and a High Court judge. They can both be described
as lawyers but the difference between them is huge.'

'I take your point.' Webster laid his notepad on the table.
'But an accountant, with certified or chartered status is still
deserving of respect.'

'Our lives seem to have mirrored each other in many ways,'
Allerton continued, 'but it was only once we started to meet
for a beer that we talked about childhood days . . . what
happened to mutual friends . . . not all of whom are still with
us; misadventure, natural causes . . . that's always worrying.
We can cope with our old classmate Charlie Hopper getting
killed in a car crash but hearing that Alex Ball, who was also
in our form at Hoytown, had succumbed to cancer . . . well
that made us stop talking for a few seconds.'

'But it's only latterly that we got to talk about *that* day.'
Middleton brought the conversation back on track. 'It was
myself who mentioned it initially but we both wanted to talk
about it . . . and so we did . . . and then we both realized we
had to report it, just in case it was what it appeared to be . . .
even if we are thirty years late . . . and so here we are.'

'And here you are,' Webster echoed, 'here you are, but thirty
years later is still not too late and that is the main thing.' He
tapped his notepad with his ballpoint. 'Can I ask you to wait
here, please, just for a minute or two. I'll have to go and talk
to my senior officer about this.'

'They are not a pair of game-playing fantasists, I hope?'
Hennessey replied after listening to what he thought was
Webster's succinct delivery. It had been, he thought, very clear,
his facts were given in logical order and very precisely.

'I don't think so, sir.' Webster sat in the chair in front of
Hennessey's desk. 'I wondered if that might be the case, but
they seem genuine. They are both professional men in their
mid forties, both family men, so they claim, and in fact do
have just that stamp about them, by their speech, their mannerisms and their dress. They really do seem to have too much

to lose by playing silly games.' Webster paused. 'They're the genuine article. I'm sure of it.'

'Very well, I think you had better ask them to take you there. Take two constables.' George Hennessey ran his liver-spotted fingers through his silver hair. 'Yes . . . two should be sufficient.'

'Yes, sir.' Webster stood. 'Two constables.'

'And separately,' Hennessey added as an afterthought as Webster was leaving his office.

'Sir?' Webster turned back to face Hennessey. 'Separately?'

'Yes,' Hennessey confirmed. 'I mean separate the two gentlemen once you are near the location, and have each of them take you there independently, that is to say take you there in the absence of the other. It will strengthen the credibility of their story if they identify the same location.'

'Yes, sir, understood.' Webster turned and walked out of Hennessey's office.

Independently, and with what Webster thought to be notable precision, and clarity and confidence, both Cyrus Middleton and Tony Allerton each placed their fingertip on the same part of the Ordnance Survey Map and indicated a location which was close to the village of Catton Hill on the A19 York to Selby Road, some two miles south of the city. It was, thought Webster, just the sort of distance that two fifteen-year-old boys would wander from their homes in Fulford, that being the catchment area of Hoytown Comprehensive School, during their last summer of innocence. It would have been a walk across flat meadows by two lads who were both buoyed up by their friendship and the recent school holiday in Scotland. Following the pinpointing of the location where the disturbed soil was observed both Middleton and Allerton were driven by Webster to the village of Catton Hill. They were followed there by two constables in a marked car.

Reginald Webster lived close to Selby and had thus often driven through Catton Hill on his way to and from Micklegate Bar Police Station, but he had never spared it a second glance nor even turned off the A19 to explore the village and its side streets. It had always been for him a settlement to drive through on his way to and from home and his place of employment. Upon reaching the village, he turned left and on to the road which was signposted towards Wheldrake and parked the car at the side of the kerb. Webster, glancing about him, saw that Catton Hill was a compact village with the buildings on either side of the road being conjoined. One or two of the buildings, unusually for the north of England, he noticed, had thatched roofs. It seemed to Webster to have changed little over the years and had not fully encompassed the twenty-first century. The telephone box, for example, was of the traditional red Gilbert Scott design. The shops were small and seemed to be independently owned, rather than belonging to a supermarket chain. There were two pubs which Webster could see from where he had parked the car, both almost directly opposite each other, and both had names which spoke of their rural location: one was called The Black Bull, and across the road from it, slightly further towards Wheldrake, was The Three Horseshoes. Webster turned to Tony Allerton who sat in the rear seat of the car. 'If you could kindly remain here, please, sir.'

'Inside the car?' Tony Allerton asked with a slight note of protest distinct in his voice. 'The car is uncomfortably warm in this weather. I mean the inside is uncomfortably warm. May I stand on the pavement?'

'Of course, sir.' Webster opened the driver's door and stepped out of the vehicle. 'But if you would remain close to the car with one of the constables?'

'Of course.' Allerton stepped out of the car and breathed deeply. Middleton also stepped out of the car and stood close to Allerton.

'So . . .' Webster addressed Middleton, 'if you could accompany me and one of the constables, or rather if you could show me and the constable where the area of recently dug soil was, as best you can recall?'

'That's a better way of putting it.' Middleton grinned. 'Because I rather think you'll be accompanying me.'

'Yes.' Webster returned the grin. 'I dare say that I have just become used to asking people to accompany me.'

'It's down here.' Middleton pointed along the road, where the pavement was dotted with villagers, adults shopping, and children running or riding bicycles. The police presence attracted a few curious glances but not any hostility that Middleton could detect. 'I'll do my best to get us there. It won't be a fool's errand but the memory does play its tricks over time, and thirty years . . . that's nearly half a lifetime.'

'We'll allow for that, sir.' Webster felt the warm glow of the sun upon his head and face. 'Summer is not giving in without a struggle.'

'Suits me,' Middleton growled. 'I care not for winter . . . those early dark nights.'

Webster beckoned one of the constables to join him and Middleton. 'You really did do the right thing in coming to us,' he said as he waited for the constable to join them. 'As I said in the police station, thirty years is not too late.' Webster's eye was then caught by a horse-drawn trap being driven along the road by a ruddy-faced young man with a cheery smile and large, farm-worker's hands, who doffed his flat cap as he and the chestnut pony passed, the hooves making a measured clop, clop, clop sound which echoed in the narrow funnel of the buildings on either side of the road. It could, thought Webster, have been an image from the nineteenth or even eighteenth century.

'We didn't do it lightly.' Middleton was also drawn to the image and sound of the horse and trap as it passed. 'I'll certainly show you the best I can, but I am now very pleased that we came forward, even if it does turn out that a farmer buried his dog, though if it was a dog it would have to be one of those horrible Japanese hunting dogs, the sort of dog that's as big as a donkey.'

'Well,' Webster replied, 'it's always as well to be safe rather than sorry, and you and Mr Allerton are clearly very well intentioned. We won't be prosecuting you for wasting police time even if your suspicions prove to be unfounded. Shall we go?'

'Yes, of course.' Middleton walked along the pavement with Webster at his side and with the younger of the two constables walking a respectable distance behind them. Middleton and Webster, followed by the constable, walked on in silence until they came to the outskirts of the village and began to enter open country. Soon after leaving the village, Middleton stopped

walking and pointed to a pathway which led off the north side
of the road at ninety degrees. 'Down there,' he said. The track,
Webster noted, was still muddy in places from that morning's
rain, but was, he saw, mainly dry. The two officers walked
behind Middleton as he and they sidestepped the occasional
pool of muddy water. Cyrus Middleton followed the path until
he entered a small wood and found a second pathway within
the trees.

'Confess I don't remember this path,' Cyrus Middleton
commented over the bird song, 'but it's the right place. Yes
. . . this is the wood we found . . . there is the stone gatepost.'
Middleton pointed to what could forgivably be taken for a tree
stump covered in ivy had it not been for its complete uniformity
of width, flat top and square shape and the two rusted hinges
protruding from one side. 'There clearly was a road or a
driveway here at some point in time. I can't remember seeing
any sign of a derelict house at all, but this is the wood all
right.' He pressed forward, and still following the path, he
eventually emerged into a field from which the crop had
recently been harvested. There he stopped as Webster and the
constable joined him. 'It's like going back in time –' Cyrus
Middleton brushed a fly from his face – 'same field and the
same time of year. Astounding.'

'Good.' Webster glanced to and fro across the field. It was,
he saw, a wholly rural setting with another field adjoining the
field in which they stood, although the steady and relentless
hum of traffic on the A19 could be distinctly heard. 'So where
was the patch of soil, if you can remember?'

'Over there.' Middleton pointed to his left. He turned and
walked in that direction and stopped when he was about ten
feet from the corner of the field. 'About here . . . yes, yes . . .
it was about here. Me and Tony came out of the wood about
here.' He pointed to a dense stand of shrubs at the edge of
the wood. 'The path we followed just now wasn't there when
we came here that day, but I remember we left the wood about
here, just where the patch of soil was and I said, "Look,
someone's been buried" and we both laughed, and then smoke
from the stubble being burned in that field –' he pointed to
his right – 'came over here and we began to choke and then

we moved hurriedly in that direction –' he pointed to his left
– 'looking for breathable air . . . but it was here . . . just about
here. I'm sorry I can't be more accurate.'

'No matter.' Webster looked at the ground though it told
him nothing. He saw only stubble protruding from the rich
brown soil. 'In fact, too precise a location would suggest to
us that you and Mr Allerton had contrived something.'

A blue tractor pulled an empty trailer along a hidden sunken
lane to their right, the driver looking with undisguised curiosity
at the three men in the field, one of whom being a police
constable. Their presence in the field would doubtless, thought
Webster, be the talk of The Black Bull and The Three
Horseshoes that evening and throughout the weekend. He
looked skywards and saw a silver jetliner crossing the blue
and, by then, cloudless sky, leaving four vapour trails behind
it. 'Well,' he said, lowering his head and turning to Middleton,
'if you and the constable would care to return to the car, I
will remain here. The second constable can escort Mr Allerton
and we'll see what part of the field he points at.'

It was Saturday, 12.35 hours.

Sunday

George Hennessey focussed his mind on the situation in hand:
the field near the village of Catton Hill, the constables in white
shirts and serge trousers, Detective Constables Ventnor and
Webster, Detective Sergeant Yellich, the ominous white inflatable tent that had been erected close to the corner of the field,
from which two SOCOs were emerging looking grim-faced
and carrying photographic equipment. The senior Scene of
Crime Officer walked slowly up to where Hennessey and
Yellich stood and said solemnly, 'All finished, sir, both colour
and black-and-white photographs have been taken.'

'Thank you.' George Hennessey slowly nodded in apprecia-
tion. He then noticed a police constable emerge from the
wooded area at the side of the field carrying a highly polished
Gladstone bag and who was closely followed by Dr Louise
D'Acre. Dr D'Acre was a slender woman, tall, and with a
well-developed muscle tone which Hennessey knew was the

result of her lifelong passion for horse riding. She wore her hair closely cropped and her only make-up was a trace of lightly shaded lipstick. Hennessey's heart leapt as he saw her and at the same moment his chest swelled with pride. Dr D'Acre turned upon emerging from the wood and walked across the stubble towards Hennessey with the constable still carrying her bag, but by then walking reverentially behind her.

'Good afternoon, Chief Inspector.' Dr D'Acre had a soft speaking voice with an accent of received pronunciation. Her manner was polite but always professional; when working, the job, and only the job, mattered.

'Good afternoon, ma'am.' George Hennessey doffed his Panama as he replied.

'Thank you for the advance notice.' Dr D'Acre glanced at the tent. 'It meant I was able to acquire an early lunch. I am always exhorting my two girls to eat and so I like it when I can set an example.'

'Of course, ma'am.'

'So,' Dr D'Acre said, 'a mass burial I am told?'

'Well.' Hennessey cleared his throat. 'Hardly mass, ma'am, that is a bit of an overstatement. I'll tell you the story of how we came to be notified of it but the upshot is that we had to wait until this morning before we could get the G.P.R. down here.'

'G.P.R.?' Dr D'Acre asked.

'Ground Penetrating Radar.'

'Ah . . .'

'Well,' he continued, 'when it arrived . . . it had to be brought down from our headquarters at Northallerton . . .'

'I see.'

'We had good information and we were able to concentrate on a small search area, and pretty well as soon as the operators turned the thing on they picked up an image of something down there, but exactly what, they couldn't say.'

'I see,' Dr D'Acre said again.

'So we brought in a mechanical digger, now returned, to get down as close as we could without damaging whatever it was that the G.P.R. had seen. We had to assume that they were human remains until we knew otherwise.'

'Of course.' Dr D'Acre brushed a persistent fly from her face and reflected how fortunate it was that the recent rain had kept the insect activity to a minimum.

'For the last foot or so,' Hennessey continued, 'we used manpower, good old mark one manpower, just one constable with a spade scraping the soil away, keeping the bottom of the pit as near horizontal as he could. He did a very good job of it.'

'Yes, I see the spoil.' Dr D'Acre glanced at the mound of soil beside the tent. 'It is very rich-looking soil.'

'It seems so,' Hennessey agreed. 'It's very wet and heavy; it was hard work for the mechanical digger and it was especially hard for the constable who dug the last few inches, and it will still all have to be thoroughly sieved and sifted, for any vital evidence it might contain.'

'I can imagine how hard it must have been,' Dr D'Acre murmured. 'I do a little gardening. It looks to be very heavy, as you say.'

'And they have to put it all back.' Hennessey laughed softly. 'I haven't told the boys yet, but they will have to put it all back with spades, the digger having been returned as I said. I couldn't justify the expense of keeping it here.'

'So . . .' Louise D'Acre said, 'what is down there?'

'At the moment, just two skeletons, ma'am,' Hennessey replied. 'They appear to be human and radar images indicated something, possibly more skeletons, beneath them, as if they were buried on top of each other.'

'Layered?'

'Yes.' Hennessey held brief eye contact with Dr D'Acre. 'That's a better way of putting it, ma'am. So once we had exposed two skeletons we stopped digging and requested the attendance of a forensic pathologist.'

'And you got me for your sins.' Louise D'Acre inclined her head. 'So hard luck you.'

'I would hardly say that, ma'am,' Hennessey replied diplomatically.

'Well, it was Hobson's choice in fact. Tom Pembroke is at an arson incident in Driffield and Clarissa Pugh is engrossed in a post-mortem. I was writing a report, so this incident fell

to me.' Louise D'Acre paused, and being out of earshot of
any other police officer, she lowered her voice and added,
'Look, George, I have to tell you that Clarissa's p.m. is looking
like a case of Sudden Death Syndrome.'

'Oh . . .' Hennessey felt as if he had sustained a blow to
his stomach.

'I am sorry, but I thought that I had better warn you, better
coming from me than for you to read about it in the *Yorkshire
Post*.'

'Yes.' Hennessey held another very brief period of eye
contact with Louise D'Acre. 'Thank you . . . I appreciate it.
It's very sensitive of you.'

'Well.' Louise D'Acre glanced around her, the vast blue
sky, the flat, rich green landscape. 'It's just one of those conditions, one of those medical conditions that will remain a
mystery until medical knowledge advances sufficiently to
explain just what it is that causes a young person in perfect
health to suddenly fall down dead in mid stride, as if the life
force within them has been suddenly extracted by some unseen
power.'

'Yes,' he sighed, 'I have puzzled that many, many times.'

'I am sure you have and I am sorry we do not have an
answer for you, and from what I know, Clarissa's case appears
typical. Just twenty years old, and just too good to be true,
non-smoker, non-drinker, active in his local scout group,
churchgoing, bank employee with a promising future, and
yesterday he was taking a stroll along the banks of the river
after attending Holy Communion and he just collapsed. He
was Condition Purple upon his arrival at York District Hospital.
And his family . . . they're still numb with shock.'

'I attended Sunday School when I was a nipper,' Hennessey
said. 'We had the most formidable teacher who told us that
"Even if we are perfect, the Almighty can still and will punish
us in some way. It is just the way of the world". I know what
he meant now.'

'Yes . . . just the way of it,' Louise D'Acre echoed. 'It's an
unidentified medical condition, so it will remain a syndrome,
until . . .'

'Until . . .' Hennessey repeated, 'until . . .'

'But anyway,' Louise D'Acre said with finality, 'we have our own job to do.'

'Yes,' he replied, 'you're right; come on, I'll show you.'

Inside the inflatable tent both Hennessey and Dr D'Acre found the air very difficult to breathe and both gave thanks that it was the slightly cooler month of September and that they were there after a morning's rainfall. They both knew that if it was earlier in the year, in the high summer, the air in the tent would be nearly unbreathable. Dr D'Acre stood on the lip of the neatly excavated hole and peered into it. She saw, perhaps four feet below the surface of the field, two skeletons, human, adult, both lying on their side as if gently facing each other. Even their arms seemed to be interlinked.

'Adult human,' Dr D'Acre observed, 'one male and one female. They are highly likely to be white European, although there is a possibility that they could be Asian. They are definitely not Afro-Caribbean. It's quite a deep grave. Unlawful disposals are usually in much shallower pits, in my experience anyway.'

'And in mine,' Hennessey growled. 'Somebody had time to dig this hole.'

'I can't tell at a glance how long they have been buried,' Dr D'Acre continued, 'but I see no flesh or internal organs, so quite some time, and no bits of non-degradable items of clothing either, such as zip fasteners or wooden toggles. So they may have been naked when buried.'

'We think they were buried thirty years ago.'

'You can be as sure as that?' Louise D'Acre glanced at Hennessey.

'Yes, we can,' Hennessey replied, and he then related the tale told by Cyrus Middleton and Tony Allerton.

'That's an interesting story.' Louise D'Acre glanced at the skeletons. 'It definitely marks the time of burial . . . thirty years ago this month. A story to dine out on and taking thirty years to come forward . . . but having said that I can understand the way memories are buried by the mind and only surface much later, often only when the person concerned is able to deal with it.' She paused. 'You know I once read an account of an incident in the United States, wherein a young girl, when aged about five years old, witnessed her father murder her friend and bury the body. She blocked the whole incident from her conscious mind, but some twenty years later the memory surfaced and she clearly felt that she owed more to her friend and her friend's family than she did to her father, and she was able to take the police to the precise location where the little girl had been buried.'

'As our two witnesses did.'

'Indeed,' Louise D'Acre continued, 'and he spent his retirement as a permanent guest of the state. Well, I'll collect my tool kit and start to earn my crust.'

'Yes, ma'am.'

'And there's more beneath those two, you say?' Dr D'Acre snapped on a pair of latex gloves.

'So we believe, ma'am,' Hennessey replied. 'The G.P.R. "looks" into the ground at a forty-five degree angle and thus provides a three-dimensional image, and there does indeed seem to be something else beneath the upper two skeletons.'

'Well . . .' Dr D'Acre prepared to gently lower herself into the grave. 'Let's see what we find.'

'I'll leave Webster and Ventnor here with you, plus the constables. I'll ask them to avail themselves to you, ma'am.' Hennessey made to leave the tent.

'That would be appreciated. Thank you, Chief Inspector.' Dr D'Acre lowered herself into the hole, taking care not to put any weight on to any part of either skeleton.

'I have a notion to pay a visit,' Hennessey added.

'Oh?' Louise D'Acre looked up at him from the grave.

'Yes . . . I have.' Hennessey smiled. 'Just a notion that I and Sergeant Yellich should pay a courtesy call to the landowner. I mean, I wouldn't want the police to dig up my back lawn without paying a call on me.'

'Well a field is hardly a back lawn.' Dr D'Acre knelt and began to scrape away soil from the head of one of the skeletons. 'But I know what you mean.'

'It's just a courtesy call really,' George Hennessey explained in a soft, calm and what he hoped was a reassuring tone of voice to the man who answered the door to himself and Yellich.

'I am Detective Chief Inspector Hennessey and this gentleman
–' Hennessey indicated to Yellich – 'is Detective Sergeant
Yellich. We are from Micklegate Bar Police Station in York.'

The man remained silent.

'We understand from the land registry that you own the
field near here?'

'Which field near here? There's plenty of fields round here,
so which one in particular? No shortage of fields round here.'
The man was in his middle years, Hennessey assessed, probably mid to late fifties. He was tall, and perhaps could be said
to be of aristocratic bearing, his near-perfect physique being
marred only by a large pink birthmark on the back of his left
hand. He wore casual but expensive-looking clothes and an
equally expensive-looking watch. His attitude was, Hennessey
found, far from aristocratic. He was, in fact, openly hostile to
the police. His attitude was more akin to that of a career
criminal, Hennessey found, than it was akin to the attitude of
the establishment.

'You are Thomas Farrent?' Hennessey asked, coping very
easily with the man's hostility, though he was grateful for
Yellich's supportive presence.

'Yes, I am,' Farrent sneered. 'That is I.'

'Good, good.' Hennessey smiled. 'We just have to be certain
that we are talking to the right man. The field in question is
the one by the wood close to the village of Catton Hill.'

'Yes, that will be mine. I own all the land round here.'
Farrent's voice was cold, suspicious, guarded.

'All of it?'

'Yes, all the land round Catton Hill. You can walk from
York to Selby without stepping off land I own. Sometimes
it's a narrow path, and the route is not direct, but it can be
done.' The man looked a little smug, Hennessey thought. 'So
yes, I will own the field you mention, and the wood, and the
leases on the properties in Catton Hill village.' Despite the
brief show of smugness Farrent continued to seem wary and
was very defensive of his house. He stood solidly in the
doorway in a manner which stated very clearly that he had
not the slightest intention of allowing Hennessey and Yellich
to enter, keeping, as he did, the door half closed behind him.

Nobody, Hennessey realized, was going to get into that house without a fight or a warrant, and most probably both. Farrent's height of in excess of six feet, plus the elevated step upon which he stood made it possible for him to look down upon his unexpected callers and he did so with the steely eyes of a hungry predator. Farrent, Hennessey sensed, was looking upon him and Yellich as if looking upon fair game, and when he did take his eyes off the officers it was to look beyond them from left to right, carefully scanning the shrubs beyond the driveway of his house as if he was searching for any lurking prey or adversaries.

'This really is just a courtesy call,' Hennessey explained. 'There is no need to be worried.'

Farrent seemed to relax, though only slightly. Hennessey still sensed, with the intuition of a very experienced police officer, that Farrent was a man with something to hide and, or, something to fear. 'We got the precise directions to your house from a farm worker,' Hennessey explained.

'Oh? Which one?'

'We never asked his name.'

'Where was he working?' Farrent snapped the question.

'We feel most disinclined to tell you,' Hennessey replied calmly.

'I see,' Farrent growled, 'but yes, the house is difficult to find, that's how my father liked it. You'd have to know this area very well in order to know the house existed. It occupies a natural hollow in the landscape.'

'Long driveway,' Hennessey commented.

'Half a mile long,' Farrent advised, 'narrow gateposts, thick shrubs and trees between the house and the road; my father planned it like that. He valued his privacy and, quite frankly, so do I.'

'Well, we won't take up too much of your time,' Hennessey reassured Farrent. 'The situation is, you see, that there has been a development, quite a significant development in fact.'

'What sort of development?' Farrent's eyes narrowed.

'A development as in the form of a discovery.'

'Like someone with a metal detector? A hoard of coins has been found?'

'No . . . nothing as lucrative, I am afraid. It is the discovery of human remains.'

Thomas Farrent's neatly chiselled jaw dropped. Blood drained from his face. His brow furrowed. 'A body? Not ancient, otherwise the police would not be involved.'

'No, two bodies in fact, at least two, and yes, recent enough for the police to be interested.'

'In my field?'

'Yes . . . though you don't seem to be like a farmer . . .'

'I am not. I own the land. I rent it to tenant farmers. They do all the work. I get paid the rent.'

'Seems like a nice, comfortable way to make a living,' Hennessey observed drily.

'Possibly it is. But that's how it should be.'

'It is?' Hennessey queried.

'Yes . . . it is,' Farrent sneered. 'In this case it is. The land has been owned by our family, the Farrents, since the English Civil War. It used to be in the possession of a Royalist family, but after the war the deed of ownership was acquired by my ancestor who was a Parliamentarian. The deed was bestowed upon him by Oliver Cromwell, no less.'

'No less,' Hennessey echoed. 'Can't do much better than that.'

'No, not much better,' Farrent continued. 'That was in 1651, and it was a fair and just reward for my ancestor for being a loyal lieutenant of the leader of the Parliamentary cause. He was a man by the name of William Farrent. The lands have been in this family, owned by this family, from that day to this.'

'Lands?' Hennessey questioned.

'Well, once an area of land becomes large enough it can be referred to in the plural, and at one point our land or lands stretched from the west of York to the coast, all one huge parcel. Over time some have been lost, sold to pay debts, or compulsorily purchased to build airfields during the Second World War or to allow motorways to be built. But once it was possible for a man to walk from York to the coast and not have to step off land owned by the Farrents . . .'

'But now you can only walk from York to Selby on Farrent-owned land?' Hennessey said with a smile.

Thomas Farrent glared at Hennessey and then continued,

'Now it's fragmented into a series of small parcels . . . and only about ten thousand acres remain all told, but once . . .' Farrent sighed at the thought of losing so much land, 'but once . . . ponder a rectangle of land, prime agricultural land, some fifty miles long from east to west and ten miles wide. That was the extent of the land conferred upon William Farrent in 1651. Say about one hundred and fifty thousand acres. So the present acreage of ten thousand is nothing to crow about. The tenant farmers pay a low rent, so the income is just sufficient to maintain this house and to provide a comfortable level of living, modest but comfortable.'

'Well, as they say,' Hennessey replied, 'one man's floor is another man's ceiling.'

'Meaning?'

'Meaning it's all relative,' Hennessey explained. 'There are folk who could not even dream about living in a lovely house like this.' He glanced at Farrent's bungalow which seemed expansive, both wide and deep.

'I see what you mean,' Farrent growled. 'The original house was a manor house; it was about twenty miles from here, but my father had it demolished . . . it was crumbling. I remember it; I was five years old when it was demolished. We saved what we could . . . old swords, paintings . . . they're in storage, and moved into this house . . . a bungalow, a bit of a come down from a seventeenth-century manor house. So, skeletons in my field?'

'Yes,' Hennessey replied. 'I am afraid so.'

'Who?'

'We don't know yet, hence our calling on you,' Hennessey explained, 'to let you, the landowner, know what we are doing. But so far we have observed two skeletons.'

'So far?' Again Farrent's voice became menacing.

'Yes, we are still digging. Our ground penetrating radar indicates something beneath the topmost skeletons.'

'I see.'

'So we'll keep . . .' Hennessey stopped speaking as a small red car, a BMW, drove up the drive towards the bungalow crunching the gravel. Both he and Yellich turned to their right and watched it approach.

'Mrs Farrent,' Thomas Farrent announced in the manner Hennessey and Yellich had often encountered of men referring to their wives. The woman, who appeared to be of the same age group as Thomas Farrent, drove past the door of the bungalow glancing curiously at Hennessey and Yellich as she did so.

'Best burglar deterrent there is,' Farrent said as the red BMW drove by. 'A cat can't even walk on gravel without making a sound. You have to be close to hear it but it's true – not even a cat.'

'Oh I wholly agree,' Hennessey replied. 'I do so wholly agree.'

The officers watched as Mrs Farrent drove the BMW into the open garage and continued to watch as moments later she reappeared carrying her shopping in two eco-friendly straw bags. She wore a blue cardigan over a blue blouse, and a darker blue three-quarter length skirt, and wore blue sports shoes.

'Mrs Farrent's colour is blue,' Thomas Farrent explained with an unexpected tone of apology in his voice. 'It's her blue eyes, you see.'

'Ah.' Hennessey nodded.

'These two gentlemen are from the police,' Thomas Farrent announced as Mrs Farrent approached. As she drew nearer Hennessey saw how powerfully she was holding on to her youth. She said nothing but both Hennessey and Yellich noticed a look of fear in her eyes and both thought her smile was disingenuous. They both sensed an insecure and timid woman.

'About something in a field,' Farrent explained. 'Nothing to fret about.'

'Can you tell us who rents that field?' Hennessey asked, turning once again to Farrent.

'Bowler rents it. Francis Bowler.'

'Where do we find him?'

'The white-painted farmhouse. A small house. Left out of our gate, then go about a mile and a half. There will most likely be an ancient VW in the drive . . . if he's not at the pub. It's all that wretched mendicant can afford, an ancient VW . . . it's red underneath all the dirt. His farm is called Blue Jay Farm.'

Mrs Farrent slid past the two police officers and entered the bungalow as Thomas Farrent opened the door a little to allow her to enter. Without saying a word Farrent turned and followed his wife, shutting the door on Hennessey and Yellich.

'Well, thank you anyway,' Hennessey addressed the solid-looking door of the bungalow. 'We appreciate your help in this matter.' He and Yellich turned and walked to where Hennessey had parked their car.

The police constable looked up at Dr D'Acre and Webster who stood at the edge of the grave. Both thought that he looked weary, and well he might. Removing skeletons from deep holes is a task which will reach even the strongest constitutions, emotionally, as well as physically. 'This is definitely compact soil now, sir . . . ma'am.' The constable wiped his brow. 'I am certain to be the first human being to get down this far.'

'Very good.' Webster nodded. 'Thank you. As you say, no point in digging any deeper. If we do need to go deeper for some reason, then we can always return. The hole isn't going anywhere. Even it it's filled in, it's still not going anywhere.'

'Yes, sir.' The constable put the spade on the side of the hole, levered himself out and brushed the soil from his overalls.

Louise D'Acre and Webster walked slowly and solemnly back to where the skeletons had been laid out, one beside the other, in a row, behind the screen.

'It's a family,' Dr D'Acre announced, as she and Reginald Webster stood side by side looking at the skeletons, as a grim-faced SOCO took photographs. 'I think we'll find that it is a family.'

'A family, ma'am?' Webster queried.

'I think so,' Dr D'Acre replied softly. 'I will be able to determine that for certain once we examine the DNA results . . . but we have five adults, as you see, two with fully knitted skulls, one male and one female, the remaining three are all female with partially knitted skulls. So, father, mother and their three teenage daughters . . . skulls do not fully knit until about the age of twenty-five years. They were a short family in terms of stature, save one who, as you see, was noticeably taller than her sisters and parents.'

It was Sunday, 15.37 hours.

TWO

in which an unpleasant tale unfolds, an identity is confirmed and the gentle reader is introduced to Carmen Pharoah.

Virginia Farrent lay awake. Her husband snored loudly beside her. Through the window of her bedroom she pondered the dark outline of the tree canopy against the lighter outline of the sky. She heard an owl hoot and then the second hoot from an answering owl. She could only recall the formidable and terrifying Sister Mary, whose bulk towered over her, the black and white of her habit and huge metal crucifix which dangled from around her neck, 'Your sins, child, will always seek you out', 'If you push a rock it will roll back on top of you', 'If you dig a hole you will fall into it' . . . 'There is no escape, no escape at all.'

A hole . . . in the ground.

A hole . . . in the ground.

The first sliver of dawn appeared in the sky. She glanced at the clock beside her bed: 06.05. She felt a terrible, very terrible dawn was breaking.

Louise D'Acre stood thoughtfully in the post-mortem laboratory of the York District Hospital and looked carefully at the five skeletons which lay in a row, each on a stainless steel table. Taking her time she studied each skeleton carefully with her practised eye. A metal bench, also like the tables of stainless steel, ran the full length of one of the walls of the laboratory, beneath which were drawers, also of metal, containing surgical instruments, a plentiful supply of starched towels and other items necessary to the conducting of a post-mortem examination. The room was brightly illuminated by a series of filament

bulbs set in the ceiling and concealed from direct view by
transparent Perspex sheeting so as to soften the glare and to
protect living human eyes from epileptic fit-inducing shimmer.
The room had no natural source of light. Also attached to the
ceiling were microphones on the end of long anglepoise arms,
one above each table. The aluminium and the stainless steel
in the room gleamed brightly under the filament bulbs; the
scent of formaldehyde was heavy and mingled with the odour
of strong disinfectant which had been used to clean the industrial grade linoleum which covered the floor. Eric Filey, of
short and rotund appearance, and who, unusual for one of his
calling, managed to approach his work with good humour and
appropriate joyfulness, was also at that moment in a subdued
mood as he stood close to the bench. At the opposite side of
the laboratory to the stainless steel bench was Carmen Pharoah,
who remained motionless with her eyes downcast as if in
reverence to the presence of the forensic pathologist, and also
in reverence to the five, as yet, nameless victims.

'I think we all feel the same.' Louise D'Acre spoke quietly.
'One victim is bad enough, all come here before their time,
but five, all found in the same hole in the corner of a wheat
field . . . I think that reaches us all.'

'Yes, indeed, ma'am,' Carmen Pharoah replied, equally
quietly.

'I expected Mr Hennessey.' Dr D'Acre turned to Carmen
Pharoah.

'He did in fact intend to observe for the police, ma'am, but
asked me to stand in for him instead. He and Sergeant Yellich
have inquiries to make.'

'I see.' Dr D'Acre turned back to the tables and continued
to observe the skeletons. 'We have,' she said, 'two mature
adults, one male and one female, plus three young adults, all
female.' She paused. 'It is a family, I'll be bound. You know
if I was a betting lady I would lay good money that what we
have here is a family with one daughter who grew up to be
significantly taller than her parents and her sisters. Such is not
unknown, and is commonly referred to as a "throwback gene",
but "dormant gene" is the preferred term. Somewhere back
along the line of this family an ancestor had congress with a

tall person and a height-inducing gene was introduced into their line. We often observe much the same in this part of England, Ms Pharoah.'

'Really, ma'am?' Carmen Pharoah allowed herself a brief but still reverential eye contact with Dr D'Acre. 'That is quite interesting.'

'Probably not so much in London,' Dr D'Acre continued, 'but up here in the frozen north, the wilderness that extends north of the River Trent, but particularly north of the River Humber, it is not at all unusual for stocky, swarthy, dark-haired people to produce a tall, blue-eyed blonde child. The Viking legacy you see. The Vikings left the beginnings of permanent settlements. They left place names and names for geographical features like "foss" for "waterfall", and they also left their genes.'

'That is quite interesting, ma'am,' Carmen Pharoah replied, 'and, as you say, no Viking influence in London, so that doesn't happen.'

'It is, isn't it?' Dr D'Acre rested her fingers on the lip of the nearest table to which she stood. 'But I will be very surprised if these five people were not related in life, and were not related in their manner and time of death.' She snapped on a pair of latex gloves and walked to the table upon which the male skeleton lay. She then reached upwards with a controlled and a confident movement and pulled down the microphone until it was level with her mouth at perhaps, estimated Carmen Pharoah, about two feet distant. 'Date . . . today's date, please, Sheila,' Dr D'Acre said for the benefit of the audio typist who would shortly be typing her words into a word processor, 'and also the next case number, please.' She paused and then commenced her commentary. 'The body is that of a mature adult male. It is completely skeletal. There is no trace of muscle or sinew, which indicates a burial in the damp, clay soil in the Vale of York of at least twenty years.' She turned to Carmen Pharoah and explained, 'Plenty of microscopic bugs in the soil to feast on the flesh. If they had been buried in a desert or in very cold areas then some flesh would remain, particularly in the cold areas.'

'Yes, ma'am.'

Dr D'Acre forced open the mouth of the skeleton and remarked, 'British dentistry is noted, and with a gold filling, no less, which indicates late twentieth and early twenty-first century dentistry, unless the victims were especially wealthy, in which case the time of death could equally be much earlier in the twentieth century, even earlier than that, but gold fillings ceased to be a symbol of wealth after the Second World War.'

'I see, ma'am,' Carmen Pharoah responded.

'Yes, courtesy of the good old envy of the world National Health Service, and were never to my taste.' Dr D'Acre folded her arms. 'I understand from Mr Hennessey that there is witness evidence which indicates a burial of about thirty years previous but forensically and pathologically speaking, I cannot find anything which would indicate a time of death so precisely.'

'Understood, ma'am,' Carmen Pharoah replied.

Dr D'Acre unfolded her arms. 'But . . . let's press on and see what we can find. No injuries seem to have been sustained by the skeleton. There is no evidence of a blunt or sharp force trauma. So, for an explanation of cause of death we are looking at drowning, or suffocation, or asphyxiation or poisoning . . . something of that nature but we also cannot rule out death by thirst or starvation . . . slower and very painful but just as effective.'

'Indeed, ma'am,' Carmen Pharoah said. 'Three days, I believe?'

'Yes, the rule of threes; three weeks without food, three days without water, three minutes without oxygen to cause death and just one minute without air to cause brain death. You know, if you want to murder someone and avoid being charged with murder you simply deprive them of oxygen for sixty seconds. The heart still beats but the victim is left in a permanent vegetative state . . . as good as dead.'

'Yes, ma'am.'

'But an awful lot more difficult to carry off than people imagine. You have to get the timing just right. Too long and you are looking at life in prison, and you've also got to incapacitate the person in question, which is not at all easy, not without evidence of same. I mean to say that I can't declare the victims to have had a massive stroke when there are ligature marks on their wrists and ankles.' Dr D'Acre smiled. 'It ain't so easy to get away with.'

'Of course, ma'am.' Carmen Pharoah returned the smile but did so briefly. 'Better not to commit the crime in the first place.'

'Which would always be my advice.' Dr D'Acre returned her attention to the male skeleton. 'I will send marrow samples to the forensic laboratory. I can obtain that very easily from the long bones. They will retain diatoms if the victim was drowned.'

'Diatoms?' Carmen Pharoah queried.

'More microscopic beasties,' Dr D'Acre explained. 'They live in water; a drowning victim inhales them into their lungs from whence they migrate to the marrow in the long bones, there to remain.'

'I see, ma'am. Diatoms,' Carmen Pharoah said. 'Diatoms.'

'The marrow,' Dr D'Acre continued, 'will also retain traces of heavy poisons of the likes of arsenic and others of that family, such as strychnine, but frankly murdering someone with arsenic went out with hansom cabs and gas street lighting and it is now practically impossible to obtain.' Dr D'Acre paused. 'So let us do what we can because we must come up with goods of some sort. Let us therefore turn to the issue of iden-tification which is always useful for the police investigation.'

'Yes, ma'am.' Carmen Pharoah grinned. 'Always very useful.'

'Well, the shape of the skull of the male skeleton indicates that he is of North Western European racial extraction, as I think I commented at the scene of the excavation. An Asian male is not impossible, although Asian skulls tend to be more finely made than the European skull which tends to be broader and more thickly set. As I have already noted, the teeth are intact and show dental work having been undertaken, so dental records may help you but don't hold out too much hope there,' Dr D'Acre added. 'Dentists, you see, are obliged by law to keep all the records of their patients for eleven years only. So any dental records in respect of this gentleman and his family might no longer be available. It depends upon the dentist.'

'Eleven years,' Carmen Pharoah echoed for want of a response, 'noted, ma'am.'

Dr D'Acre turned to Eric Filey. 'Can you hand me the tape measure, please, Eric?'

Filey turned to the stainless steel bench, opened a drawer and extracted a yellow retractable metal tape measure, walked the short distance to where Dr D'Acre stood and gently handed it to her.

'If we could turn him, please, Eric?' Dr D'Acre slipped the tape measure into the pocket of her white laboratory coat, moved to the end of the table and took the skull of the skeleton in her hands, whilst Filey silently went to the other end of the stainless steel table and took very careful hold of the ankles. Then with an ease and a sense of care which reached Carmen Pharoah, Dr D'Acre and Eric Filey, with a clearly well-rehearsed manoeuvre, rotated the skeleton through 180 degrees and carefully laid it face down upon the polished metal table. Dr D'Acre took the tape measure from her pocket and extended it, laying it the length of the skeleton from skull to heel. 'There are,' she said, smiling at Carmen Pharoah, 'certain rules which we can observe if we are dealing with bits of a human body to estimate height. The spine, length of, is the same length as hip to ankle, approximately speaking, and if the person was of normal proportion. The femur is one third of the height, also approximately, but here we have the whole skeleton, so no need to estimate.'

'Yes, ma'am.' Carmen Pharoah stood back against the wall of the laboratory.

'So . . . so . . . not a tall man . . . quite short in fact.' Dr D'Acre read the measurement of the tape. 'We have a measurement of five feet two inches, or one hundred and fifty-seven centimetres tall, when he reached adulthood. He was not the sort of bloke to attract admiring glances from females as he walked along the pavement.'

'Not a tall old geezer then, ma'am,' Carmen Pharoah offered.

'Nope.' Louise D'Acre grinned. 'You know I like the word "geezer". We don't ever seem to hear it up North. It is a London expression, I believe?'

'Yes, ma'am.' Carmen Pharoah returned the grin. 'I believe it is.'

'Where are you from? In London, I mean, Miss Pharoah.'

'Leytonstone, ma'am,' Carmen Pharoah replied in answer to Dr D'Acre's unexpected question, 'in the East End.'

'Ah . . . can't say I know it. Can't say I know London at all well, in fact. Anyway, to continue.' Dr D'Acre returned her attention to the skeleton. 'So, a small but all in proportion old geezer . . . How old when he died is the next step. I will extract a tooth, cut it in half, and that will provide us with evidence of his age at time of death plus or minus one year. It is really a very accurate recording we achieve using that method. I will do so for all five skeletons.' She paused. 'But once again I repeat that I am not going to be of much help when it comes to determining the cause of death, unless we find diatoms in the marrow of the long bones. However, even finding diatoms will not be absolute proof of drowning *per se*, it will only prove the inhalation of water was peri-mortem, but not certain to be the cause of death.' She paused again. 'Sorry, I ramble.' Dr D'Acre drummed her fingertips on the rim of the table. 'You know what puzzles me . . . what foxes me, is the complete absence of anything which is not biodegradable; apart from the gold filling, there are no zip fasteners, no bra hooks, no belt buckles, no wooden toggles or plastic buttons, et cetera, and with a burial of just thirty years earlier you would expect such items to be found with the skeleton as any clothing decayed around the bones . . . shoes also . . . There should be a trace of remnants of their footwear. So there is only one inescapable conclusion . . .'

'They were naked when they were buried, ma'am?' Carmen Pharoah suggested.

'Yes,' Dr D'Acre replied. 'Unless a sifting of the soil removed from atop the skeletons reveals such items as I have mentioned, then that is the inescapable conclusion, so yes, naked when buried, all five victims. You know I have the distinct impression that a very unpleasant tale is beginning to unfold here, a very unpleasant story indeed.'

'Seems so, ma'am,' Carmen Pharoah replied as she too surveyed the five skeletons. 'It does certainly seem so.'

'Well, let's crack on, let's look at the other skeletons.' Dr D'Acre spoke with forced good humour as she added, 'We have our daily crust to earn.'

In the event, the other remaining four skeletons did not reveal anything new. None of them exhibited any sign of trauma; all had dentistry which was both British and contemporary. Four of the five skeletons were short of stature but were in proportion, none having abnormally short legs or abnormally long spines. One of the five skeletons would have been a significantly taller person when alive than the other four persons. The male would have been five feet two inches tall or one hundred and fifty-seven centimetres tall. The three shorter females would have been about five feet or one hundred and fifty-four centimetres tall. The fourth female, on the other hand, would have been a lofty five feet eight inches or one hundred and seventy-two centimetres tall. Dr D'Acre stroked the back of her hand under her chin in a seemingly absent-minded gesture. 'You know, these people, these goodly folk will have been noticed to be missing. A missing family . . . there will definitely be a missing person report filed somewhere in the country in respect of those five people.'

'Yes, ma'am,' Carmen Pharoah replied.

'The older female skeleton had given birth; pelvic scarring is evident, so at least two breech deliveries, being the minimum required to cause such scarring, which fits in neatly with the impression that these five persons were a family. And again, I repeat, no injuries are noted. Can you see anything, Eric?'

'No, ma'am,' Eric Filey replied quickly, 'and I have been looking.'

'A second pair of eyes is always useful and you don't need to be an MD to be able to identify a hairline fracture in the bone or bones of a skeleton,' Dr D'Acre explained, 'and Eric has been useful before.'

'Yes, ma'am.' Carmen Pharoah smiled approvingly at Eric Filey who shifted uncomfortably at the compliment and approval.

'So,' Dr D'Acre continued, 'all these five people died without damage to their bones, which is how the great majority of us meet our end if you would care to think about it.'

'I suppose so, ma'am,' Carmen Pharoah replied. 'I confess I have never thought about it like that before.'

'Well, death by old age or serious illness takes most of us in the Western world anyway. But five wholly intact and undamaged skeletons is . . . is . . . what would you call it, Eric?'

'Unusual, ma'am.' Eric Filey beamed in response to his opinion being sought. 'I'd say it is unusual.'

'I would say so too, unusual in the extreme.' Dr D'Acre leaned on the table upon which lay the skeleton of the oldest female, the skeleton assumed to be that of the wife and mother. 'None of the other female skeletons show signs of having given birth, though they are quite old enough to have done so. Late teenagers I would say, probably early twenties. My findings will be spartan and wholly inconclusive, though we must wait for the DNA and diatom test results, as I said.'

'Yes, ma'am,' Carmen Pharoah replied. 'I will inform Mr Hennessey.'

'Yes, please do . . . please do . . . but we are looking at death by poisoning, suffocation, exsanguination, but that is unlikely because it's too messy, forty pints of blood will leave quite a trace . . . or drowning or asphyxiation . . . and possibly thirst or even starvation. Definitely some form of death which did not involve trauma.'

'They were not large,' Carmen Pharoah said, 'apart from one. I mean it would not have taken a great deal of strength to overpower them, tie them up and then leave them in a garage where there is a car with its engine running, something like that.'

'Yes, that's the sort of death we . . . you should be looking for and, yes, their lack of stature might indeed have been a factor which worked against them.'

'It was quite a deep hole,' Carmen Pharoah observed, 'or so I am led to believe.'

'It was,' Dr D'Acre replied, 'it was a deep grave in heavy soil, believed to have been buried in the September of the year. It gets light at about five thirty a.m. these days and dark at nine thirty p.m., approximately. I can't see a grave being dug during the hours of daylight unless some form of subterfuge was employed.'

'Nor can I, ma'am.'

'Mind you,' Dr D'Acre continued, 'here I encroach on your territory.'

'Mr Hennessey won't mind, ma'am,' Carmen Pharoah replied, 'he won't mind at all, not the Mr Hennessey I know.'

'Nor the one I know; he is a very open-minded police officer,' Dr D'Acre said, 'not at all jealous of his remit. Mr Hennessey's response would be "encroach all you like, all help gratefully received".' She paused and then added, 'Hardly remote.'

'Ma'am?' Carmen Pharoah queried. 'Remote, ma'am?'

'The field, the scene of the burial. You haven't been there but I can tell you that it is hardly remote. It is a rural location, that I grant you, but the rooftops of the nearest village are easily visible from the field to one side of a wooded area. The hole must have been dug and the victims brought to the graveside already deceased, and already naked, and conveyed in the sort of vehicle which is capable of driving over a field without getting bogged down.'

'A tractor and a trailer,' Carmen Pharoah suggested.

'That sort of thing. My heavens!' Dr D'Acre gasped then fell silent as she put one hand up to her mouth.

'Ma'am?' Carmen Pharoah stepped forward as did Eric Filey. 'Are you all right, ma'am?'

'Yes . . . yes, I am all right . . . I am all right.' Dr D'Acre raised her right hand and pointed to the larger of the female skeletons. 'In myself I am all right but I am wrong, very wrong.'

'Wrong, ma'am?' Carmen Pharoah asked.

'Yes, wrong, how wrong I am. You know,' Dr D'Acre said quietly, 'after twenty years of cutting corpses and examining skeletons you develop an eye for detail. You see, all human skulls look the same at first glance and often remain to look the same to the untrained eye, but in fact they have minute differences that are accentuated by the overlaying of layers of flesh and muscle, which explains why human faces look so different from each other.'

'Yes, ma'am?' Carmen Pharoah replied curiously.

'But, just now, in running my eye along the line of skulls, three of the females have the sort of familial similarity that you would expect in people who are related, but the fourth, the taller female, is different. Two females grew up to look like their mother, but the third female, she is taller because she is not a relative. Her height is not the result of a dormant gene, it is because she is, or was, wholly unrelated. The DNA results will confirm whether I am correct or not, but now I think that this is not a family of five, but a family of four plus a fifth unrelated person who was murdered and buried with them. Of that I am sure, as sure as I can be without the DNA results.'

'Oh,' Carmen Pharoah gasped as she looked at the skeletons, 'but the fifth skeleton, the tall girl, she is or was of the same age as the daughters I think you said, ma'am.'

'Yes . . . prior to tests confirming age . . . but yes,' Dr D'Acre replied, 'the younger three females were of the same age group, late teens to early twenties.'

'So a family plus a friend of the daughters?'

Dr D'Acre nodded. 'Yes, possibly, possibly. The tall girl was just in the wrong place at the wrong time or she was murdered for another, unconnected motive, and since a grave was being dug anyway . . . As I said, a very unpleasant tale is unfolding and it's just got a little bit more unpleasant.'

If anyone, if any single soul on this planet, thought Hennessey – even before he and Somerled Yellich saw the farmhouse of Blue Jay Farm – harbours the illusion that farming is a pleasant and a romantic occupation, then let him or her come here to Blue Jay Farm with its delightful but wholly misleading name. Blue Jay Farm might sound, he felt, as if it belonged in a children's book but the first thing that met Hennessey and Yellich's gaze was a wooden building, just one storey high, which was of such misshapen appearance because of age and rottenness that Hennessey felt it would collapse in the next strong wind or at the push of a man of but average strength. For his part, Yellich was astounded that the structure was still more or less upright. Two rusting motor cars stood in the long grass beside the building and clearly had not moved in many, many years, and which equally clearly would never move again. Beside the cars stood rusting bed frames, an old-fashioned wood burning stove and an equally ancient mangle. Strewn about amid the weeds and the long grass were rusted metal buckets, the bottoms of which had long vanished with decay, old prams and old bicycle frames. A hollow-cheeked, sunken-eyed youth stared at Hennessey and Yellich with what seemed to the officers to be an attitude of detached curiosity, as if wondering who the officers were and what their business at the farm was, but not questioning them or seeming threatened or concerned by their presence. It was, thought Hennessey, as if the youth was looking at a rare bird which had lighted there, the arrival of which might merit a passing comment over that day's evening meal.

George Hennessey and Somerled Yellich walked silently onwards, nodding to the youth as they passed. The youth, for his part, remained motionless to the point that he reminded Hennessey of one who was held in a passive catatonic state. Only the sunken eyes of the youth moved as Hennessey and Yellich made their cautious and unsteady way across the farm-yard. The youth made no response to Hennessey's cheery, 'Hello there,' and Yellich's equally cheery, 'Good morning to you; lovely day.' Not a sound passed the lips of the youth, not a fraction did his head even nod in response to either officer, but yet his eyes remained fixed upon the visitors. Hennessey and Yellich walked onwards, past the rotten wooden shed, beyond which, to the right-hand side, was the farmhouse. When seen, the house revealed itself to be a low, squat-looking building which, by its state of disrepair, blended neatly with the wooden shed and general detritus of the yard that had greeted Hennessey and Yellich upon their arrival. The wood of the door and the window frames were clearly rotten, badly so, with peeling paintwork. Many of the black tiles on the roof, which sagged in the middle, were loose, dislodged and, in some cases, missing altogether.

The officers walked slowly up to the door of the house and Hennessey knocked on it with a certain respect and a certain, quite unusual, gentleness. It did not seem to him to be at all appropriate that he should knock loudly, despite being a police officer conducting a murder inquiry. Hennessey intuitively felt that neither the house was structurally strong enough, nor the family emotionally strong enough for either to withstand a sudden and an aggressive declaration of the presence of two police officers. Further, they had, after all, been seen by, he assumed, one member of the household and he further sensed that the farm had an atmosphere of wariness, of being hostile to strangers, and said atmosphere reached him, strongly so.

The woman who opened the door, and did so slowly and cautiously in response to Hennessey's soft tap, tap, was middle-aged, short and stocky, with large hands, so observed Hennessey. The woman's hair was an unkempt mop of grey and black and her eyes a matching steel-grey colour. Her woollen cardigan was grey, her blouse was grey, her tweed skirt was grey and her legs ended in a pair of faded red carpet slippers. The lady of the house held eye contact with Hennessey and then with Yellich, and did so with evident coldness and aggression.

Just as Hennessey was about to introduce himself and Yellich the woman turned and yelled into the gloom of the house, 'Father! Father!' She then turned and walked into said gloom, leaving Hennessey on the doorstep being stared at from behind by the sunken-eyed youth, who had followed the officers as they had walked towards the house but who had always retained a wary distance. Moments later a man appeared at the door, emerging slowly from its interior and he, like the woman, Hennessey and Yellich noted, was also short and squat. He wore baggy brown trousers, an unclean white shirt and a black waistcoat. He wore heavy industrial footwear. The man was, evidently, thought Hennessey, 'Father', and speaking in a thick Yorkshire accent he said gruffly, 'Mother said you wanted something?' He then reached into his trouser pocket and retrieved a small pipe which he placed in his mouth and commenced to suck it loudly.

'Yes, we do.' Hennessey produced his ID and showed it to the man. 'I am DCI Hennessey and this gentleman is DS Yellich, of Micklegate Bar Police Station, of the Vale of York.'

'Aye.' The man scrutinized Hennessey's warrant card and gave but a cursory glance at Yellich's warrant card. 'Micklegate Bar, that be in York itself.'

'Yes, quite right, sir, it is just without the walls at the top of Queen Street, at the junction with Blossom Street.'

'Them road names mean nothing to me, but I do know the
bars . . . the gateways in the walls. Mind, I have not been in
York since . . . well, since I don't know when. You'll be here
in connection with the goings on in the five acre?'

'The five acre?'

'The field by the wood near Catton Hill village, the police
vehicles, the equipment, the mechanical digger, the blow-up
tent and the screen, and the men with cameras. So what is
happening?'

'We have unearthed human remains,' Hennessey replied, relieved
that the man, unlike the youth, was obviously willing to talk.

'I thought as much and I told mother as much. Either dead
bodies or digging up the loot from a bank robbery. Not much
else would cause the bobbies to dig a big hole in the ground,
especially in a wet field like the five acre, hard work that would
be. So, human remains . . . a grave? Well, dare say you wouldn't
be knocking on my door if you had dug up a dead dog.'

'Hardly, sir.' Hennessey forced a smile.

'I did wonder,' the man replied. 'Thought it had to be
something important.'

'You saw us, I assume?' Yellich asked.

'Aye . . . the country is like that. You might not see anybody
but it would be wrong to think that you were not being watched,
or heard. You know the old saying, "The fields have eyes and
the woods have ears"? It's very true is that old saying. So yes,
I saw you, so did a few others. So why come here? Why knock
on my old door?'

'Mr Farrent told us you rent that field . . . so we came here
to pick your brains.'

'Farrent . . .' The man made a low, growling sound.

'You are Mr Bowler, Mr Francis Bowler?'

'Aye, that I am.'

'And you do rent that field, the five acre?'

'Aye, that I do . . . and another two hundred and fifty more
on top of that.'

'A large farm?'

'Only a townie would think that it was large. You need to
farm the best part of a thousand acres to make a decent living.
I rent the land and the house but will Farrent put up any money

towards the upkeep?' He tapped the door frame. 'See . . .
rotten . . . it'll fall down on top of us any day now.'

'Yes . . .' Hennessey replied.

'Farrent owns a lot of land round here, we rent it, me and
tenant farmers like me. We rent it and we work it. Prices for
produce are going down and Farrent still puts up the rent.
You'll have been to his house?'

'Yes, we have, yesterday.'

'Aye well, I haven't ever been there but they say it's a nice
bit of brickwork . . . so that's what you live in if you own the
land and sit back while others work it.' Francis Bowler raised
a finger and indicated the interior of his house. 'I'd invite you
in but you're safer out here. You can see better out here as
well; it's a bit dark in there.'

'So I see,' Hennessey replied as he noted the dim and gloomy
interior of the house, and as he and Yellich both detected the
strong smell of questionable hygiene mixed with the unmistak-
able odour of damp. 'Thank you anyway.' Hennessey paused.
'We have information which suggests that the body or bodies
were buried about thirty years ago. In fact we can be more
precise and say that they were buried thirty years ago this
month. Were you the tenant of Blue Jay Farm then, thirty years
ago?'

'Aye . . . we took over the tenancy ten years before he were
born.' Francis Bowler made a slovenly indication to the youth
who still stood some distance behind Hennessey and Yellich.
'Don't mind him, gentlemen, he's harmless. The doctor said
something about oxygen starvation when he was born, but if
you give him a job he'll do it; can't drive the tractor though,
or any vehicle but he carries his weight. He's my son, he's
part of the farm . . . he's twenty-two years old now . . . so
yes . . . we came here thirty-two years ago.'

'I see,' Hennessey nodded.

'He's our last born, mother and I had two before him. Both
left home now but he's all the help I need. I contract out the
harvesting, that really eats into any profit I make, but it's all
we can do . . . we being me and the other tenant farmers round
here. We don't have a lot of money coming in and we have
to pay for the harvest.'

'Still cheaper than buying a combine harvester and having it stand idle for fifty weeks of the year,' Yellich commented.

'Aye . . . possibly,' Bowler growled.

'So . . .' Hennessey asked, 'were you aware of any activity in the five acre field thirty years ago this month? It is a long time ago, but a large hole was dug. It would seem to me to be an obvious thing and would not have gone unnoticed.'

'Aye . . . you'd think so, I'll grant you that and it could only have been done at one of two times of the year, that is just after the winter wheat has been harvested and before the summer wheat is sowed, and just after the summer wheat has been harvested before the winter wheat goes in. We have two wheat crops a year, you see, so any hole like that would be dug after harvest and before the next ploughing and sowing. September, after the summer wheat is harvested, is when I used to take my family on holiday; low season you see, cheaper rates, much cheaper. We went to a holiday camp in Skegness.'

'I see.' Hennessey felt the damp from within the house grip his chest, making it difficult to breath even outside the building. 'So you would not have been here then?'

'Unlikely, chief, not very likely at all in fact, and I wouldn't have noticed anything when I returned from Skeggie because the five acre is a wet field, like I just said, and any disturbance would not be seen after a day or two. I mean by that that it wouldn't seem to be seen . . . might be a gap in the stubble but that would be all and then it would be ploughed over and you know, quite honestly, when a farmer ploughs his old field, you don't look forwards all the time like when you're driving a car, you look backwards at the plough. That's the only way to make sure that you're ploughing a straight furrow, just glance forwards once every few seconds or so but mostly you look backwards, keeping the plough level with the edge of the field or level with the previous furrow. Every old farmer likes his straight furrow, take it from me.'

'So,' Hennessey said, 'you'd likely drive over the disturbed soil and not see it because you'd be looking backwards?'

'Yes.' Francis Bowler sucked on his empty pipe. 'That's exactly what I am saying, chief, exactly what I am saying.'

'And once the plough has gone over the disturbed soil,'

Hennessey continued, 'it is then indistinct from the rest of the field?'

'Indistinct?' Bowler raised his eyebrows. 'You have a good way with words, sir, I like that word . . . indistinct . . . but yes, it would be indistinct from the rest of the field. You put it very well, sir.'

'Thank you.' Hennessey inclined his head at Francis Bowler's compliment, 'Your information is very useful. The grave was about four feet down . . . deeper in fact . . . the topmost bodies were four feet below the surface. There were others beneath them.'

'Deep,' Bowler growled, 'a proper grave . . . proper depth.'

'Yes, it seems so,' Hennessey replied. 'We thought the same. Not a shallow grave . . .'

'Proper grave,' Bowler repeated, 'a final resting place. We all get one.'

'Probably not as final as the person who dug it might have hoped.' Hennessey smiled wryly. 'So, tell us, how long do you think it would take to dig a hole as deep as that?'

Francis Bowler shrugged. 'Well . . . wet field . . . even in the late summer and the early autumn it's a wet old field . . . heavy soil. My wife's father was a gravedigger for the council in York all his days. He dug graves in Fulford cemetery and used to dig graves in churchyards also, because he was a Christian and helped out the vicar when there was a funeral and a burial to be done. Anyway, he once told me that a grave is a day's work for a good gravedigger. From peeling back the turf to getting six feet down, keeping the sides vertical and the bottom level . . . very important to do that . . . so you "sink" a grave, do you see? You work it down into the ground, down into the soil, so one grave is one day's work. Now the five acre, heavy, wet soil, there's a lot of work there I would think.'

'So nine a.m. to five p.m. with an hour for lunch, seven hours actual labour?' Hennessey suggested.

'That sort of time, but it would be sunk at night, you can be sure of that, gentlemen.' Bowler tapped his pipe stem against his teeth which appeared blackened with decay.

'You think so?' Hennessey asked.

'Certain,' Bowler replied. 'No thinking about it in actual fact . . . certain as certain can be, there's eyes about at night, just the same, but not as many.'

'The fields have eyes,' Hennessey said, 'as you just mentioned.'

'Yes . . . so you'd need to be finished by dawn. It would take all night.' Bowler fumbled some tobacco from an old leather pouch into the bowl of his pipe and then lit the tobacco with a match. He then blew strong-smelling smoke towards, but not at, Hennessey and Yellich. 'Dark at nine these nights, but a fit man with willing hands would have done the job in a single night, including the filling in.'

'Yes,' Hennessey murmured, 'I was thinking of the filling in, that would take time. Not as much as the digging, but still it would take some time.'

'That's an hour's job at least.' Bowler drew lovingly on his pipe. 'And a very good hour. It would tire a man well out.'

'Just one man with a spade, you think?' Hennessey queried.

'Could be done . . . be better with a team of men, but if it were me, I'd use a digger, a mechanical digger.'

'Really?' Hennessey sensed a possible lead.

'Aye.' Bowler once again drew on his pipe and glanced upward. 'This is a lovely old time of the year, September . . . lovely.'

'I am inclined to agree.' Hennessey too enjoyed the blue sky and the lush green foliage.

'So,' Bowler continued, 'if I wanted to get six feet down and six feet long and two or three feet wide into the five acre, dump the body or bodies, then fill in and be away before dawn I'd use a mechanical digger, that I would. The five acre is not too far from Catton Hill. Farming, even thirty years ago, was almost fully mechanized and so sounds in the night wouldn't seem too unusual, but there's the risk that someone might chance on you . . . a poacher . . . that still goes on, or an old boy walking home across the fields. So you'd not want to waste time and hang around any longer than you had to.'

'Interesting.' Hennessey nodded. 'Very interesting and a good point you make, sir.' He paused and then asked, 'So who owned a mechanical digger in these parts about thirty years ago?'

'No one,' Bowler grinned, 'no one . . . no . . . you rented them, you still do . . . you rent the things.'

'Really?' Yellich asked.

'Really, chief, and they are not cheap. I can tell you no one, no tenant farmer could afford to buy one, even renting is expensive.' Bowler re-lit his pipe.

'Who would rent out in this area?' Hennessey asked.

'Marshall and Evans Plant Hire, they're in Catton Hill village. They're the people to talk to.' Bowler pulled strongly on his pipe. 'They've been in the plant hire business for years now. Whether they keep records going back thirty years, well, that I don't know, but it's a slim chance that they might.'

Hennessey sighed. 'Slim or not, it's a chance we have to take. Thank you for your time, sir.'

Carmen Pharoah carefully and methodically trawled the missing person files held at Micklegate Bar Police Station which were between twenty-eight and thirty-two years old. She was searching for a report of a missing family, comprising parents plus two and still possibly three daughters. She had reasoned that if such a report did exist then it would not be hard to find. Not hard at all, pretty well unique, in fact, so she had told herself. Carmen Pharoah knew that it was most often the case that missing persons turn up alive and well within twenty-four hours of being reported as missing. Very few missing persons actually remain missing, usually if the person in question is not found alive, then their body is, but for an entire family to be reported as missing and to remain missing is, she believed, most newsworthy and pretty well unheard of. The file, when she very easily found it, contained just one sheet and had been sent to the Vale of York Police for their information by the Metropolitan Police, the family having been reported as missing by the mother's brother in London, where the family home was. The missing family was investigated because of the unusual nature of the case and because evidence indicated that the family had vanished when visiting York. One Detective Constable Clough was recorded as being the 'interested officer' but his investigation had come to nought and the inquiry was suspended after just ten days.

Carmen Pharoah found herself to be more than a little disappointed that a case of a missing family was allowed to go 'cold' after such a remarkably short period of time. The family, she read, were given as being Gerald and Elizabeth Parr and their two daughters, Isabella and Alexandra, of the Camden area of London, and who had disappeared when visiting York on 'business', rather than as tourists, though the exact nature of said 'business' was not disclosed. Just two daughters. Carmen Pharoah sat back in her chair and glanced out of the window of her office, along the backs of the houses along Blossom Street, being a ribbon of nineteenth century terrace development. So, she thought, Dr D'Acre was correct, two daughters and a third non-related female of the age group of the daughters of Gerald and Elizabeth Parr. That meant more searching to be done. Somewhere in the pile of missing person files was a file in respect of a young woman who had been reported missing at approximately the same time as the Parrs.

Carmen Pharoah returned her attention to her desktop and the pile of dusty manila folders. 'So this is how it was before the days of the microchip,' she said to herself, 'all written up in copperplate long hand.' It was, for her, like touching history. 'But ten days,' she whispered, 'surely there must be something within those days? It's in there somewhere, girl, it's in there somewhere, so look for it. Then . . . then,' she said, 'a visit to DC Clough, if he is still with us. Human memory is often better than dry details in an old file.'

'There was just nothing, nothing at all, and so nothing else I could do. I wasn't best pleased about closing the case after just ten days but the order to do—'

'Close . . . close the case?' Carmen Pharoah questioned. 'Close it?'

'Sorry.' Adrian Clough smiled. 'A slip of the tongue; of course it wasn't closed but it was left to go cold. The order to let it go cold came from the top floor, pressure of work; it was just a very busy time.'

'I see.'

'I wasn't happy, none of us were. With the suspicion . . . no . . . no . . . the real certainty of foul play we felt we should

keep the case in the media, but with a lot of work to do . . .
and . . . well, you're a copper and you know you can't act on
just nothing, and that's all we had . . . nothing. So I dare say
the top floor was correct. They took the hard decision, and
the case of the missing Parr family was consigned to the vaults,
"to await developments", was the official line.' Ex-Detective
Constable Clough, by then just plain Adrian Clough, was a
gentleman in his seventies. He sat in an old, deep leather-bound
armchair in the living room of his modest three bedroom,
semi-detached house in Bishopsthorpe. He had, as Carmen
Pharoah noted, reached the stage in life where he had begun
to smell old, as some elderly people are wont to do, some
earlier than others. Adrian Clough, she saw, had heavily liver
spotted hands and a gaunt, drawn face as if, she sensed, he
was fighting an internal growth. He also seemed to her to have
some difficulties in his breathing and to have lost much weight,
being in her view much too slight to be taken for the police
officer he had once been. Carmen Pharoah discreetly read the
room with a series of glances and saw the room was very
neatly kept. She thought that she detected a woman's touch,
as in that of a dutiful daughter, or a kindly granddaughter.
There certainly was no evidence of the presence of a Mrs
Clough.

'Is there a Mrs Clough?' Carmen Pharoah braved to ask the
question.

'No . . . sadly, not any more, our Mabel went before, she's
passed on, our lass. She saw me get my promotion to Detective
Sergeant and she saw me collect my pension, and we had a
couple of years together in my retirement before she went in
her sleep. She was still only in her fifties, no age at all. These
days it's no age at all. God rest her.'

'I am so very sorry.' Carmen Pharoah found herself beginning to warm to Adrian Clough, Detective Sergeant (retired).

'Thank you, miss, but I have come to get used to being
alone and I wouldn't want to share my house . . . not now.'
Adrian Clough glanced adoringly at an alcove beside the chair
in which he sat and in which were many framed photographs
of many men and women and children of varying ages. 'That's
my rogues' gallery,' he said proudly, 'more in the pipeline.

They keep a good eye on the old man and it helped me that I grew up in a large family, and so I learned from an early age that I am not the centre of anyone's world and that has helped me cope with solitary living.'

'Good . . . good.' Carmen Pharoah smiled approvingly. 'I am pleased you are coping.'

'Well, you know, I had a good life. I dare say that I never amounted to much as a police officer. I got worried about my lack of advancement for a few years and eventually settled into the routine of being a low-ranking CID officer and stopped worrying about the young, thrusting high-fliers shooting past me. I just settled into my post and consolidated. I had my family and I began to look forward to my retirement. I never got to be part of the team investigating the million pound jewellery raids, or the large-scale fraud, but someone has got to look into the theft of tools from the old lady's garden shed and the lifting of Yorkshire stone paving slabs which occurs during the hours of darkness, and I made a respectable number of arrests which led to a respectable number of convictions. I pulled my weight. I did my duty.'

'Good for you, sir.'

'Oh . . . don't call me, sir. You know, I was very pleased to receive your phone call, very pleased indeed. The only calls I get these days are from my family checking up on me, which I don't mind, or from double-glazing companies, which I do mind, so a phone call from my old station, good old Micklegate Bar nick . . . or Mickie Bar as we used to call it.'

'Mickie Bar?' Carmen Pharoah grinned. 'I have never heard it called that before. Mind you, I am fairly new.'

'It used to be the nickname until a new station commander arrived and he put a stop to it. Sent an angry memo round to all hands; it was unprofessional he said, so after a while it fell into disuse. I dare say he was correct in his attitude.'

'I confess I quite like the sound of it,' Carmen Pharoah replied. 'I think it has quite a homely ring to it. It speaks for a police station which had a good level of morale among the officers. I seem to have noticed that when a place of work is known by a nickname among the people who work there, then it has a happy working atmosphere.'

'You are probably right, miss, in fact I know what you mean.' Adrian Clough struggled with a difficult breath and then continued. 'We used to feel that way about it, homely, as you say, but I wouldn't reintroduce the nickname if I were you; dare say it was unprofessional, dare say we did have the wrong attitude.'

'I won't,' Carmen Pharoah replied, 'but I do like the name, I really do. So, the missing family?'

'Yes, the Parrs, very, very strange, a real mystery, like the missing Roman legion. What was it?'

'The Ninth.' Carmen Pharoah glanced out of the window and noted a small but neatly kept garden. 'I think it was the Ninth Legion. I read about it before I came up here.'

'Yes, it was the Ninth, an entire Roman legion, some five thousand men; they just vanished without a trace. They left Eboracum, the place of yew trees, which was the name of the original settlement which became York.'

'I see how you have been using your retirement, sir.' Carmen Pharoah smiled.

'Yes.' Adrian Clough returned the smile. 'I developed a passion for history, particularly local history. The Ninth Legion left Eboracum to go north to Caledonia . . .'

'Scotland?'

'Yes, now called Scotland, to quell an uprising of the Picts and just vanished . . . but that was about one hundred AD. Four people, a complete family disappearing in this day and age, well, it is probably not to the same scale but the mystery is still as powerful. Something happened to the Ninth Legion and something clearly happened to the Parr family of Camden, London. It made quite a media splash as you might well imagine.'

'Yes.' Carmen Pharoah sensed the gentle scent of air freshener in the room. 'I saw and read the newspaper cuttings which were attached to the missing person report. Quite a splash, as you say, local, regional and national newspapers all carried the story.'

'Yes, I remember.' Adrian Clough glanced up at the ceiling of his living room. 'And no one heard or saw anything. You know it's that which I find the most difficult thing of all to comprehend about the whole case. The hotel the family were staying in initially reported the family as doing a runner, absconding without paying the bill, which was quite a large bill because they had been staying at the King Henry, no less.'

'So . . . monied,' Carmen Pharoah commented, 'that's not a cheap hotel. They were very comfortably off.'

'Yes, they were no fly-by-nights.' Adrian Clough nodded briefly in agreement. 'Then their car was found abandoned. It was a top of the range Mercedes Benz, which then scotched any notion that they had run off without paying the hotel bill and confirmed that something untoward had happened. I mean, parents and their two daughters with no known links or connection to York disappear in the night . . . as if abducted by aliens . . . sinister, passing sinister.' Again Adrian Clough took a deep breath which seemed to Carmen Pharoah to cause him great discomfort.

'Are you all right, Adrian?' Carmen Pharoah could not restrain her concern.

'No, I am not.' Adrian Clough forced a smile. 'But all that can be done has been done. It's just pain relief now, this is my last lap. Comes to all of us and it's come to me. Let's just talk about the Parrs.'

'Of course.'

'You have to put it into context. I lived to have my three score and ten plus a year or two on top. I reproduced . . .' He inclined his head towards his 'rogues' gallery'. 'The two daughters of the Parrs were barely in their twenties when they died. I mean they had to have been killed, so sinister.'

'Yes, sinister is just the word.' Carmen Pharoah spoke softly. 'This is something that you probably don't know, sir, but we will be making it public in the press release, and at the press conference, and that is that the grave in which the Parr family was found . . . it seems certain it will be them . . . there was also a fifth body buried with them.'

'Oh . . .' Clough gasped, 'that is news to me . . . that really is news, a fifth body?'

'Yes, I'm sorry, I thought that it might come as a surprise.' Carmen Pharoah sat back in the armchair she occupied. 'It deepens the mystery somewhat.'

'I'll say.' Adrian Clough shook his head. 'I'll say it deepens it. A male or female?'

'Female, of the same age group as the daughters. The forensic pathologist has a very finely developed eye. At first she thought that she was dealing with a family of five with one daughter being significantly taller than the others because of a dormant gene carried in the family line, four of the skeletons being quite short in terms of stature. I was observing the post-mortem for the police, you see.'

'Yes.' Adrian Clough adjusted his position in the chair. 'Yes, I remember the hotel staff remarking that they were a short family, I remember that quite well.'

'But the fifth body, the tallest of the skeletons, was of average height and Dr D'Acre, that is the forensic pathologist I mentioned, she at first thought it was because of a dormant gene, which can happen apparently.'

'You're telling me.' Clough smiled. 'You should see the height of one of my grandsons. He is taller than both his brothers and he has to bow his head when he stands up in this room to avoid cracking it against the ceiling. Huge boy. He's at Newcastle University now.'

'Good for him,' Carmen Pharoah replied, 'he's on his way in life . . . but the forensic pathologist then noticed a slight difference in the shape of the skulls.'

'You can do that?' Clough sounded surprised. 'They have all looked the same to me. You've seen one, you've seen them all.'

'And to me.' Carmen Pharoah grinned in reply. 'But it was explained to me that, apparently, there are minor differences from skull to skull which get accentuated by the layers of muscle and skin and which make human faces appear different from one another.'

'I see, that is interesting.' Adrian Clough raised his eyebrows. 'So skulls are not all the same after all. You still learn things even at my time of life.'

'Yes, sir, seems so.' Carmen Pharoah continued to speak in a soft, reverential tone. 'Anyway, the forensic pathologist was able to discern a difference in the skull of the tallest skeleton, which indicated to her, prior to tests being carried out, that we were looking at a family of four plus a fifth victim who is . . . or was . . . of the same age group as the daughters. Tests will confirm it, of course, but the missing person report of a family of four and the press coverage at the time seems to confirm that the fifth victim was not related. She was probably an unconnected victim who was murdered at the same time and whose wretched body was dropped into the same grave which had been dug for the Parr family.'

'How convenient,' Adrian Clough growled.

'Yes,' Carmen Pharoah agreed, 'convenient. Her skeleton probably has a wholly different tale to tell, could be linked in some way . . . but, equally, it may be wholly unconnected.'

'Only time will tell,' Adrian Clough wheezed.

'Yes.' Carmen Pharoah began to feel uneasy about visiting a man who was in such clear discomfort. 'So far we have yet to identify a likely victim from the missing person reports of about thirty years ago, but the mis per report on the Parr family leapt out at me.'

'As it would do.' Adrian Clough smiled. 'As it would do.'

'Yes, as it would do . . . hence my phone call,' Carmen Pharoah explained. 'I felt it necessary to follow it up with the interested police officer at the time.'

'Yes, seems a sensible thing to do.' Clough once again took a difficult breath.

'I am sorry, Mr Clough, is this a good time?' Carmen Pharoah enquired. 'I can return later.'

Adrian Clough grinned. 'No, it's not a good time but it's the only time you'll get; you had better gather ye rosebuds while ye may. I was given six weeks, seven weeks ago.'

'I am sorry . . .'

'Thank you . . . but you won't escape, so ask away.'

'Thank you.' Carmen Pharoah held eye contact with Adrian Clough. 'It is very generous of you to give your time . . . very courageous.'

'One last useful thing,' Adrian Clough replied. 'It will make me feel better about myself this evening.'

'If you are sure . . .' Carmen Pharoah pressed.

'Sure.'

'So tell me what you found out about the Parrs?' Carmen Pharoah asked. 'It sounds like an old name . . . it rings a bell.'

'One of Henry Tudor's wives perhaps, Catherine Parr? The sixth and final one, I think. She was the last one.'

'Of course, English history lessons.' Carmen Pharoah beamed. 'And yes, you are correct, she was the last one. She survived him and lived to tell the tale.'

'English history?' Clough enquired. 'We just had history.'

'I grew up in St Kitts,' Carmen Pharoah explained, 'so at school English history was taught as a separate subject to West Indian history.'

'I see.' Clough paused. 'That's interesting. So the Parrs, well, what can I say? I must search my memory for anything that might not have been reported in the file. I contacted the police in London, the Parrs' home being in London, in north London . . . Camden, I think.'

'That's quite posh,' Carmen Pharoah commented.

'Really? Mind you, their car and staying at the King Henry Hotel, I shouldn't be surprised that Camden was and still is posh, but I don't know London. I have rarely been there.'

'It is posh, you can rest assured,' Carmen Pharoah said. 'Me and my husband used to live in Leytonstone . . . down the East End . . . it is very unfashionable.'

'So what brought you north?' Clough asked.

Carmen Pharoah sank back in her chair and after a pause said, 'A car . . .'

Adrian Clough scowled at her reply.

'I am sorry,' she explained, 'I am not being facetious. I actually travelled north by train, following my husband being knocked down and killed in a road traffic accident. So in a sense it really was in fact a car which made me come north, which made me feel I had to get away from London.'

'I am sorry to hear that,' Clough wheezed. 'I understand your reply now. I am very sorry; you are too young to have to cope with a loss like that.'

'I am coping.' Carmen Pharoah smiled.

'Courageously so.' Adrian Clough returned the smile. 'So, the Parrs. I remember that they once had a double-barrelled name, Parr-Keble . . . Keble with a single "e", but in fact it was pronounced "Keeble" as if it had a double "e".'

'Sounds posh, as I said.'

'I think that they were once quite wealthy, suffered a slide but not yet quite – what's the term? – "distressed gentlefolk", those born into money who then fall on hard times and expect handouts to keep them in a manner to which they are accustomed. Well try being born into poverty, I say,' Clough said angrily.

'I believe the term is "downward social mobility", but, as you say, it's hard to find sympathy for them.' Carmen Pharoah nodded in agreement. 'Distressed and gentle as they may be.'

'But the impression I had, Ms Pharoah, was that they were clearly still monied.'

'Carmen.' Carmen Pharoah smiled warmly. 'You can call me Carmen.'

'It is just the impression I had, Carmen. I should really offer you tea. I feel like a cup. Would you care to join me? I am told I make a passable cup of tea.'

'Please.' Carmen Pharoah made to stand. 'I will make it.'

Adrian Clough extended his hand palm outwards. 'No . . . no, I want to, today has been an unexpected pleasure.' He levered himself up from his chair. 'Last chance to do some police work . . . last chance to make tea for an unexpected guest. The only people who visit me are my family and the district nurse who gives me this day my daily morphine. No, you stay seated, Carmen, let me do something knowing I am doing it for the last time.' Adrian Clough walked unsteadily out of the room, leaving a slight but pungent odour in his wake.

Later, and over what indeed proved to be a very passable pot of tea, Adrian Clough, once again seated in his armchair, continued. 'Yes, no recollection of the Parrs being financially embarrassed, no recollection at all.'

'Well, they lived in Camden and they don't sound like they rented . . .' Carmen Pharoah stirred her tea which, to her surprise, was served in daintily decorated cups and saucers rather than the half-pint mug she had expected a retired police officer to have favoured. 'And the Mercedes Benz you describe . . . not cheap. So, do you know . . . did you find out why the Parr family came to York? It would seem very relevant to the inquiry.'

'As you say, Carmen, very relevant; we thought the same and asked just that question but the hotel manager and staff were unable to help. The Parrs never mentioned to the hotel staff what their reason was for visiting York, not even in passing. When we searched their rooms at the King Henry we found only age and gender appropriate clothing, sufficient for the week they had booked the room for, plus a little jewellery, but no documents of any kind . . . no business cards, nothing that could throw any light as to their reason for coming to York.'

'Where did you put their possessions?' Carmen Pharoah sipped her tea.

'It all went into police storage, as you'd expect, and it remained there until it was claimed by the next of kin.'

'Mr Verity, Mrs Parr's brother?' Carmen Pharoah consulted her notebook.

'If that was the name.' Adrian Clough also sipped his tea. 'I can't recall his name at all. I recall him presenting at Mickie Bar looking very solemn. I didn't get any sort of bad feeling about him, which is the sort of thing I would remember. He was quite short, like the Parrs, and he kept muttering about it all being a "fool's errand".'

'A fool's errand?'

'I am sure that it was what he said.' Adrian Clough looked down at the carpet. 'Yes, he did say that, "all a big fool's errand".'

'Did you ask him what he meant by that?' Carmen Pharoah closed her notebook. 'It sounds like he knew the reason for the drive north.'

'No . . . no, I didn't . . . confess I didn't.' Adrian Clough looked uncomfortable. 'I remember he was bustling about, anxious to get out of the door and back down south with the Parr family's belongings bundled into three cellophane evidence bags. I dare say I should have asked him to explain, but I just seemed to respond to his eagerness to get home to London and so I didn't hinder him any. That attitude of mine probably explains why I was slow to rise and why I never made it beyond Detective Sergeant.'

'Don't reproach yourself, Adrian, hindsight is twenty-twenty vision.' Carmen Pharoah paused and then said, 'So it would seem that the Parrs had a purpose in visiting York and they were not on a family holiday.'

'Yes . . . but a week is a long time to conclude business.

They might have been intending to do a little tourism. York being York even a week is insufficient time to see all that there is to see, that is if ancient history is your area of interest. And the time of year . . . you can visit York any time of the year but September, when they visited, is a good month to do sightseeing, still warm and dry. So they may have chosen to extend a business trip with a small holiday.'

'Yes . . . their car, the Mercedes,' Carmen Pharoah asked, 'it was found in Leeman Street car park, I understand?'

'Yes,' Clough replied confidently, 'yes, it was a day or two later. The car park attendant alerted the police. When the vehicle hadn't moved for two days he inspected it and found the driver's door window was half wound down and the ignition keys still in place. It was quite suspicious, he thought, and so he called the police . . . quite rightly.'

'Really!' Carmen Pharoah gasped. 'I mean, was the car really left like that?'

'Yes, really.' Adrian Clough raised his eyebrows. 'Really, really left like that.'

'Suggesting what?' Carmen Pharoah asked. 'What is in your mind, Adrian?'

'Well, in my mind . . .' Adrian Clough seemed pleased his opinion was sought. 'Suggesting the possibility that leaving the window open would destroy any fingerprints that might have been left by a felon or felons that had not been wiped. It's an old dodge, as you will likely know, exposure to the atmosphere, the moving air, will cause latents to degrade much more rapidly than those in enclosed spaces.'

'Yes.' Carmen Pharoah smiled. 'An old dodge, as you say.'

'But quite frankly,' Adrian Clough continued, 'I think the more likely explanation was that the Mercedes Benz was left like that so as to be an open invitation to car thieves, in the hope that joyriders might come across it and take it for a spin and then set fire to it, that would really cover the tracks of any felon.'

'Yes.' Carmen Pharoah nodded in agreement. 'It certainly would, especially if it was torched, as you say.'

'If not joyriders then car thieves, it was an open invitation to one or the other. You could have sold that car in the Arab market or the Russian market with no questions asked, that would get it well out of the reach of the British police.'

'Certainly would.' Carmen Pharoah put her empty teacup down on the hearth tiles. 'That was a lovely cup of tea, just what I needed. I can understand that reasoning.'

'And Leeman Road car park was a good place to leave a car if you wanted it stolen,' Adrian Clough added. 'A gang or separate groups of car thieves were active in central York at the time.'

'Thus implying local knowledge?' Carmen Pharoah suggested.

'Possibly,' Adrian Clough agreed, 'but only possibly. May just be coincidental, but in the event we were lucky because we acquired it before it could be stolen. We phoned the address of the owners and a maid answered.'

'A maid?'

'Yes . . . so further indicating that the Parrs were monied. She told us the family had gone to York for a few days. It was just about then that the hotel phoned us to say a family had done a moonlight, giving the name of the family. So we linked that to the abandoned Mercedes and then Mrs Parr's brother phoned.'

'Mr Verity?'

'Yes, so we opened the missing person report and appealed to the media. A missing family . . . quite a splash it made, as I said, but we heard not a whisper. We heard not a dicky bird, until now.' Adrian Clough sighed. 'I'm glad I lived to see this development.'

'And now with an extra body thrown into the mix,' Carmen Pharoah added.

'Yes.' Clough raised his eyebrows. 'As you say, Carmen, with an extra body thrown into the mix.'

Taking her leave of Mr Clough with no small measure of thanks, Carmen Pharoah walked away from his house feeling a most profound sense of humility, combined with a great sense of privilege that she had met the gentleman, and she felt pleasure in having made a small contribution to his life as it was drawing to its close.

'Thirty years.' The man grinned. 'Seriously? In excess of a quarter of a century?'

'It's a bit of a long shot,' Hennessey replied, sharing the
man's humour, 'but I've shot longer shots in my time, and,
yes, I am afraid that we are serious, very serious.'

'And long shots have paid off before,' Yellich added, 'in
fact they have paid off most handsomely. Frankly, the thought
of letting an investigation grind to a halt for the sake of turning
over a stone is . . . well . . . shall I say, it is a thought which
provides me with no comfort.'

'Nor me,' Hennessey echoed. 'I don't have the fortitude to
withstand such guilt and despair.'

'That I can well understand, very well understand,' the man
replied, 'and in fact I might indeed be able to help you,
gentlemen. Do please take a pew.' John Bateman by the nameplate on his desktop, of Marshall and Evans Plant Hire Co.
Ltd, was a tall, thin man whom, both officers noted, was
immaculately dressed, though not wholly to the taste of either
Hennessey or Yellich. The plum coloured suit, the yellow tie,
the small, almost ladylike watch he wore, it was a dress sense
which did not appeal to the officers. The man, the officers also
noted, had only one arm. The left arm seemed to have been
lost just above the elbow, and the left sleeve of his jacket was
hitched up to the shoulder and held in place with a large safety
pin. He tapped his left arm as he saw the officers, noting the
image he presented. 'They offered me a prosthetic arm but I
declined, I mean, everyone can tell it's plastic. I have the same
attitude to false teeth. If they had any medical value I would
wear them, but they are just cosmetic. If I had lost my leg I
would have used a crutch. I just have no time at all for
cosmetics, no time at all.'

'I confess I have the same attitude.' George Hennessey
adjusted his position in the chair in front of Bateman's desk,
which had looked soft but in the event had proved itself to be
surprisingly hard. To his right he observed Yellich, who sat in
an identical chair, making the selfsame discovery.

'Yes, I believe that I must have inherited that attitude from
an elderly relative of mine. He left one of his legs behind him
during the retreat to Dunkirk and I have early memories of
him powering along the pavement with a crutch under each
arm and me running behind him trying to keep up with him.

He just seemed to carry all before him, and he once told me that he walked much more powerfully with two bits of wood under each arm than he had ever done with two good legs. He drank like a fish and he had a wild temper, and if he got into a fight he'd sort out the whole pub with his crutches, or so I was told in later years. I never really knew him. He died when I was still very young but his legend lived on after him, it still does in fact. Folk in our village still talk about him. I lost my arm in a motorcycle accident, nothing so heroic or patriotic in my tale of woe.'

'I'm sorry,' Hennessey replied, as a pain stabbed at his emotions.

'Well, the old "put it into context number", I suppose. I was the pillion, the driver lost his life. My Great Uncle Benjamin Bateman lived without a leg for seventy of his ninety-three years. I dare say I can live without half of one arm, and, like I said, at least I am still here . . . and my friend is in his family plot. You must put these things in context and just knuckle down and get on with life.'

'Is the correct attitude.' Hennessey rested his hat on his knee. 'Quite the correct attitude.'

'Your long shot may just pay off, gentlemen; it just might well pay off. This modest little company keeps all of its records for the five years required by the Inland Revenue and we continue to keep them out of interest, thus forming a company archive, although it is not a complete historical record. There are some gaps, I have to warn you of that. Some have been lost, inexplicably vanished, and we once sacked an employee for gross inefficiency together with an offhand and abusive attitude towards customers. So she walked out and when she had gone we found out that she had removed a few old ledgers with her, just out of spite. We wondered what was in the large shopping bag she carried. She took them because she knew how much we valued them. She probably burned them. Other ledgers were thrown out by an over zealous employee who was just "making room", she said, for more recent documents. Either way, ledgers have been lost . . . taken, thrown away or just vanished as if we have a poltergeist on the premises.' Bateman paused and held eye contact with Hennessey and

Yellich, 'So all I can do is check . . . September, thirty years ago . . . I'll see what I can find.'

'If you'll be so good.' Hennessey inclined his head.

Bateman stood. 'I'll go a few years either side, see what I can find.' He walked out of his office.

Hennessey and Yellich relaxed in their chairs as best they could. They both read a neatly kept office which spoke of efficiency. A large green vase of flowers on Bateman's desk softened the room, as did a colour photograph of the Yorkshire Dales landscape in high summer in a wooden frame which hung on the wall behind his desk. Framed photographs of yellow and green painted earth-moving machines of various sizes hung on the walls of cream-painted plaster. The room smelled powerfully of air freshener, despite an open window, which looked out on to the main street of Catton Hill village. Within ten minutes Bateman returned carrying six slender ledgers, still glistening from evidently being wiped with a damp cloth.

'They were very dusty, as you might expect, so I wiped them down.' Bateman handed three of the ledgers to Hennessey and three to Yellich.

Hennessey took hold of the ledgers he was given. 'Thank you, appreciated.'

'Just the covers,' Bateman added, 'the pages might be a bit dusty still.'

'We'll cope with that.' Hennessey opened the topmost of the ledgers at random and saw entries in neat, copperplate letters and numerals. He thought it to be very Victorian in appearance and commented upon it.

'Yes.' Bateman resumed his seat behind his desk. 'I dare say you could say that, Victorian . . . quite appropriate. I think we must have been the last plant hire company to introduce new technology and the last to computerize our records. My father didn't like the new machines, as he called them. He was very conservative by nature and he didn't trust what he couldn't understand.'

'Your father?' Hennessey queried.

'Yes, my father. Why, is that a problem for you, sir?'

'No . . . no.' Hennessey shook his head. 'It's just your

nameplate, Mr Bateman; I assumed that you were an employee of Marshall and Evans.'

'Oh no.' Bateman grinned. 'It does confuse people at times but you see Messrs Marshall and Evans retired and my father bought the business, and as part of the sale he was allowed to keep trading under the good name of the company. It is quite a standard business practice. So we then continued to trade as Marshall and Evans and they sold the company for more than it was actually worth on paper; the good name counted for something, you see. You can sell a good name.'

'I see.' Hennessey thumbed through the ledger. 'Beautiful handwriting.'

'Indeed . . . we have had our lean years. I mean, which company hasn't? But unlike the majority of plant hire companies we are not tied solely to the building trade. Our customers include farmers and the agricultural industry as a whole. The building of houses might come to a stop from time to time as the national economy rises and falls but there's always wheat to be harvested, potatoes to be scooped up in huge quantities and loaded into the back of huge bulk-carrying lorries, you'll have doubtless seen the like . . . and there's always ditches to be cleared. All used to be done manually, but nowadays it's all done by machine, most of which are hired for the purpose.'

'I see,' Hennessey said again. 'That's interesting.'

'So,' Bateman continued, 'it is because of our agricultural clients, and only because of them, that we have kept afloat in the inevitable lean times.'

'You are indeed fortunate.' Yellich also leafed through the ledgers.

'Yes, we are.' Bateman nodded. 'And we are not unappreciative. We have a wide client base and farming has meant that this is a stable local economy. It takes a lot to bring agriculture to a standstill.'

'Dare say that's true.'

Bateman leaned back in his chair. 'So . . . if you would like to examine the ledgers at your leisure, gentlemen, I can let you have a small office. It has a small desk and a lovely view of our backyard,' he added with a grin.

Hennessey and Yellich gratefully accepted the offer of the

small office and settled down to leaf through the ledgers while
fortified by cups of tea provided by the smiling receptionist.
Looking at the entries for September of the year in question,
one entry caught Yellich's eye and he drew Hennessey's attention to it. It was a very significant entry because it was the only
entry to record that the hire had been paid for in hard cash. All
the other entries read either 'cheque', 'credit card', or 'charge
to account'. Laying the other ledgers to one side Hennessey
and Yellich carried that particular book to Bateman's office.
Upon tapping on the door they were warmly invited to enter.

'Can you tell me anything about this entry here, Mr
Bateman?' Hennessey rotated the ledger and laid it on Bateman's
desk. He indicated the relevant entry.

'Cash,' Bateman read, 'that is quite unusual, pretty well
unique in fact.'

Hennessey stood upright. 'That is why we are interested in
it, from a police officer's point of view.'

'Can't be traced.' Bateman glanced up at Hennessey and
Yellich. 'Is that the reason for your interest?'

'Yes,' Hennessey replied, 'yes, it is. All other forms of
payment leave a paper trail but hard cash . . . hard cash . . .
the good old folding brown and blue, especially if used and
untraceable, has always been a favoured method of doing
business in the criminal fraternity.'

'So I believe . . . so I believe.' Bateman looked at the ledger.
'So what does the entry tell us? Well, the first thing it tells us
is that it dates from the time before we took over the business,
just by a couple of years, so we won't be able to tell you
anything about it other than what is in the ledger. The handling
agent is given as "E.E.", that would be Edward Evans, of
Evans and Marshall. He is still with us.'

'Still alive?'

'Yes, very much so. The plant in question, a Bobcat 322
. . . it's a mini digger, the smallest design of digger there is.'

'I think I know the type,' Yellich observed.

'Yes.' Bateman glanced at Yellich. 'Small, green-painted
machines. They are very popular with gangs who dig up the
pavements or the roads to access gas and/or water mains. The
operator often looks to be quite cramped in the cab but they

really are a very handy bit of kit, they have a long "reach", as we say, they can get a long way down into the ground. They are designed for digging long, narrow trenches rather than excavating holes or large, deep foundations, and we often hire them to farmers who use them to clear their ditches. They also have a small shovel under the cab at the front, and so can be used like a very small bulldozer.'

'So good for digging graves,' Hennessey asked, 'and also good for filling in of same?'

'Ideal, in fact some of the larger local authorities have bought them for that purpose. They can do in less than an hour what a gravedigger would take a working day to do.'

'We have an interest in a hole about three feet wide and up to six feet deep.'

'So, a grave.' Bateman raised his eyebrows. 'You were not joking?'

'Nope.' Hennessey retained a serious expression. 'Not joking at all. Police inquiries rarely are a laughing matter. You will shortly hear about it in the regional news bulletins and read about it in the press. I dare say it will be the talk of the local pubs this evening.'

'I see. Well I live to the north of York so I won't hear anything in the pubs . . . but yes, three feet wide, six feet deep . . . that size hole is well within the capacity of that type of machine, the Bobcat 322.'

'So what can you tell us about the other vehicles hired out about that time, particularly on that same day?'

Bateman leaned forward and read the ledger. 'All larger types . . . scoopers, the ones used to lift grain into the back of bulk-carrying lorries, as I mentioned earlier . . . just the right time of year to hire those things out to the agricultural sector.'

'So the cash hire stands out?'

'Yes, yes, it does; not only is it the method of payment which makes it stand out but it is not the sort of machine we would hire to farmers in September.' Bateman leaned back in his chair. 'It's a bit too close to harvest time for ditching.'

Hennessey sensed the beginning of a lead in the investigation. 'And the hire charge is what you would expect, not unduly inexpensive or unduly expensive?'

'No, it's about right.' Again Bateman consulted the ledger and turned the page back. 'Look, here is a similar machine . . . a Bobcat 322, hired out in the previous March . . . that would be for clearing ditches . . . and the fee is the same, but . . . but you know there would be a huge cash deposit involved, so much more money would be involved than appears here in the ledger.'

'There would?'

'Oh yes, take it from me, gentlemen, take it from me.' Bateman smiled. 'It is a necessary insurance against theft.'

'Theft of plant?' Yellich confirmed.

'Yes,' Bateman explained, 'plant, you see, is in great demand and it is very expensive, with a long waiting list for new stuff, and about that time, just as we took over the business, there was a spate of plant thefts.'

'Plant thefts as well . . .?'

'As well.'

'It's just that one of my officers interviewed a retired police officer who reported that thirty years ago there was a spate of car thefts, hence my comment of "as well",' Hennessey explained. 'I doubt they would have been linked.'

'Doubt it too.' Bateman nodded. 'Plant theft tends to involve organized crime, not teenagers looking for kicks. People . . . gangs would hire plant and just didn't return it, even when they left a deposit up to the value of a replacement machine because they could sell it for more than its value, even its value when brand new, because builders, especially overseas builders, will pay more than the list price of an earth mover if they can have it in a few days' time, rather than wait eighteen months for a new one.'

'I see,' Hennessey replied quietly, 'that explains a lot.'

'Yes, and it helps the thieves that plant is very easy to conceal,' Bateman added. 'Unlike stolen cars it is rarely driven on the public highway and when it is it is often only for a very short distance. Usually they are carried on roads on low loaders which are always street legal, or are kept on farms or building sites so they don't look out of place, or in the yard of a dodgy plant hire company . . . even less out of place. So anyway, we put a stop to that form of theft by charging a massive deposit, about twice what the vehicle would cost new, and when the word got round that we were doing that we got no more requests for cash hires.'

'So we need to talk to Edward Evans. Where can we contact him?' Hennessey asked. 'I assume he hasn't retired to Spain?'

'No . . . no.' Bateman smiled. 'He retired locally. He's a member of the York and Malton. They went early in life, just forty years old when they sold up and retired. He's a sprightly seventy now, very sprightly. I have found that people age at different rates. Mr Evans has retained much of his youth . . . even if only in his attitude.'

'So, still *compos mentis*?'

'Oh yes, he still has all his marbles.'

'So,' Hennessey queried, 'the York and Malton?'

'Sounds like a building society, doesn't it?' Bateman mused. 'In fact it's a golf club . . . very upmarket, him and his 1960s' Bentley. They are a right pair of characters, him and his old car.'

'You sound like you belong to the same club,' Yellich commented.

'I do . . . my family does.' Bateman shrugged. 'So perhaps it's not so posh after all.'

Carmen Pharoah walked homewards and she did so slowly. She chose not to heed her colleagues' advice and 'walk the walls' as the speediest way to transit the ancient city; rather, on that warm, September afternoon, she walked the pavements. Her route when she walked the pavements took her down Micklegate, over the Ouse Bridge, into Low Ousegate and left into busy commercialized Coney Street, thence on to Blake Street with its solid Victorian buildings, into the graceful curve of St Leonard's Place and finally to Bootham Bar and Bootham itself, perhaps a pleasant forty-five minute stroll, York being small as well as ancient. Yes . . . a car brought her North . . . not untrue, and she was pleased to have been able to explain to the warm and helpful Adrian Clough that her reply to his question was not facetious nor sarcastic. It was a car that had carried her husband's life away one night as he was crossing the road. He was late, the night was dark, the driver was drunk. Both she and her husband had been so very proud to be

Afro-Caribbean employees of the Metropolitan Police. She a Detective Constable and he an accountant, both still in their twenties and both learning the great truth of her father-in-law's edict, 'You're black, that means you've got to be ten times better to be just as good, ten times faster to remain level with the competition, ten times more intelligent to be just as brainy. 'It is,' he had said, 'just the way of it'.

It was little comfort to be told that he wouldn't have known anything, it was instantaneous, nor was it any comfort to know that the driver was to be prosecuted, 'We'll throw the book at him'. It was not just that she had been robbed of the man she loved, and she knew him to be the only man she ever would love, but he had been robbed of his life . . . all that glittering future . . . his career, his fatherhood . . . all . . . all taken away so cruelly, the familial line which had come to an end, the children that will never be . . . and their children, and their children.

The guilt had come a few days later, the guilt of surviving, the sense of shame that she was alive and he was not, and with it the sense of a debt to be repaid, a penance to undertake and so she had transferred to the north, where it is cold in the winter, where the people are insular and do not like strangers. The sort of place where a stranger might get invited to take part in a game of darts, but only if they had been going to the pub every night for the last ten years. Here she had come, and here she will stay until she felt her debt had been fully repaid. She let herself into her small flat on Bootham and showered and changed into casual, comfortable clothes.

A car . . . a car, yes, it was that had brought her north to York.

It was Monday, 15.41 hours.

THREE

Tuesday, 11.10 hours – Wednesday, 01.10 hours

in which a jovial man in a time warp is encountered,
Somerled Yellich makes a worrying connection and
Thomson Ventnor is at home to the most urbane reader.

Third Georgian, thought Webster, as he and Ventnor slowly and purposefully approached the building, though he would stand corrected, fully conceding he was no architectural historian. It was, he thought, a proud and a confident-looking building, standing four square and solid with a protruding entrance way, the roof of which was supported by two large stone columns. The building was of three storeys, he noted, with a steeply angled roof. In front of the building was a wide expanse of pale pink gravel, which gleamed and glittered in the sunlight, and upon which were neatly parked motor cars of the ilk of Rolls Royce, Bentley, Porsche and Range Rover. Both officers saw what George Hennessey had meant when he had said, 'Mind how you go, gentlemen, it's reportedly a posh golf club, very well-to-do'. It was thus with some tongue-in-cheek insolence, wholly approved of by a grinning Ventnor, that Webster parked the small two door police Ford between a Ferrari and Daimler. Leaving the car with one window wound partially down to allow the interior to 'breathe', the two officers walked across the car park, noisily crunching the gravel surface, and entered the cool hotel-like interior of the clubhouse of the York and Malton Golf Club.

'If you have identification, please, gentlemen?' The steward of the golf club wore a dark-coloured blazer with a military association badge on the breast pocket, a neatly pressed blue shirt and tightly knotted black tie, which was held to his shirt with a gold tiepin. He wore sharply creased grey flannel trousers and highly polished black shoes. His hair was close cropped and he was clean-shaven, smelling gently of after-shave. The steward was, guessed Ventnor, about fifty years of age, but he still enjoyed a trim and enviable athletic build. He inspected Ventnor's card closely but politely declined to look at Webster's saying that if one is genuine then so will be the other. Then he added, 'Yes, gentlemen, Mr Edward Evans is indeed a member here,' speaking with a slight trace of a Welsh accent pronouncing 'here' as 'yur'.

'Is he here at the moment?' Ventnor slid his warrant card back inside his jacket pocket and glanced around him at the highly polished wood surfaces of the furniture and the wall panels, and he savoured the scent of furniture polish.

'I don't believe he is, sir,' the steward replied briskly. 'He is expected, though. I do hope there is no trouble?'

'Oh, always plenty of trouble.' Webster smiled, keeping eye contact with the serious-minded steward. 'Enough to keep us gainfully employed, but we seek only to pick Mr Evans' brains. He is not under any suspicion, we can assure you.'

'Yes,' Ventnor added, 'you may rest easy on that score.'

'I see.' The steward inclined his head. 'I am relieved to hear that, for Mr Evans' sake as anyone else's. I have always found him to be a kindly gentleman, a little flamboyant and without the sense of reserve of the greater part of the membership, but kindly, and a gentleman of ethical steadfastness when it comes to the important things in life. I ask because the committee will not like the police coming to the clubhouse for any other reason than the reason you gentlemen have given.'

The police, thought Ventnor, can go anywhere we damn well please, and beside him he sensed Reginald Webster stiffen as he too contained his anger, but he said, 'We seek only his advice on a matter, nothing more.'

The steward smiled. 'Well, perhaps you two gentlemen would care to wait in the lounge? A tray of coffee or tea perhaps?'

'Tea,' Ventnor replied, 'tea for me, please.'

'Same please,' Webster added. 'Thank you.'

The steward showed the officers into the lounge of the clubhouse which they found looked out over the car park and the approach road beyond. The view being obtained through two rectangular sash windows which Ventnor estimated to be probably twelve feet high, reaching almost from floor to ceiling and each about three feet wide. The lounge was at that moment occupied by just six other members, all men, Webster noted, all reclining in leather armchairs, one or two of whom glanced at the officers once and then forgot them, but most of the members ignored Webster and Ventnor completely. In response to their icy reception, the two officers glanced at each other and smiled as they sat in a corner seat, near the door, in front of a highly polished low, circular, wooden table. A bar ran the length of the lounge opposite the windows and the elderly barman, in a white shirt, black tie and scarlet waistcoat, looked at the officers curiously. Ventnor and Webster sat in silence, growing to enjoy the library-like quiet which had developed in the room. It was, they felt, a silence of mutual respect rather than the highly stressed silence of things unsaid. It was, they found, a very relaxing atmosphere and both Webster and Ventnor saw then the attraction of spending a weekday after-noon at the golf club if one had the luxury of sufficient time to spare. A young woman in a long-skirted maid's outfit with a starched white apron approached Webster and Ventnor carrying a tray upon which was a large teapot, milk, two cups and saucers and a plate of biscuits. 'With the compliments of the club, gentlemen,' she said as she lay the tray upon the circular table and then quietly withdrew.

Webster and Ventnor enjoyed the tea and biscuits whilst relaxing in the leather-bound armchairs looking out at the view the window offered.

'Red Kite.' Webster indicated a bird wheeling above the field adjacent, to the right of the approach road, against a backdrop of blue sky.

'I'll take your word for it.' Ventnor helped himself to another chocolate digestive biscuit, pleased that they were the darker, plain chocolate, variety. 'It's a hawk of some sort though, that I can tell.'

'It's the fan-shaped tail,' Webster advised, 'that's how you can tell the Red Kite from other similar sized raptors.'

'Didn't know you were a birdwatcher.' Ventnor reached for a copy of *Yorkshire Life* which lay on the wide window sill.

Webster also took a biscuit from the plate. 'I'm not, not

any more. I used to dabble when I was a teenager, so I still remember things, but I never got to see a Peregrine Falcon in flight. They're the fast jets of the avian world. They can fly at in excess of two hundred miles an hour. That's on the list of things to do before I sleep my final sleep . . . to see a Peregrine Falcon in flight.'

'Still plenty of time . . .' Ventnor stopped talking as the steward approached.

'This is Mr Evans now, gentlemen –' the steward indicated towards the car park – 'the Bentley.'

'Thank you.' Ventnor glanced out of the window as did Webster. They watched as a two-tone Bentley, black over bronze, of late 1950s' vintage, entered the car park and was parked neatly between two Volvos. A portly, golden-haired man dressed in a light-coloured suit with 'plus four' trousers got out of the car, as did a noticeably younger woman who tottered round the rear of the Bentley on four-inch heels, hooked her arm into his, and then together they walked across the car park towards the golf clubhouse.

'I will introduce Mr Evans.' The steward turned and walked towards the foyer.

Webster grinned at Ventnor. 'Methinks I am going to like Mr Evans muchly.'

'Methinks likewise.' Ventnor returned Webster's wide grin. 'Methinks likewise and, as you say, muchly so.'

A few moments later the steward of the golf club returned in the company of Edward Evans and his younger, much younger, lady companion. Webster and Ventnor stood smartly and shook Mr Evans by the hand as he was introduced. Evans then introduced his lady friend as Molly. Molly, guessed the officers, was in her mid-thirties, slender, but yet should, they both thought, be in the next larger dress size. Evans despatched Molly to the bar with a wholly politically incorrect, though playful, slap on her bottom, saying, 'Men talk, sweetheart.' Molly tottered obediently and indignantly towards the bar in her wasp-waisted, below the knees, red dress.

'It's all part of the game,' Evans explained. 'Couldn't act like that these days but that's the joy of the people I mix with . . . the clothing, the old car . . . the floozy of whom the wife would not approve. I tend to introduce Molly as my niece, but I know it wouldn't wash with two worldly-wise officers of the law.'

'Probably wouldn't,' Webster replied, 'but it wouldn't be any of our business anyway.'

'Whatever . . . Shall we sit down?' Evans took a seat by the table. Webster and Ventnor also sat. 'I like to feel I am in that era, the late 1950s, when rock and roll was the thing, Macmillan was the prime minister, the Suez Crisis, Cold War, and me, at my age, with a floozy of her age.' Edward Evans glanced at Molly who was by then perched on a bar stool in front of a gin and tonic and seeming to Webster and Ventnor to be growing in indignation. 'She's a lovely lady but the dragon would not approve.'

'The dragon?'

'The wife,' Evans explained with a sigh. 'She's a little highly strung and capable of throwing real tantrums. I mean it is "Bikini State Red . . . real DEFCON One" if she gets even a little bit angry, so I have to be discreet, even making a detour before I pick up Molly in case the Dragon has put a private eye on my trail. She'd do that, you know, she really would. The Dragon lost all interest in our marriage years ago . . . on every level . . . but does all she can to keep me reigned in. But, a blessing is this: she is not interested in the Fifties set.'

'The Fifties set?' Ventnor queried.

'It's a group of eccentrics . . . I belong to the Yorkshire chapter. We meet once or twice a month or so dressed in 1950s' clothing and drive 1950s' cars if we can. My car is actually a 1962 model but the design dates from the 1950s . . . so we "jive" the afternoon away. We go on outings every now and again and once hired a 1950s' double-decker bus and went to Scarborough for the day. The owner of the bus wouldn't drive her "baby" as she called it, at more than thirty miles an hour . . . and this was a Bank Holiday Monday . . . so by the time we arrived at the coast we had quite a stream of angry motorists behind us . . . really quite a following. We had an afternoon in Scarborough, all the boys in baggy trousers and double-breasted jackets and all the girls in long flowing skirts and dresses.'

'Sounds fun.' Webster was encouraged that Evans seemed willing to relax in the company of himself and Ventnor. He thought it augured well for a cooperative member of the public.

'It's great fun, it's what the Brits are good at, producing eccentrics, and I get to pat Molly on her bottom . . . 1950s' attitudes you see. So, the steward said that you wanted some information from me, want to pick my brains, what's left of 'em. So I'll just go and get myself a nip.' Evans indicated the bar. 'You two gentlemen don't want . . .?'

'Can't, sir,' Webster replied warmly, 'we are on duty, but thanks anyway.'

'Very well.' Edward Evans stood and walked confidently to the bar, next to where Molly was sitting, ordered a whisky with dry ginger and another gin for Molly, with whom he exchanged a few words and then returned to the table where Webster and Ventnor waited. Seated once more, he asked, 'So how can I help you? Pick away.' He sipped his drink. 'Pick, pick away.'

'We understand you used to own Evans and Marshall Plant Hire Co.?'

'Yes, founded the business, built it up from scratch and sold it for our retirement money. That's the way to really make money, start a business and build it up, then sell it as a going concern. The Batemans will have to work for longer than we did before they recover their investment, but if they play the game they'll sell it on for their retirement money.'

'Yes, we met Mr Bateman junior, or rather our boss did. He put us on to you.'

'Nice young fella. He's a member here but he doesn't play . . . one arm you see. He or his father can't help you? I am well out of touch these days.'

'No, unfortunately they can't.' Webster leaned forward. 'You see, this is the tricky bit, or as our boss would say, "this is a long shot", but as he would also say, "they've paid off before".'

'So shoot away.' Evans grinned. 'Let's see where we get. I do so love an adventure. I'm in my seventies now but I'm still game for an adventure.'

'Well, sir.' Webster opened his notebook. 'This is going back a way but we would like to know if you can recollect a particular transaction, a hire of machinery some thirty years ago this month.'

'Thirty years ago this month . . .' Evans pursed his lips. 'That would be just before we sold the company. I might recall a particular transaction but only if it had some distinct aspect to it, or if it had some personal significance for me or my partner, or for the company as a whole . . . or if it was memorable in some other way . . . unusual sort of customer, for example, that sort of thing.'

'All right,' Webster replied, 'we might be able to help you there. Can you go back thirty years . . .?'

'I think so . . . I'll try . . . I like going back in time, the Fifties set and all that. So, thirty years ago I was a sprightly forty-seven years of age, our marriage still had a semblance of life about it . . . the old flame of passion . . . hot, hot passion had not been entirely extinguished. Heavens, we even slept in the same bed in those days. Now it's not just separate beds but separate rooms for us. We still eat together, though, we manage to do that. The children were still at home, just. I can recall that period . . . it's beginning to come back. I recall that period, not as halcyon days, though. I recall the bad weather, the flooding . . . I remember the car breaking down. I ran an old Vauxhall in those days; the Bentley out there is or was a pre-retirement present to myself. I saw her advertised as a "classic", so called, in a specialist car magazine and drove down to Devon to collect her. I brought her back on a trailer pulled by a company Land Rover, but I paid the diesel out of my own pocket . . . that kept it legal.'

'Good for you.'

'Well, it was that time; we were selling to the Batemans. The discussions were at a very early stage and it was a year or two before we completed, but we wanted them to purchase clean books. So, yes, I recall the era quite well . . . it's all coming back. So, the transaction you are interested in, what can you tell me about it?'

'It was the hire of a small digger, a Bobcat 322 we believe.'

'Yes, I know the type, used for entrenching or ditch clearance.' Evans sipped his whisky. 'It's the smallest type of plant available.'

'So we believe,' Ventnor said.

'Yes, we had those machines. We had six; they were, probably still are, very popular little beasts. In fact, we soon recovered our purchase price on the Bobcats, which fact might be a hindrance to you.'

'Oh,' Webster asked, 'in what way?'

'Well, their popularity you see. We had many customers wanting to hire those things,' Evans explained. 'They came in and they went straight back out again. They were in such demand that we barely had time to give them a quick hose down and basic service before they were hired out again. I mean, they were in such demand that it was not at all unusual for a customer to say "don't bother washing it, we need it yesterday".'

'I see . . . could complicate things as you say.' Webster tapped his ballpoint on his notepad. 'Can I ask how your customers paid?'

'Cheque, or credit card . . . or sometimes charged to their account.'

'Always?'

'Always.' Evans nodded. 'Always any one of those three methods.'

'This customer didn't,' Webster replied. 'If he hired from you and didn't go out of the area to hire plant from another company, then this customer, the one who interests us, paid in cash, hard cash, and our boss saw one such entry in the ledger. It is likely to be our man.'

'So a hard cash transaction, thirty years ago this month,' Ventnor prompted.

'There will be a name in the ledger,' Evans queried, 'surely that would be a logical trail for you to follow?'

'It will be a false name,' Ventnor explained. 'The Bobcat was used . . . so we believe . . . in respect of a commission of a crime.'

'Oh.' Evans sat back in his chair. 'I see, so hence the police interest?'

'Hence the police interest,' Ventnor echoed. 'That's why we are here.'

'Yes.' Evans took another sip of his whisky. 'Do you know,

I do think I am able to recall that hire . . . it was, as you say, unusual in that the payment was in hard cash.' He moved his right hand in a slow, circular motion. 'Let me see if I can bring it back.'

'Take your time, sir,' Webster encouraged, 'but details are crucial.'

'Of course, the Devil is in the detail and all that, but I need more of this stuff though.' He raised his empty glass of whisky. 'You know the most untrue thing of all? Shall I tell you?'

'Tell us,' Ventnor replied.

'That you can drink to forget, because just the opposite happens, believe me. If you drink enough booze you start to remember things. That's true, take it from me.' Evans stood. 'I'll be back in just one little jiffy.'

Edward Evans once again walked across the carpeted floor to the bar, ordered a drink and chatted to Molly, who was observed to shrug her shoulders at whatever it was he said to her, and he then returned, drink in hand, to the corner table where Webster and Ventnor sat. Evans sat down looking pleased with himself. 'Do you fellas know, I do think I can recall that hire.'

'Really?' Ventnor smiled. 'It would be very useful, crucial in fact, if you can.'

'Yes, really, it was . . . it really is the unusual nature of payment that makes it stick out in my old mind.' He took a long, loving sip of his drink. 'Plant hire is a risky business; a lot of folk want to hire plant in order to sell it, usually overseas.'

'So our boss told us.'

'Yes, hurts the business, the inconvenience of having to wait eighteen months before a new piece of kit can be delivered and of course the insurance premiums rocket.'

'So we understand,' Webster commented. 'An unfortunate business all round.'

'Hence the need to be able to identify our customers.'

'Of course.'

'So, the customer who wanted to pay cash . . .' Evans glanced out of the window. 'What can I remember about him?'

'Alarm bells?' Ventnor suggested. 'Dare say the request to pay cash in hand made you suspicious?'

'Yes . . . I am remembering now. I seem to remember that although we were doing good business overall at that time, and the Bobcats were in particular demand, we had two of them sitting in the yard. Both nice and clean and fully serviced because we had had time to wash them, so it must have been a bit of a quiet time for trench digging.' Evans took another sip of his drink. 'I recall that we were not happy with the cash payment but the customer was most insistent . . . and he wanted it in a hurry.'

'That's interesting,' Webster commented.

'Is it?'

'Well, possibly the crime had been committed by then, rather than being anticipated.'

'I see. Now I kid you not, it was only when he agreed to deposit not only the full cost of replacing the machine but also agreed to add fully thirty per cent on top as surety that we agreed to hire it for cash. He was unlikely to steal it and try to sell it then you see. Cost of replacement plus thirty per cent, he wouldn't get his money back if he sold it on, no questions asked.'

'That's not cheap,' Ventnor commented. 'So the customer was monied?'

'Must have been,' Evans agreed.

'So you hired it on those terms?' Webster confirmed.

'Yes.' Evans nodded. 'He said he would send his man in.'

'Ah,' Ventnor interrupted, 'so you never saw the customer?'

'No, the negotiation was done by phone.'

'All right . . . sorry I interrupted.' Ventnor smiled. 'Please continue.'

'Yes, so the next day a gentleman arrived carrying a suitcase. Said suitcase was full of twenties and fifties . . . the sum agreed . . . all of it.'

'No wonder you remember it,' Webster gasped.

'Yes, it's coming back to me and is doing so with great clarity.' Evans grinned. 'We were still a little wary so we offered him a cup of coffee while we counted it.'

'Fingerprints?' Ventnor guessed. 'Get his dabs as a bit of extra insurance?'

'Yes, exactly.' Evans tapped the side of his nose with his

right forefinger. 'Softly, softly, catchee monkey, as they say. We wiped the mug down first and handed the coffee to him on a tray.'

'Clever.' Ventnor winked at Evans. 'Good move.'

'Yes, we thought so. When he left with the Bobcat we picked the mug up using a ballpoint pen through the handle, put it in a large manila envelope and left it on one side, but he returned the digger on time the next morning and said, "You can wash my prints off the coffee mug now". So he was just as clever as we thought we were. Anyway he collected the suitcase full of cash and drove away. We washed the mug and that was that.'

'Were there any indications that you recall as to where he used the machine,' Webster wondered. 'I emphasize, that you recall?'

'None that I can recall, as you say.' Evans stroked the knee of his plus four trousers with a large, fleshy hand. 'Like I said, he returned the Bobcat the following forenoon so whatever it had been used for it wasn't a big job. Thereafter I am afraid the memory merges with other returned hires, no details about the return have stayed with me.'

'Fair enough.' Webster nodded briefly. 'We believe that it was used overnight so it could have been a larger job than you might have thought.'

'No reason why it shouldn't be used during the hours of darkness. Plant is often used at night, to minimize disruption of traffic, for example.'

'I see. How did he transport it?'

'A trailer, he brought a suitably sized trailer behind his Land Rover . . . ran it on to the trailer and towed it away, nothing of note about the Land Rover or the trailer . . . metal frame, aluminium ramps. We did take a note of the number plate of the Land Rover.' Evans held his hand up. 'Sorry, don't get excited, we did it as a safeguard and when the Bobcat was returned we destroyed the paper with the number plate on it, just as we washed the mug with the man's prints on it. The man and his boss had played the game, you see, kept to the agreement.'

'Fair play,' Ventnor mumbled, then he asked, 'What can

you tell us about the two guys, the one on the phone first . . .
the customer?'

'The customer, as I recall, he was old money, posh . . .
relaxed . . . used to getting his own way but relaxed with it.
Calm authority I seem to recall. He wasn't brassy, excited,
overbearing new money, or like someone who had just scooped
the jackpot on the football pools, nothing like that. Male, as
I have indicated. Couldn't put a finger on his age range,
possibly younger adult rather than older adult, you'll appreciate
that my memory is clouded by the mists of time.'

'Yes, fair enough,' Webster conceded. 'The second man, the
one who picked up the Bobcat . . .'

'Yes, him, I remember more about him, helped by the fact
that I set eyes on him and spoke to him. So . . . so . . . well
he, on the other hand, was not monied, not as I recall, by his
manner nor by his appearance, though appearances can be
misleading . . . the bankrupt who dresses well and the million-
aire who wears denims . . . but I thought him to be scratching
his pennies, again as I recall. He struck me, if I remember
correctly, as a factotum, but a factotum who could be entrusted
with a great deal of money. It was the case, I thought, that he
was a most reliable and trustworthy employee, as if an old
family retainer, or somebody who had a gun pointed at his
head so as to dissuade him of the notion of doing a runner
with the money, or perhaps he just didn't know what was in
the suitcase . . . but the third option would have been a risky
one for the customer, I would have thought, but who knows?'
Evans raised his eyebrows. 'Who knows?'

'We hope we will get to know,' Ventnor replied drily. 'Do
you recall anything else about him?'

'Well, I doubt he'll still be alive, I can tell you that. He was
older than I was, much older, and this was thirty years ago.'
Evans sipped his whisky. 'I do remember calling him "sir",
not just because he was a customer but also . . . in fact more
so, because of my natural deference to age. I am the product
of a very traditional childhood and was brought up to show
proper respect to my "elders and betters". Mind you, as I grew
up I found myself challenging the logic of that notion. I mean,
are our elders necessarily our "betters"? You know my grandson

has the correct logic, if you ask me; he has a sign on his bedroom door which reads, "Why should I tidy my room when your generation has made such a mess of the world?"'

Webster and Ventnor laughed softly.

'Mind you.' Evans raised a finger with a gleam in his eye. 'I countered that,' he continued with an equally gentle laugh. 'I got hold of a sticker which read, "Grab yourself a teenager while they still know everything", and next time I visited my daughter and her husband, I stuck it on his door above his sign. He was not amused by all accounts, my grandson I mean, he was not amused. My son-in-law thought it was a huge joke but my grandson tore it off his door and shredded it.'

'I can understand that,' Ventnor replied. 'Teenagers take themselves very seriously.'

'That's true.' Evans continued to grin. 'They don't like being put right, teenagers don't. But if the old factotum is still alive, he'll be a hundred up by now and we men don't live forever, not like women. They just go on and on.'

'We can try and find him,' Webster said. 'We can but try.'

'Yes, that's the right attitude, you can but try. I remember he was of stocky build . . . and –' Evans raised his finger again – 'he was a Scotsman, that I suddenly remember.'

'Scottish?' Ventnor sat forward. 'That is useful, that will narrow the field down considerably, quite considerably indeed.'

'Imagine it would.' Evans swilled the whisky round his glass. 'The Scots gave us this stuff and he was a Scotsman. Strange how it all floods back. I recall in my mind's eye a stocky, ginger-haired bloke, short but barrel-chested. He wore a tartan cap. I remember I commented on his accent. I really was trying to get as much information about him as I could . . . still suspicious, you see. So I commented on his accent.'

'Yes,' Ventnor replied, 'understood.'

'I was still wary of criminal intent on his behalf and I remember he looked away and down at the floor and said, "Aye, I made a lassie pregnant when I was down here with the army and so I stayed". So I thought, good for you, Jock, squaring up to your responsibilities like that. Any other guy would have gone home and left the lass struggling alone with a newborn infant. Confess I might have done just that if I was in his situation. I mean, if I had been up in Scotland and I had made a Scots girl pregnant, then knowing me I would have likely said, "I've heard the poem darling, and your heart might be in the Highlands, but mine isn't".' Evans paused. 'Well, I don't know, possibly I would have stayed, my seed and all that, or brought her south with me, but I doubt that I could tear myself from my roots because of a single moment of indiscretion. I love this part of the world you see, just love it, but I do recall feeling a little more reassured when he told me that.' Evans shrugged. 'He was evidently an honourable man, so I felt a little safer letting him take the Bobcat away. Even though I had the suitcase full of money, I still felt more reassured by his attitude to that girl all those years earlier.'

'So he was a Scotsman who had a wife and child and who lived in this area?' Ventnor confirmed.

'Yes, he seemed to be familiar with the area, drove here and drove away again quite confidently,' Evans replied. 'Didn't seem to have a map, didn't ask directions. I thought him to be in his sixties then.'

'And ginger haired?'

Evans glanced out of the window. 'Yes, fiery ginger hair, if not red haired . . . more like red hair really, very Scottish.'

'Would you recognize him again?' Webster asked, and then added, 'Allowing for the passage of time?'

'I can only say possibly,' Evans replied. 'Possibly.'

'Photographs.' Webster turned to Ventnor. 'I was thinking of photographs.'

'Yes.' Ventnor smiled. 'He might have been known to us, so by the passage of time, you mean going back?'

'Yes.' Webster nodded. 'Mr Evans here might be able to recognize the gentleman in an earlier phase of the man's life. Could you look through our albums, sir?' Webster turned to Evans.

'I could, certainly won't do any harm but he didn't seem like a felon. As I said, he seemed to me to have a sense of duty and a sense of ethic about him.' Evans held eye contact with Webster. 'But, yes, I am willing to look at your photograph albums; might be worth a flutter. When would you like me to call in?'

'A.s.a.p.' Ventnor replied.

'Well, you'll need me more sober than I am now.'

'You're not driving any more today, sir?' Ventnor enquired with a note of caution in his voice.

'Just onwards from here to the Fifties club . . . just had two and mostly it was ginger. I'll be all right. I'll have lunch, then three or four more of these lovely little gems. After that the pretty little popsie will take the wheel. She'll have lime juice and soda for the rest of the day, I've got that bit covered, got it well covered. I couldn't get by without being able to drive. So you see the popsie has her uses. So shall we say ten of the clock upon ye morrow forenoon? Suit you, gentlemen?'

'Suits admirable.' Webster smiled. 'Thank you, sir.'

'Good, that's settled.' Evans grinned. 'That will take me very nicely to yardarm time, lovely, lovely yardarm time. I'll have the dragon drive me into York.'

'Micklegate Bar Police Station, sir,' Ventnor added.

'Yes, I know it. So I'll look at the photographs then I'll call in at the old pub, have lunch, stroll over to the popsie's. You know it sounds like a good day is about to shape up for me tomorrow. Retirement is like a long holiday, I can tell you. I can't recommend it too highly. You two young fellas should look forward to it. You know I was talking to a popsie just the other day, not my floozy over there –' Evans indicated Molly who was still perched upon a bar stool, still looking indignant – 'but another popsie, and when she asked me how old I was, I said twenty-five, and she laughed out loud and said, "Come on", so I said, "I mean it, I'm twenty-five. If you are as old as you feel, I am twenty-five".' Evans stood. 'Life is good, it is still very good.'

George Hennessey read and then carefully re-read the report which had been faxed to Micklegate Bar Police Station, for his attention, from the forensic science laboratory at Wetherby. He relaxed back in his chair as he read with a great deal of interest that, as Dr D'Acre had surmised, four of the five skeletons were related: parents and two daughters who were full siblings. The fifth skeleton, a young adult female, had no genetic link to the other four skeletons. He glanced up at

Webster and Ventnor who sat in front of his desk patiently
waiting for him to complete reading the report. 'So,' he said,
'the fifth victim, who is she? A friend of the family who was
in the wrong place at the wrong time? An unconnected victim
of a second wholly unconnected but contemporary crime?'

'I dare say that is for us to find out.' Webster smiled.

'Yes.' Hennessey returned the smile. He found over time
that he liked Webster's attitude, he had an enthusiasm, a
go-getting attitude which seemed to be lacking in Ventnor.
Ventnor, it had always seemed to Hennessey, would work if
he was given a job to do, Webster on the other hand had the
initiative to find work. 'Yes, it is as you say, Webster, up to
us to find out.' He laid the report down. 'So, do you fancy a
trip to the Smoke?'

'The Smoke, sir,' Webster queried, 'where is that?'

'London, the Great Wen, also known in medieval times as
the Great Maw.'

'Wen? Maw?' Webster was puzzled.

'A wen is a cyst . . . so it is a great blot on the landscape,
large and unsightly, and a maw . . . a maw, also from medieval
English, is a stomach.' Hennessey patted his stomach 'That's
your maw. London is a huge thing which swallows other
smaller things.'

'I see, sir, thank you for the history lesson, but frankly,'
Webster replied, 'I do not fancy a trip to the Smoke, or the
Great Wen, or the Great Maw. London is not my favourite
place. I could never understand the draw it has, the magnetism
that holds folk there. I find far-famed London Town to be dirty
and untidy and smelly.'

'And overcrowded.' Hennessey grinned. 'I'm with you all the
way, even as a Londoner myself. I am in complete agreement
with you, complete agreement, but someone has to go and talk to
the surviving relative of the missing family, the Parrs.'

'Yes, sir,' Webster replied with a groan. 'Essential . . . has
to be done.'

'I've already broken the bad news to DS Yellich; he'll be
going with you.'

'Yes, sir, I'll be glad of the company.'

'Ventnor.' Hennessey glanced at Thomson Ventnor.

'Sir?'

'Missing person reports of thirty years ago, trawl through them, link up with Carmen Pharoah if you have to. We have to identify the fifth victim.'

'Yes, sir.'

'As for me, I have a press release to prepare: witnesses to a crime sought, possibly two crimes, over a quarter of a century old.' Hennessey reached forward and picked up his telephone. 'Ah well, I am advised needles have actually been found in haystacks. Oh, thank you for digging up Mr Evans this morning. I read your recording, potentially very interesting . . . a Scotsman with a suitcase of readies. We'll see if he can pick out a photograph tomorrow. I'll ask Carmen Pharoah to show him the albums.'

Thomson Ventnor calmly and methodically read the missing person reports from thirty years previously which had been collated by Carmen Pharoah. There had been many people reported missing in York during that period but only three files remained open. Three persons in the Vale of York had disappeared thirty years previously and who still remained missing. The greatest number of missing person reports of that year had been closed within twenty-four hours of the 'mis per' in question having returned home, or had been found alive, either safe and well, or found injured or seriously ill, but nonetheless alive. A smaller number had been closed when the missing person had been found deceased, either through misadventure, natural causes or foul play. Those latter cases were tragic and often traumatic for the family of the victim, but at least those families had some closure once they knew what had happened to their relative. But three families, whose loved one disappeared in the Vale of York thirty years earlier, still, after all that time, had no closure. Of the three open missing person files dated thirty years earlier only one was female. Thomson Ventnor sipped his tea as he read the report.

Michelle Lemmon was twenty-one years old when she was reported missing in the April of the year in question. She was five feet eight inches tall, dark haired and at the time had been unemployed. She did though, it was reported, sometimes take employment as a part-time barmaid. She had been reported missing by her parents who provided a 'very recent' photograph of her, showing her to be an ordinary, plain-looking woman. She was, in Ventnor's eye, no head-turning beauty, but neither did she seem to be the sort of girl who would have struggled to find a partner. It was, though, the eyes which reached Ventnor; Michelle Lemmon's soul was, he thought, an angry soul. A very angry soul indeed. Ventnor had observed just that look in the eyes of criminals who had been photographed upon their arrest and charging, as if they had been served some dreadful injustice. The photograph of Michelle Lemmon seemed to Ventnor to be a perfunctory photograph, clearly taken at a photo booth for a passport or bus pass or similar. Yet the anger in the eyes could not be concealed. Her address was given as 197 Third Avenue, Tang Hall, York.

Ventnor signed out at Micklegate Bar Police Station, leaving a note as to where he was visiting and commenced to walk the short distance – about, he thought, one mile as the crow would fly and perhaps half as much again on foot – to the last given address of Michelle Lemmon. It was, he found, a good walking day in terms of the weather, not too warm, a near clear blue sky with just a hint of cloud at high altitude, and no indication of imminent rainfall. It was, he also thought, a good opportunity to refresh in himself the feel of the city. He believed that the police should not lose touch with the community they served, for policing does not, he thought, only mean controlling and investigating, but it also means caring for, being guardian of, and only by walking, he would argue, can a police officer retain the sense of being in touch. Once he had, for a very brief period, been a postman and he never felt closer to any streets anywhere than he had felt close to the streets of his 'walk'. Even on his beat as a junior constable he had never experienced the level of contact he felt that he had experienced with the streets, the cul de sacs, the front gardens and letterboxes of his 'walk' as a postman.

And so he walked, observing the broad sweep of the urban landscape, observing details closer at hand, always observing. As he turned into the Tang Hall estate he began to attract hostile glances from idle youths as though he had the word 'police' stamped in large letters upon his forehead. He walked through the narrow streets of the housing estate; low-rise council accommodation, narrow streets, small gardens, very second-hand cars and motorcycles chained to lamp posts. He turned into the common entrance of number 197 on Third Avenue and climbed the stairs, two at a time, until he read 'Lemmon' and also 'Parkes' on the nameplates on a door on the second floor. He knocked twice, tap . . . tap . . . using the metal knocker attached to the bronze letterbox. Ventnor's knock was calm, methodical, and with a distinct pause between each tap. It was a police officer's knock.

The door was flung open almost the instant he tapped on the door for the second time by a small, finely built, waif-like woman, who glared up at Ventnor with undisguised hostility. 'What!' she demanded. 'What do you want?'

'Police.' Ventnor showed his ID while remaining calm and composed in the presence of the woman's aggression.

'What?' The woman repeated her demand with no notice-able abatement of her anger, which by then was suggesting to Ventnor that the woman was mentally unwell. Certainly she was emotionally unstable. Behind her Ventnor could see the disordered state of the interior of her flat.

'Mrs Lemmon?' Ventnor asked.

'No!' And with that, the angry, waif-like woman slammed the door shut.

'Where does she live? Do you know?' Ventnor spoke softly to the closed door, not expecting a reply but he was clearly heard because the woman replied angrily from within her home, 'Don't know, don't know . . . don't know, don't care. I don't know and I don't care.'

'Well, thanks anyway,' Ventnor whispered.

Behind him the other door on the second floor opened. Ventnor turned. A late middle-aged woman stood on the threshold of her flat. 'Did you say you were the police?' she asked of Ventnor, softly, pleasantly.

'Yes . . . yes, I did.' Ventnor showed the woman his ID. 'DC Ventnor, Micklegate Bar Police Station.'

'And you are looking for the Lemmons? Sorry I was in my hall by the door and I could not help but overhear.'

'Yes, ma'am,' Ventnor replied. 'Yes, I am.'

'You're a little late.' The woman smiled. By her wedding ring Ventnor noted she was 'Mrs', and by the name on her door he noted she was 'Wheatley'. 'They don't live there any more, Mr and Mrs Lemmon. Bit sad that time was. Nice couple. She –' Mrs Wheatley pointed to the door across the landing – 'Hilda Parkes, she is just too lazy to take their name off the door, and as you might have guessed, she bounces in and out of the mental hospital, and I think she's about ready for another bounce in there. That'll give me peace and a quiet life for a few weeks. Anyway, the Lemmons, they never got over the loss of their daughter. She disappeared twenty-five . . . no . . . more than that . . .'

'Thirty,' Ventnor said. 'She disappeared thirty years ago.'

'Yes . . . I remember her, quiet sort of girl, but horrible for her family never knowing what happened to her. It's worse than her predeceasing them, that would be bad, but the not knowing . . . horrible way to have to live. It would gnaw away at me . . .' Mrs Wheatley sighed. 'Horrible for them.'

'Yes,' Ventnor agreed, 'I'd feel the same. I'd rather know than not know, even if it is bad news . . . I'd still rather know than not know.' Ventnor paused. 'Are there any relatives of Michelle Lemmon living?'

'Just her brother, Harry Lemmon.'

'Is he close by?'

'Yes, he's on the estate, he's "tangy" born and bred.'

'Do you know his address?'

'Well so long as it didn't come from me.' Mrs Wheatley smiled. 'He's still a bit of a wide boy . . . even at his age.'

'Deal.' Ventnor winked. 'Mum's the word.'

'OK. He lives just two streets away on Eighth Avenue.'

'That's two streets away? But this is Ninth Avenue?' Ventnor queried.

'Turn right as you leave this address . . . go right at the end of our street and just follow your nose.' Mrs Wheatley was a portly lady, smartly dressed with a neat hairstyle and with, Ventnor thought, eyes which had a real warmth about them. 'You'll see what I mean.'

'OK, thank you, ma'am. Appreciated.'

'Second entrance on the right on Eighth Avenue, first floor, no name on the door. I visit that stair, you see.'

'Got it. Thanks again.' Ventnor turned away as the door to Mrs Wheatley's flat was gently closed. He walked down the stairway, which he found to be cleanly swept and smelling of disinfectant. He reached the street and followed the directions to Eighth Avenue. He climbed the narrow stairway of the second address up to the first floor and on finding the door with no nameplate he knocked upon it, using the same authoritative police officer's knock that he had used just a moment ago. He noted that the door had a battered and a scarred surface, as if, Ventnor mused, it had been used for knife throwing practice. He knocked on the door a second time after there was no response for thirty seconds to his first taps.

'Wait!' The shout came from deep within the flat and had an irritated ring to it: an angry man. Ventnor waited, noticing as he did so that the stair had a musty smell but was nonetheless cleanly swept. Eventually the door was opened in a calm, casual manner.

'Yes! What?' The man had a hard face with cold, blue piercing eyes.

'Mr Lemmon?' Ventnor asked. 'Mr Harry Lemmon?'

'Aye.' Lemmon spoke with a chilling voice and he seemed to be openly hostile.

'Police,' Ventnor explained.

'I know . . . I know who you are, I can tell. But just one of you? You usually come in threes and fours when I am to be lifted . . . at least four. Once it took six of you to get me in the back of the van.'

'I can believe that.' Ventnor smiled, trying to calm the situation. 'But I am not here to arrest you.'

'You're not?' A note of relief crept into the man's voice.

'Nope.' Ventnor continued to smile. 'Why? Should I?'

'Well, let's just say you could if you knew,' Lemmon replied icily. 'Mind you, I dare say you could arrest half this estate if you knew what they'd been up to.'

'It's often . . . in fact, always the way of it.' Ventnor spoke softly and was pleased that Lemmon's manner appeared to be relaxing. Ventnor noted the man to be short but powerfully built, barrel-chested, a weightlifter of a man, and he could understand why it had once taken six constables to get him into the back of a police van. 'You know, if we knew all that's been did, and all that's been hid, well, there just would not be enough prison space, we'd be arresting half the population.'

'Seems that way to me, so why pick on me? Why knock on my door?'

'I . . . well, we need information.'

'Hey . . . listen . . . I don't grass.' Lemmon began to close the door. 'Not for anyone . . . not for any money . . . and no matter how much is in it for me.'

'About your sister,' Ventnor explained quietly. 'We need information about your sister.'

'My sis—' Lemmon gasped.

'Michelle, about your sister, Michelle.'

'She disappeared.' Harry Lemmon relaxed fully and became curious.

'We know,' Ventnor replied. 'We might have some news but I am afraid it's not good news.'

'Any news of Michelle is good news, even if it's bad.' Lemmon stepped slowly aside. 'You'd better come in, boss.'

Ventnor entered a small, two bedroomed, untidily kept flat. Harry Lemmon, barefoot, padded after him, clad only in faded denim jeans and a saggy, baggy blue tee shirt.

'It's not Buckingham Palace,' Lemmon said, 'and I am not expecting a visit from *Ideal Home* to do a photo shoot, not until next week anyway, but it's where I live, comfortably . . . as comfortably as I can on what the Government allows.' Lemmon shook his head slowly. 'Job Seekers Allowance, no one can live on it. No wonder we doley's have to bend the law.'

'Not break it?' Ventnor grinned.

'The old black economy in the main, boss, work for hard cash and on the hush-hush.' Lemmon shrugged.

'Are you sure that you want to tell me that?' Ventnor began to warm to Harry Lemmon, detecting an essential honesty about the man, 'wide boy' that he may be.

'Somehow I don't think you'd be very interested, boss,' Lemmon replied. 'It would be a cheap conviction for you. I mean if I told you I burgled houses or stole cars for the extra money then . . . then I reckon you might be interested, but washing up at the Indian restaurant three nights a week for a free meal and a few pounds cash in hand, somehow I think that would be too small beer for you.'

'And you'd be right, that is illegal, and I am very not interested despite it being against the law.' Ventnor glanced round the flat. He saw nothing that could be of interest or concern to the police. 'Very not interested.'

'It's all I get up to these days.' Lemmon sighed. 'My crooking days are gone, well behind me. I'm in my fifties now. A bit of extra cash and a quiet life, that's all I need . . . all I want, and when I said it took six cops to put me in the back of a van, well that did happen, but it was twenty years ago.'

'Didn't think I knew your name.' Ventnor grinned. 'Not a recent or a regular customer of ours.'

'Hope it stays that way . . . and working the black economy . . . well the government snoopers have to catch me at it and who's going to follow me home at two a.m. on a winter's night? I mean, not many, Benny, not many.' Lemmon paused. 'And I take a different route to work and a different route home from the routes I used two days before.'

'I reckon you're safe,' Ventnor said, 'as safe as houses.'

'I can't work on a building site or wash cars in the second-hand car garage but, in the kitchen of an eatery, at night, no one will see me. So, my sister, Michelle . . . sorry, boss, where's my manners? Take a seat.'

'Thank you.' Ventnor sat on a plastic upholstered armchair and read the room which was inexpensively furnished, with a small television standing in the corner. Harry Lemmon sat opposite him and grappled to his left for a packet of cigarettes and a yellow disposable lighter. He took a cigarette and offered one to Ventnor.

'No thanks, I don't smoke. But your sister . . .' Ventnor looked at Lemmon. 'So, as you say, Michelle disappeared.'

'And now her body has been found?' Harry Lemmon lit the cigarette.

'Possibly,' Ventnor replied, 'but only possibly. We'll need a sample of your DNA to be certain.'

'You're not getting that.' Harry Lemmon grinned as he exhaled smoke through his nostrils. 'I might need to make a bit more money than I make at the Indian eatery and so far my DNA is not on file.'

'You've been lucky.'

'Careful . . . I've been careful, covered my tracks and any convictions I have had were before DNA was invented.'

'Discovered.' Ventnor smiled. 'It was discovered, but, anyway, so you are withholding your DNA even if it means making a positive identity of your sister?'

'I can let you have a lock of her hair.' Lemmon grinned. 'That's even better than my DNA. I would think that will suit us both.'

'Agreed, and I will take it with pleasure and gratitude.' Ventnor sat back in the armchair. 'So can you tell me anything about your sister's disappearance . . . anything that might not be in the missing person file?'

'Such as?' Lemmon also reclined in his chair.

'Well, for example, any difficulties at home, within the family, any boyfriend harassing her . . . that sort of thing?'

'I remember her disappearing, I remember it so well. What brother wouldn't, even after thirty years?' He drew deeply on his cigarette. 'But what was happening at the time?' Lemmon paused, looking down at the carpet. 'She had a fight with our dad, she packed her bags and went away, but after a few days she didn't contact us . . . it was then when we reported her missing.'

'She went to London. I read that in the file.'

'She said she was going there . . .' Lemmon corrected Ventnor, 'and that's what we told the police. It seems that everyone who runs away runs to London. I mean, who runs away to Belfast or Glasgow? And she did go there . . . sent us a card. So she made it. She got herself there.'

'You didn't report that,' Ventnor said accusingly.

'No, we didn't. That was our dad's idea. He said if we told you we had received a card then you wouldn't have taken the report, or you would have closed the case. Our dad thought that it was better if she was listed as a missing person; he thought it was better if the police . . . you guys, had an open file on her. You see, I think he thought that would mean that you would search for her, but I knew you don't search for adults, but I never told him that.'

'In exceptional cases we have in fact been known to search for adults,' Ventnor replied, 'but do carry on.'

'OK . . . I think it helped him to think that our Michelle was being looked for,' Lemmon explained, 'that the Metropolitan Police were organizing search parties, that sort of thing.'

'I see.'

'That's why he never reported the cards.'

'Cards?' Ventnor queried. 'You mean that there was more than one?'

'Yes, there were seventeen in all, they all were from London. You know the type . . . tourist cards . . . Tower Bridge, Nelson's Column, and the message was always the same just, "Still OK", that's all she ever wrote, "Still OK", and signed "M" for Michelle. We recognized her handwriting so they came from her all right.' Lemmon leaned forward and flicked ash from his cigarette into the empty fire grate. 'Then we got the last one, still in her handwriting which said, "This is not working, I am getting a lift up next week".'

'A lift?'

Harry Lemmon gave the thumbs up sign. 'Hitching, boss.' He smiled. 'That's what I assumed she meant; it was the only way she could get back up north unless she made some money. She had no skills to get a job and she wouldn't have sold her body, not our Michelle, she was too proud to do that. She had too much self-respect.'

'Getting a lift,' Ventnor quoted. 'Sounds like she had met someone who was giving her a ride up here, don't you think? Rather than taking a gamble on hitching a ride, she sounded very certain of returning on a particular day.'

'Aye, that's a possibility, come to think of it.' Lemmon glanced upwards at the ceiling. 'She hitched down to London, so we just assumed she meant she was going to hitch back . . . and she just got in the wrong car, it happens . . . such happens. So why are you interested after all these years? You said you want to make a positive identification.'

Ventnor told him.

Harry Lemmon fell silent, then he said, 'You mean she made it? She got back to York only to be done in, murdered when she was practically home, right on her own doorstep?'

'That would seem to be the case,' Ventnor replied softly. 'I am very sorry.'

'And she was found with the family who vanished? I remember the news about them disappearing and now they've been found –' Lemmon pointed to the small television set – 'I saw it on there.'

'The Parrs?' Ventnor replied. 'Yes, if it's her she was found with the Parrs.'

'So that means that she was in their car.' Lemmon slowly stood, turned his back on Ventnor and walked to the window of his flat and looked out over the back gardens of Tang Hall Estate.

'It's now a distinct possibility,' Ventnor confirmed, 'but the identification still has to be made. How long was she in London?'

'Sixteen – seventeen weeks. We got a card once a week. It always arrived on a Saturday, posted second-class, so she would have posted the card each Thursday.'

'Do you have the cards?' Ventnor asked.

'No . . . no . . . we let our dad take them.' Harry Lemmon fell silent and then said, 'He pined for our Michelle once the cards stopped arriving and he carried those postcards with him wherever he went . . . poor old guy. He loved Michelle . . . father and daughter . . . there was always a closeness between those two despite the arguments. So we let him take them with him, put them into his coffin . . . poor old soul. Might sound a bit daft but it's the sort of thing you do when a loved one dies.'

'Yes,' Ventnor replied softly, 'I can understand that. I can see myself doing the same thing.'

'It made us feel better.' Lemmon forced a smile and half turned to Ventnor.

'Oh believe me,' Ventnor replied, 'I fully understand.'

'You know . . . you know.' Lemmon raised a finger and fully turned towards Ventnor. 'You could try Mary Emery.'

'Mary Emery.' Ventnor took his notebook from his pocket. 'Who is she?'

'Her school friend,' Lemmon explained. 'They were very close; it was Mary who told us that our Michelle had probably hitched to London. They were as thick as thieves were those two lasses. Don't know where she is now. She'll be a married woman with a different name, but her mother still lives in the same house Mary grew up in. She's getting on now is old Mrs Emery.'

'She would be.' Ventnor took his pen from his jacket pocket.

'Well, she was young when she had Mary, so I reckon she'll be in her seventies now, well into them, but she still has it all upstairs.' Lemmon tapped the side of his head. 'She's still as sharp as a tack. She's at number 113, Ninth Avenue. That way –' he pointed to his left – 'so back towards Third Avenue, but not as far as Third Avenue.'

Ventnor wrote on his pad and then stood, smiling as he did so. 'So, Ninth Avenue is between Third Avenue and Eighth Avenue? That makes a lot of sense.'

'That's Tang Hall.' Harry Lemmon shrugged. 'You get used to it if you live here. I'll get that bit of our Michelle's hair for you then I'm going out. I've got a bit of cash . . . I need a drink.'

Somerled Yellich, who often had to explain that his Christian name is Gaelic and pronounced 'Sorely', did not at first recognize the woman. He was strolling slowly through the city of York, along Davygate which, as was normal, was thronged with shoppers, with two sets of street entertainers engaging modest crowds, when the woman suddenly stepped in front of him. The first thing he noticed was the look of fear in her eyes. 'Can I help you, madam?' Yellich asked.

'You don't recognize me, do you?' the woman said. 'You came to my house a day or two ago, you and the older officer. I'm Mrs Farrent.'

'Of course,' Yellich replied. 'Sorry, it was seeing you here, different context. I would have recognized you—'

Thomas Farrent suddenly appeared, stepping out of the crowd as if from nowhere. He grabbed his wife roughly and tightly by her upper arm. He glared at Yellich and pulled her away with him, and they both seemed to vanish, seemingly swallowed by the throng of people.

The woman was elderly, frail-looking, short and she could so very easily be overpowered, Ventnor assessed, yet she seemed to open the door to her flat with all the confidence of a Royal Marine Commando. She exhibited no fear as to who might have rung her doorbell. She just flung it open wide and demanded, 'Yes?'

'Police.' Ventnor showed her his ID.

'Yes, thought you might be.' The woman spoke with a local accent. 'I watched you walking up the road towards my flat, looking around you all the time, unconcerned for your own safety, then that knock . . . not too loud but it had an authority about it.'

'Ah.' Ventnor inclined his head. She had, he thought, just gone some considerable way to explain her fearless manner of opening the door of her flat. 'You are Mrs Emery?'

'Yes.' Mrs Emery was smartly dressed in a yellow blouse and a dark grey skirt.

'With a daughter, Mary?'

'Yes, though she is a married woman now, but, yes, she is still my daughter and she is called Mary.'

'Good . . . we would like to talk to her. Can you tell me how I can contact her?'

Mrs Emery scowled. 'She's not in any trouble, I hope?'

'No, none at all, I assure you,' Ventnor replied, 'really, but we believe she can be of assistance to the police.'

'Good, I am relieved. She married well, you see.' Mrs Emery seemed to Ventnor to stiffen with pride. 'Her husband's a solicitor, you see, very proper.'

'I see . . . very good.' Ventnor again inclined his head. 'Where can we contact her?'

'She lives at Stockton-on-the-Forest in a house called "The Mill".'

'"The Mill",' Ventnor repeated.

'I'll have to let her know that you're on your way,' Mrs Emery explained.

'Of course. We'll call tomorrow. "The Mill", Stockton-on-the-Forest.'

'I see, so not an urgent case for you?' Mrs Emery surmised.

'Serious.' Ventnor turned to go. 'Very serious, but, no, not urgent. One day won't make a deal of difference.'

'Can I say what it's about?' Mrs Emery queried, and did, so Ventnor thought, as much for her own sense of curiosity as it was to forewarn her daughter.

Ventnor paused. 'I don't see why not,' he replied, 'it's in respect of Michelle Lemmon.'

Mrs Emery caught her breath. 'Michelle . . . she went away and never returned. No one knew what happened to her. Her poor father, he was sick with worry . . . so were all her family . . . but her father especially.'

'So I understand.'

'Mary and Michelle were very close,' Mrs Emery advised, 'really good friends. Neither my husband nor I cared much for the family as a whole but Michelle was a very pleasant girl who grew into a pleasant young woman, unlike her brother, Harold, though he's calmed down now. He's almost respectable.'

'Well, if you could tell your daughter I'll be calling on her tomorrow. Who do I ask for?'

'Mrs Fleece. Mrs Mary Fleece.'

'Thank you.' Ventnor turned and went back down the stairs and into Ninth Avenue thinking, Fleece . . . Fleece, what an appropriate name for a lawyer.

The man stood in his living room staring out of the wide window at the crimson sunset. 'Keep calm,' he told himself, 'keep calm. So they have been found, after thirty years, but there is still a long way to go before anything can be proved. The important thing is not to panic.'

Behind him, the woman lay on the floor, conscious but motionless, utterly motionless, too frightened even to breathe.

Thomson Ventnor returned home in a quiet, calm manner. He chose to travel to and from work by public transport. Living, as he did, just outside the city centre in suburban Bishopton, a car, he felt, was a needless extravagance. He entered his modest, he thought, three bedroomed semi-detached house with a small garden, which, like the washing-up and the house-work, stubbornly refused to do itself. His garden, he freely acknowledged, was the least tidy in the whole street, the pile of dirty dishes never got higher, but never diminished either, and the bed linen should have been changed days earlier.

He put a ready cooked meal purchased from the supermarket into the microwave and listened to the mellifluous tones of the Radio Four newscaster while he waited for the meal to cook. After eating his meal, which he took in the kitchen, rather than in his dining room, he changed into a grey, light-weight Italian suit, and wearing a lightweight summer raincoat and hat he left his house and took a bus to the outskirts of the city. Alighting the cream single-decker Rider York bus at a stop in a leafy lane, he walked a hundred yards in the pleasant early evening, then turned into an imposing stone gateway and walked up the driveway to a large Victorian era house. He opened the porch door and signed in the visitors' book, and then opened the main door of the house and was met by a blast of warm air. He removed his hat and walked across the deep-pile maroon carpet in the foyer, before nimbly climbing the wide staircase. A young woman in uniform came down the stairs and they smiled at each other as they passed. Ventnor had noticed before that the superstition about it being a bringer of bad luck to cross another person on the stairs does not extend to institutions.

At the top of the stairs Ventnor walked across a landing and entered a room where elderly people sat in chairs placed around the walls of the room, where a television set, tuned into commercial television, was playing in the corner, and where carers in uniform appeared concerned and busy. A resident seated in the corner of the room smiled as he recognized Ventnor, but by the time Ventnor had crossed the carpet to sit beside the elderly man, the elderly man had become expres-sionless and stared into the middle distance. 'Hello, father,' was all Ventnor could say. He remained for a few minutes sitting beside his father then went to see the matron to enquire about the old man's welfare. He then left the building and took a bus into York, where he went from pub to pub not wanting to settle in one for too long a time in case he was recognized by either colleagues or felons as being a lone drinker, and then went to Augusta's night club where it was dark within. He therein got into conversation with a woman of indeterminate age who seemed obsessed with package holidays and who insisted that Portugal was always the better destination than Spain. He bought her a drink and then, mumbling his excuses, he walked home.

Alone.

It was Wednesday, 01.10 a.m.

FOUR

Wednesday, 09.30 hours

*in which Somerled Yellich and Reginald Webster travel
south, Thomson Ventnor meets a lady who is much befitted
by means of upward social mobility and George Hennessey
is at home to the too kind reader.*

Somerled Yellich and Reginald Webster took the East Coast
Mainline service from York to London. Yellich, as the
senior officer, sat facing the direction of travel with
Webster sitting opposite him with his back to the southwards.
They were, they felt, fortunate to be able to acquire seats on
the east side of the train which, at any time after ten a.m. is
the 'shady side', thus their enjoyment of the view of passing
landscape was not ruined by the glare of the sun. Upon arriving
at King's Cross station, the officers, as all passengers, were
amused by the jovial train manager announcing over the public
address system, 'Well, as you can see ladies and gentlemen,
we have managed to find London', and continued expressing
his hope that all customers had had a pleasant journey and
urging people to ensure that they take all their belongings with
them when they leave the train.

From King's Cross Yellich and Webster took the tube the
short, two stop distance, to Camden. The distance in question
they both accepted was walkable, easily so, but they both feared
losing time by taking a wrong turn here and there, and were
keen to keep their appointment. The officers duly arrived at
193A Delancey Street, NW1, a few minutes past midday, finding
the address in question to be that of a Victorian era terraced
property on four floors, set back from the pavement by just a
matter of a few feet and which had, by its twin doorbells, been
separated at some point into two independent properties.

Yellich pressed the doorbell above the name 'Parr' which

was displayed on a plastic tablet in black letters on a pearl-grey background. The front door of the house was opened within a matter of seconds by a middle-aged man. He was tall, almost as tall as the two officers and casually dressed in a blue tee shirt and denims, with his feet looking to be very comfortably encased in moccasins. His hair had greyed but was long and he wore it tied behind his head in a ponytail. He was, thought the officers, very Camden, very Camden, indeed. 'Mr Yellich and Mr Webster?' He extended his right hand.

'Yes, sir.' Yellich accepted the man's hand, finding Nigel Parr's handshake to be manly, firm, but not overly compressing. 'I am DS Yellich. This is DC Webster.' Yellich showed Parr his ID as Parr and Webster engaged in a short shaking of hands.

'You made good time, gentlemen.' Parr stepped to one side. 'Please do come in.'

'Yes, sir.' Yellich stepped over the threshold of the property. 'It is an excellent service from York to London, just above two hours.'

'Well, do come in, please, gentlemen. A nice day for September though rain is forecast, or "called" as my Canadian friends would say.'

Reginald Webster followed Yellich into the corridor which he found surprisingly narrow and where he noticed mail was left neatly piled on the floor. At the far end of the corridor was a door which was at the moment shut and had the number 193B attached to it. As if reading Webster's mind, Nigel Parr explained, 'We'd like a table in the hall, even just a small one to place the post on, but as you see, there just isn't room. Even a small table would not allow an adult to squeeze past it, so the mail goes on the floor. All we can do is to undertake not to walk on each other's mail.'

'I see,' Webster replied. 'I dare say that's as good a reason as any for the post to be left on the floor.'

'Yes.' Parr closed the front door. 'I visited a house in Glasgow once; it was a conversion, like this house, but very upmarket and very spacious, very, very spacious. Sufficient space for a huge nineteenth-century dining table to be accommodated in the hallway upon which all mail could be laid to await collection.'

'Nice,' Webster commented.

'It was, but it had a downside. Apparently someone buzzed into one of the flats, so as to gain entry upon some subterfuge or other and the beautiful table was stolen. I recall it from a previous visit; large, beautifully made, highly polished. It could have been Georgian, but I thought Victorian. Anyway, a team of wide boys with a vehicle clearly found out that it was there and it vanished . . . in broad daylight. It was there when the residents went to work that morning and when they returned that evening the thing had vanished, just four lighter-coloured marks on the floor where the four legs had rested without being moved for the previous half century.'

'Damn shame,' Webster lamented. 'That sort of theft is always very annoying.'

'Yes.' Parr shook his head in agreement. 'Annoying, as you say. The residents didn't think the theft was worth reporting. Well, do come in gentlemen.'

Parr led Yellich and Webster into his part of the conversion, which was accessed by a door to the right of the door labelled 193B, his door being labelled 193A. The door accessed a small vestibule, beyond which was a sitting room at street level. Quite small, thought Yellich as he entered, but he found it tastefully decorated with comfortable-looking furniture and with books placed in neat order on shelves each side of the original sash window, and a Galileo thermometer on the mantelpiece about the fireplace. The room though was polluted with the sound of traffic on Delancey Street.

'You get used to the noise from the road,' Parr said, again as if reading the thoughts of his visitors. 'The fumes are worse than the noise. Can't open the basement door because carbon monoxide drifts in.'

'That's dangerous,' Webster commented.

'Yes.' Parr nodded. 'Especially since that is where I sleep. My bedroom is below this room . . . downstairs front, the street side. The house is all upside down, well my part is. I live above the bedroom and I go downstairs to bed each evening. In the summer it gets very hot down there but I can't open the door to let heat out because fumes get in. It's pretty well burglar proof, even cat proof, but fumes know no boundaries. On hot nights it can be difficult to breath in the front rooms of the house but fortunately I have a small back garden. I can leave the back door open an inch or two, sufficient to let air in but keep the gap narrow enough to keep the neighbour's cats out. I am able to ventilate the house by such means and thus can survive the summers. So . . . can I offer you gentlemen something? Tea? Coffee?'

'Tea, please,' Yellich replied, 'that would be most welcome.'

'And most appreciated,' added Webster.

'Earl Grey, English Breakfast, Jasmine, Lapsang?'

'Whatever.' Yellich smiled. 'We really don't know one tea from another.'

'We're just used to canteen tea,' Webster explained.

'English Breakfast, I think.' Nigel Parr looked out of the window to the sky above the roofs of the buildings on the opposite side of Delancey Street. 'It is an English Breakfast tea sort of day methinks. Please –' he indicated the chairs with an upturned palm – 'please do take a pew.' He then turned and walked softly out of the room.

Yellich sank deeply into the wide armchair beside the bookshelf to the right of the window. Webster sat on the settee which stood against the adjacent wall facing the window. Glancing at the titles of the books he gauged that Nigel Parr was not a learned man. There was, he noted, a very wide range of books indicated by their titles, but none seemed to him to have any depth, many were even relics of childhood days. Presently Parr returned with a tray of tea and a generous plate of bread rolls and pâté.

'Oh my.' Yellich welcomed the unexpected food. 'And we reproached ourselves for not getting some breakfast on the train.'

Parr grinned. 'Well, tuck in, gentlemen, it's about lunchtime anyway.' He poured the tea from a large white teapot decorated with a floral pattern, and served it correctly, Yellich observed, unadulterated with either milk or sugar. He handed a steaming cup of tea first to Yellich and then a second cup to Webster. He took a third cup for himself and sat in the vacant armchair. 'So –' he scented the tea before sipping it – 'how can I help you, gentlemen? How can I be of assistance to the Vale of York Police?'

'It is in respect of your late parents and their daughters, as I explained on the phone,' Yellich replied.

'It could only be that.' Parr sighed. 'That is the only connection this family ever had with York. The family who disappeared, the family who vanished without a trace. The press gave the story an awful lot of coverage, as they would do I suppose. Individuals who vanish are worrying enough, but an entire family at the same time, that was and still is newsworthy . . . and in the middle of the city, no less. I have agonized during many sleepless nights. It's the not knowing, you see, it is that which is difficult.'

'Yes, sir.' Yellich held eye contact with Parr. 'Yes, that I can so well imagine.' And then fell silent as a red double-decker bus whirred loudly past, causing the lightweight ornaments to rattle and shake.

'You are not used to noise from the street?' Again, Nigel Parr seemed to read the officers' thoughts.

'Not I.' Webster smiled. 'We live in a small village adjacent to woodland.'

'A home in the country.' Parr inclined his head. 'Very nice.'

'Well . . . no,' Webster explained, 'it's actually a new-build housing estate which has been tacked on to a village, but it is still very quiet . . . wood pigeons during the day and an owl during the night.'

'I too live in a quiet area,' Yellich advised.

'I see.' Parr reached for a bread roll. 'But, as I said, you get used to the noise and I like living in the city, so I choose to put up with it and other things besides. So . . . my parents . . . I read about skeletons being found in a field in the York area; are you putting two and two together?'

'Let's just say we are moving in that direction,' Yellich replied.

'Well I have always thought they were murdered.'

'That's interesting.' Yellich sipped his tea. 'Why do you say that?'

'It's just that it is the most likely explanation, don't you think? If indeed the only explanation? Four adults, they vanish in the middle of a city. I mean, it isn't as though they were particularly adventurous and disappeared whilst rafting down the Blue Nile or whilst trekking in the Himalayas.' Parr paused. 'They were . . . we were, Camden people, well into the Camden Town lifestyle, you see; café culture and live music in bars . . . small, local restaurants, walking along the canal towpath where folk live in houseboats, and we hunted for bargains in Camden Lock Market, so misadventure is unlikely. An accident? Well, if an accident had befallen them their bodies would have been found. So foul play, it has to be a question of foul play, by process of elimination. So I have concluded that murder is the cause of death and the motive for person or persons unknown making a thorough job of hiding the bodies is also unknown. It's really quite easy to make a human body disappear.'

'You think?' Webster also helped himself to a bread roll.

Parr shrugged. 'Well I wouldn't argue with two police officers but I do believe it isn't difficult . . . if you have privacy and time . . . two big "ifs". I watch crime programmes on TV, fiction and non-fiction.'

'I see,' Yellich growled. 'I often think that such programmes put dangerous ideas into people's minds.'

Webster sipped his tea. 'In fact it is actually very difficult to get away with murder. We throw all our resources into solving that crime above all the others, and people so often trip themselves up, or are caught out by a microscopic drop of blood.'

'Or,' Yellich added, 'somebody, a fellow conspirator, sees a chance for themselves and they turn Queen's Evidence.'

'Always a sensible thing to do,' Webster agreed and held eye contact with Parr whilst he did so, noticing Parr to have become very serious-looking.

Yellich also noticed Parr's sudden serious demeanour and he told himself, Look at the in-laws before you look at the outlaws, and their visit to Nigel Parr of Camden Town took on a new, unforeseen significance. Nigel Parr had suddenly become very, very interesting.

'But, yes,' Yellich continued, 'you are in fact correct; we do believe that we have located your parents and sisters.'

'Oh,' Parr groaned.

'Yes, as you read, a grave in a field just outside York. We

learned your name from the file. Seems lucky that you did not
travel north with them.'

'Yes. I was on holiday with friends at the time on the
south coast, out of touch. It was my mother's brother who
informed the police they were missing . . . collected their
possessions.'

'Mr Verity?'

'Yes . . . Uncle George, sadly no longer with us.'

'I see. The remains were found with the skeletal remains
of a young woman who we have identified as being one
Michelle Lemmon. Do you know anything about her?'

'Oranges,' Nigel Parr gasped, 'oh, not Oranges as well. She
was going north, returning home. She asked for a lift when
she found out that the family was going north, not just north
but to York, no less, which is where she came from. She asked
if she could go with them. I just assumed Oranges went home
and rejoined her parents.'

'Oranges?' Webster queried.

'It was her nickname, from the nursery rhyme. You know
the one . . . "gay go up and gay go down, to ring the bells of
London town"?'

'Of course.' Yellich beamed. '"Oranges and Lemons sing
the bells of St Clements".'

'That's the one,' Parr confirmed.

'"You owe me five farthings say the bells of St Martin's",'
Webster enjoined, sensing the need to introduce a slight sense
of jocularity into the occasion, so as to gloss over the officers'
sudden suspicion about Nigel Parr.

'"When will you pay me? Say the bells of Old Bailey".
Yes,' Parr continued, 'that is the reference . . . and when she
came to live with us we called her "Oranges" after her surname
of Lemmon . . . spelled differently than the fruit but pronounced
the same. So her nickname was an obvious choice and she
didn't mind at all. So the name stuck.'

'I see.' Yellich paused.

'How did you find me anyway?' Parr asked.

'Telephone directory,' Yellich explained. 'There are not
many N. Parrs in Camden. We just assumed you'd stay in the
Camden area, hence my first question after I introduced myself,

asking if you were related to Mr and Mrs Gerald and Elizabeth Parr of Camden.'

'I see.' Parr sipped his tea. 'I did wonder, once I had put the phone down.'

'Well,' Yellich continued, 'we really need your help in respect of confirmation of the identity of the deceased family . . . a sample of DNA for example.'

'Can't help you there I'm afraid.' Parr shrugged.

'Oh?'

'Well, you will have heard about the skeletons, if not seen them?'

'Yes, heard reports,' Yellich replied.

'Doubtless their stature or lack of will have been remarked upon?'

'Short . . .'

'Very short.' Parr smiled. 'And look at me, I am just shy of six feet tall . . . well, tall enough to be a police officer.'

'Ah . . .' Yellich sat forward.

'Perhaps you thought some form of anomaly within the family?' Parr relaxed in his chair. 'I am fostered. I am not of their bloodline.'

'Oh.' Webster allowed his disappointment to show.

'I was a Victorian-style foundling. I was wrapped inside a blanket and placed inside a telephone box, or so the story goes, very late one night. I was just a few days old. The person who left me there, probably my mother, just seemed to have laid me on the ground and dialled three nines and then vanished into the night. It was during the winter months, so I was told, but I was left there well wrapped up and the police responded to the emergency number very quickly.'

'As they would,' Yellich replied.

'Yes.' Parr nodded. 'As they would.'

'So I was found with a note pinned to my blankets.' Parr shrugged again. 'It was apparently written in a rounded female hand and it read, "Please look after him, I can't".'

'Not a good start in life,' Yellich observed.

'There have been better starts but it was probably all for the best,' Nigel Parr replied. 'I wouldn't have had the best of childhoods with a mother who could not care for me, no matter what reason. So I was fostered by the Parrs after a few years in an institution. They were a mad, happy, strange family. Mad, but mad in a harmless way; eccentric, a little off centre . . . just . . . just . . .'

'Dotty?' Webster suggested.

'Yes.' Parr beamed. 'Dotty, that's the very word to describe them. Utterly harmless, and they created a very stimulating house, if artistic expression is your thing. You know . . . children's paintings pinned up everywhere, branches of trees steam cleaned and then varnished or painted for decoration, "art trouvé" I think it's called . . . and a veritable zoo of pets, not just cats and dogs but hamsters and a rat.'

'A rat!' Yellich gasped.

'Yes, a tame rat. Believe me.' Parr grinned widely. 'It had a personality. It really was a very intelligent creature. Tortoise in the garden . . . tropical fish in a heated and illuminated tank . . . horses in stables north of London. They were very warm and eccentric, and I grew up feeling fully part and parcel of the family; They never once reminded me that I was fostered. Not once.'

'Good for them.' Webster took another bread roll.

'I was indeed lucky.' Parr glanced at the floor. 'But what a family, the girls would bring stray dogs home and the dogs would stay. All the dogs were strays in fact. And the whole family smoked cannabis.'

'You did what!' Yellich gasped.

'Smoked dope,' Parr confirmed. 'I kid you not, as a family we smoked dope. I mean liberal minded is just not the word to describe that lifestyle. The Parrs valued education but were suspicious of formal schooling, and so they never minded much if we played truant, as we often did. They believed that the thrill of escaping and the hours of freedom were much better for our development than was sitting in a stuffy classroom and not really absorbing anything, and I have to say that they were probably correct. I was not damaged by it because I still went to college, which is where I got my real education.'

'I have indeed heard that observation –' Webster glanced at Yellich and then addressed Parr – 'that what you use in your day-to-day life you had acquired by the age of eleven and from what you learned in your professional training, but you use very little of what you might have learned from the ages of twelve to sixteen.'

'Yes, I think that applies to me.' Parr smiled. 'The square of the hypotenuse of a right-angled triangle is equal to the sum of the squares of the two adjacent sides; all very interesting but I never needed that knowledge to pay the gas bill. In fact all that taught me was the correct use of the words "sum" and "adjacent". I still don't know anything about triangles. I really was much better off truanting in Regent's Park Zoo, or exploring London . . . right out to the East End, sometimes for nothing.'

'How did you manage that?' Webster was intrigued.

'Can't do it now because you have to pay on entry, one man operation now.'

'Same everywhere,' Webster replied, 'hence the question.'

'Yes, but the operative word is "now",' Parr explained. 'Back in the day when there were conductors we'd get on a bus and run upstairs, and when the conductor came to collect the fare we asked for a destination in the opposite direction and he'd say, "You're going the wrong way, boys", so we'd get off at the next stop and wait for the next bus and pull the same stunt. You'd get at least one stop in the direction you wanted to go, at least one stop, sometimes two or even three depending on how crowded the bus was or how hard the bus conductor wanted to work. Very occasionally we'd get on a bus where the conductor was having a bad day or had a grudge against London Transport and who felt disinclined to take any fares at all . . . not from anyone. When that happened we rode for free without having to change buses. That was a rare occurrence, though. But I'd come home and tell my parents what I had done, and they thought I had done well and wholly approved of it. Eccentric, as I said.' Parr fell silent. 'There was always a lot of laughter in the house . . . a lot of care . . . a lot of acceptance, but . . .'

'But?' Yellich prompted.

'But . . . but . . . when I reached my teenage years I began to feel different, especially when the growth spurt occurred. I shot up over my sisters and then my mother and then my father, and all in the space of just a few months. I enjoyed the nick-name of "Rocket Man" for a while, rocketing up, you see.'

'Yes,' Webster replied, 'I understand . . . we understand.'

'So, suddenly I was the tallest person in the house. We joked about it but I began to feel different and gradually less and less part and parcel of the Parrs of Camden. I eventually left home to go to art college and managed that because of the Parrs' influence and encouragement. I then worked as a commercial artist, which is what my father's occupation was, painting book covers or posters for advertising products; that sort of thing. I also took the photography option with the idea of becoming a photo journalist.'

'It must pay well,' Yellich commented.

'You mean that I can afford a two bedroomed conversion in Camden?' Parr smiled. 'These don't come cheap.'

'Well . . . yes . . . as you say, this house will not have come cheap.'

'My inheritance.' Parr smiled. 'I couldn't afford to buy it, not on the money I make. I am not as successful as my father was.'

'The Parrs left something to you?' Yellich asked.

'No . . . no . . . they left me nothing. They used to tell me that being fostered meant nothing at all in terms of belonging to the family, but they were not wholly accurate. You see, being fostered meant that I inherited nothing by right.' Parr raised his eyebrows. 'I took their name by deed poll but that's all I took.'

'Yes.' Yellich nodded. 'I see.'

'So, it was the case that when the Parr family was deemed to be deceased and their estate was wrapped up we found that they had died intestate. Then, in that case, I was not going to inherit anything.'

'I see,' Yellich said again with growing curiosity.

'So their house, which was much, much larger than this, my modest little property, and all the contents therein, and all the money in the bank and all the stocks and shares went to Mr Verity.'

'Mrs Parr's brother?' Yellich confirmed.

'Yes,' Parr replied, 'to him, now sadly deceased. It was explained to me that the mechanism of inheritance is like a cross or like a lift in a building; it goes up and down then from side to side. So in the case of someone who dies intestate, the first beneficiaries are any issue, any children. If there is no issue it then goes up to the person's parents. If there are no parents still alive, which, in my parents' case, they were not, then it goes from side to side.'

'To brothers and sisters?' Yellich clarified.

'Yes, to siblings. So down, then up, then from side to side and it stops at the first legal beneficiary, who in this case was Mr Verity, my maternal uncle.'

'I see,' Yellich replied.

'I never really knew Uncle George,' Nigel Parr explained, 'not when I was growing up, but I was to find that he was of the same stuff and stock as my foster parents in that he was a very generous man, generous beyond measure.'

'I see.' Yellich remained intrigued.

'So what happened,' Parr continued, 'was that he and I sat down about two years after my foster family had disappeared and were then presumed deceased and Uncle George said, "Look, Nigel, I know Gerald, your father, and your mother was my sister, and I know that they would have wanted you to have something, in fact they told me that they intended to include you in their will. I am a solicitor with a firm in the city and I am doing reasonably well, and I want to use the money from Gerald and Elizabeth's house and their estate as a whole to start trust funds for my three children. I don't want anything for myself." So the upshot was that he sold the home and the contents therein, sold all the stocks and shares . . .'

'He liquidated the estate,' Yellich said.

'Yes,' Parr continued, 'that's the word, he liquidated my parents' estate and instead of dividing the proceeds by three to start trust funds for his children, he divided it by four, giving me an equal fourth of my foster parents' estate.'

'That was good of him,' Webster commented, 'very good of him indeed.'

'Yes, I thought so too.' Nigel Parr paused as another red double-decker bus whirred loudly past the window, drowning any conversation. 'Legally he was not obliged to give me anything, but what I did inherit was enough to buy this small conversion, well almost enough. I had to take out a small mortgage but that's paid off now. So it's mine, lock, stock and barrel, worth well over a million, being much more than what I paid for it.'

'Dare say it would be,' Yellich growled.

'Well, London prices . . . I plan to retire to the country. Dorset, I think, but somewhere in the beautiful south.'

'So,' Yellich asked, 'do you know why your parents went to York, taking Michelle Lemmon with them?'

'No, in a word, I don't . . . neither did Uncle George, but we thought it might be in connection with a property dispute, that is a dispute about the ownership of a parcel of land.'

'I see,' Yellich replied. 'Do you know who their solicitors were?'

'Oldfield and Fairly,' Parr replied confidently. 'They still are. Oldfield and Fairly have been the Parr family solicitors for a long time.'

'Where are they?'

Parr paled. 'Well, last I heard they were in the Camden area . . . but exactly where . . .'

'We'll find them,' Yellich smiled.

'Why would you want to speak to them?' Parr seemed to the officers to have become agitated.

'They might be able to shed light,' Yellich explained.

'Well, I have told you all there is to know.'

'You've probably told us all you know.' Yellich smiled. 'They might know something else. They might be able to shed fresh light.'

Parr did not press his objection further but he could not conceal a look of worry to cross his eyes which was clearly noted and registered by both officers.

Yellich was aware of the need to keep Nigel Parr talking so as to avoid him getting too defensive. 'So tell us, how did Michelle Lemmon arrive at the Parrs' house?'

Parr opened his fleshy palms in a gesture of despair, though he was also evidently relieved to have to answer a non-threatening question. 'What can I say? I don't wish to be patronizing but Oranges was brought into the house like the dogs were brought in, like she was a stray. She came home with my sisters one afternoon who all but said, "Can we keep her? Please, please, please can we keep her?" Anyway, it turns out that Oranges had been sleeping rough in Regent's Park which is where my sisters found her.'

'Is that possible?' Webster asked. 'I thought it was illegal and there are park wardens to stop that happening.'

'Yes.' Parr nodded his head slightly in agreement. 'It most certainly is illegal and, yes, it's also not easy, not easy at all. The park wardens turf the dossers out, helped by the police, and they walk every inch of the park footpaths once the gates are locked. I am told that that is a very pleasant duty during the summer months, having the whole park practically to yourself, but Oranges was a clever old soul and she had apparently found a huge rhododendron bush. She would crawl in there an hour or two before the park was shut and lay there still and quiet. Then, once the park wardens had gone, she settled down for the night, having eaten whatever she could find in the rubbish bins during the day.

'My two sisters apparently found her in the rhododendron bush. Oranges got a little careless and my sisters saw some movement and investigated.' Parr paused. 'Well, the long and the short of it is that they, the three of them, got to chatting and they persuaded her to come back home with them, with the promises of food, a hot bath and the opportunity to wash her clothing, of which she had very little. So then it was, "Please, please can we keep her?" time. The girls were allowed to "keep" her and so Oranges joined the family. She was very gauche at first, north of England working-class, but the Parrs made allowances for her and eventually, quite rapidly in fact, she found her niche in the household as a sort of "maid of all work". She became like a stowaway on a ship and she worked her passage; cleaning, laundry, washing up, shopping. She actually became a great help to my foster mother. She just wanted food and accommodation, but she also seemed to realize that she couldn't settle, and that she couldn't get comfortable. She knew she had to leave at some point. It was about then that my parents announced their plan to drive to York for some reason and Oranges seemed to take that as a sign that it was time for her to go, and so she probably asked them for a lift.'

'Probably?' Webster queried.

'Yes,' Parr replied, 'probably. I wasn't at home then, I had gone to the coast with friends. What happened was that I left a noisy, vibrant, happy house and when I returned it was quiet, cold and empty. Even the animals looked confused. They had been fed and watered and the dogs had been walked by a neighbour. By then Uncle George had reported them as missing to the Metropolitan Police who had also contacted the Vale of York Constabulary.'

'Yes,' Yellich replied, 'we collated the information, ourselves and the Met that is. The family had already come to our attention as being suspected of running off without paying their hotel bill, but later their car was found in a car park in the city centre, as if abandoned. It was about then that they became the family who vanished.'

'And Oranges was with them.' Parr reclined in his chair. 'Poor Oranges. I grew to like her. She just wanted to say "thank you" to the family by working her fingers to the bone. She was that sort of girl.'

'Yes,' Yellich replied, 'it does seem that she was with them after all, but she had not booked into the hotel, nor had she gone home to her parents. So where she went remains a puzzle to be solved.'

'Staying with friends perhaps,' Parr suggested, 'as a halfway house before returning home?'

'It's a possible explanation,' Yellich conceded. 'So if you can't help with a DNA sample do you have anything we could use to confirm the identity of Mr and Mrs Parr and their daughters?'

'Are their passports good enough?' Parr asked with some reluctance.

'Ideal.' Yellich smiled. 'Full-facial photographs. Ideal.'

'I kept them, don't know why. George Verity didn't seem to want them so I kept them as keepsakes, I suppose. I'll get them for you.'

*   *   *

'Oh, Michelle.' Mary Fleece put her long-fingered hand up to her forehead. 'Do you know, sir, I think about her near daily, so near daily that with all honesty I can say every day – practically every day, anyway – especially as I have grown older. Michelle who vanished, went south and vanished, just when she was set to return home, just at that point. I also think of another girl from Tang Hall and schooldays, skinny Jenny Noble who was killed in a car crash on the York bypass. She was just twenty-four, more or less the same age as Michelle when she disappeared. Both her and Michelle, they come to mind virtually every day.' Mary Fleece glanced up at the low ceiling of her house. 'And the television news, those bodies dug up in a field, an entire family plus a young woman . . . that other woman . . . that was Michelle?'

'It does seem that it might very well be so,' Ventnor replied softly. 'It all points that way.'

Mary Fleece sighed. 'Poor Michelle.' Mary Fleece revealed herself to be, in Ventnor's eyes, a handsome woman who had aged well. Now in her fifties she looked younger and healthier than some women in their thirties whom Ventnor had encountered. But, he thought, that is often the way of marriage. If you marry into poverty you will age; poor diet, stress, limited horizons, the tendency to give up on life, all can make a woman age rapidly, but, he also thought, if the selfsame woman was to marry wealth, as Mary Fleece had clearly done, then, whatever the emotional quality of her marriage, she is nonetheless still free of all those factors which make low-income women succumb rapidly to the years. Mary Fleece was the wife of a successful lawyer; she was expected to look the part and had evidently been given the means to do so. She had come up with the goods: a trim figure brought about by twice, perhaps thrice, weekly visits to the gym, expensive clothing, a maid to do the housework. A maid who had opened the door to Ventnor and who had asked him to kindly wait whilst she fetched 'the mistress', and when 'the mistress' had arrived, in her own time and at her own pace, she dismissed the maid, who was of at least sixty summers, guessed Ventnor, with an imperious, 'Thank you, Pearl, you may carry on'. Mary Fleece née Emery had come a long way, a very long way from a

second floor flat on the Tang Hall estate in York. The mannerisms of the English upper middle-class had clearly rubbed off
on her, as she had clearly allowed and encouraged them to
do, and, Ventnor felt, that Mary Fleece could now be taken
for the daughter of a senior army officer and the product of
an expensive boarding school education.

'So how can I help the police?' she asked.

'By assisting us to piece together Michelle Lemmon's life
at about the time she left home and by throwing any light on
where she might have gone when she returned to York.' Ventnor
glanced round the room in which he sat. It was, he saw, an old
house, eighteenth century by the date of 1756 carved in stone
above the fireplace. The roof beams were low and had been
lovingly painted in black gloss paint, and had then been treated
with a coat of varnish. A few pieces of wood burned in the
grate and gave off gentle heat and created a homely feel.
The chairs in which they sat were deep and leather-bound. The
large coffee table which stood on the floor between Ventnor
and Mary Fleece had magazines of the ilk of *Yachting Monthly*,
Classic Car and *Country Life* resting upon it. The dark blue
carpet was deep pile. Mary Fleece was casually dressed but
still looked fetching in a brown and yellow horizontally striped
rugby shirt, faded blue jeans, blue socks and Nike training
shoes. She wore a small but expensive-looking gold watch and
wedding and engagement rings. The wedding ring was broad
and the rock in the engagement ring was, Ventnor thought,
huge, and far, far beyond anything he could have afforded. The
room smelled of wood smoke mingling with the scent of furniture polish, as if it had been visited by Pearl moments before
Ventnor's arrival. The broad window of the room looked out
on to a large area of landscaped garden at the rear of the house.

'She was following Dick Whittington's footsteps,' Mary
Fleece explained. 'The boy from York who became the first
Lord Mayor of London. She grew up in an unhappy, highly
stressed and quite dysfunctional family.'

'Really?' Ventnor queried.

'Yes.' Mary Fleece raised her eyebrows. 'Really.'

'I met her brother, yesterday,' Ventnor said. 'He seemed to
be quite calm and relaxed, and sane and sensible.'

'That is probably because he lives alone and has calmed down now, or so I hear. I bump into people who know him, people from the estate, York being the big village that it is. A few years ago I even bumped into him, the boy himself, and, yes, he does seem to have matured . . . but once he could start a fight in an empty house.'

'Interesting,' Ventnor commented, 'it helps explain why a girl would leave home for the bright lights of London.'

'Yes,' Mary Fleece replied, 'unappealing but nonetheless interesting. A psychologist would have his or her work cut out trying to unravel the dynamics of the Lemmon family. Michelle wasn't much for fighting; she was quite a meek girl in fact. I think she tended to try to make herself invisible when her brother and mother and father were screaming at each other . . . and eventually she had had enough and went to London to seek her fortune. I think she must have found out how hard the ground is when you have to sleep on it and how the cold and rain down south is just as cold and as wet as it is up here in the north.'

'As many have also found out,' Ventnor replied drily, 'and doubtless will continue to find out.'

'As you say.' Mary Fleece smiled at Ventnor. 'I assume you know she sent her family a few postcards?'

'Yes.'

'She sent me some as well . . .' Mary Fleece glanced upwards. 'As I recall one said something like, "I want to come home but I can't" or "I want to give in but I can't". Yes . . . yes, that was it, "I want to give in but I can't come home".'

'"I want to give in but I can't come home"?' Ventnor echoed. 'She was not a happy young woman.'

'No . . . and she was also proud, too proud to admit defeat. It is a dangerous attitude if you ask me.' Mary Fleece wound up her watch in an absent-minded manner. 'Sometimes you just have to admit that you can't go on and that you have bitten off more than you can chew.'

'Yes.' Ventnor raised his eyebrows. 'That is a lesson we must all take on board.'

'Over time,' Mary Fleece added, 'the messages got fuller.'

'Fuller?' Ventnor queried.

'Yes . . . more in them. In one she told me that she had
been taken in by a family who take in stray dogs and homeless girls.'

'Do you still have the postcards?' Ventnor sat forwards.

'No.' Mary Fleece gave a slight shrug of her right shoulder
and smiled apologetically. 'I regret that, whatever my faults,
I will never be accused of hoarding.'

Ventnor returned the smile. 'I am of much the same attitude,'
he said.

'The last postcard she sent, she said she was coming home.
So she must have arranged to travel up with them.'

'Must have,' Ventnor agreed. 'We think the family had been
in York for a day or two before they vanished. Do you know
where Michelle slept if she didn't return home?'

'No,' Mary Fleece said softly, 'no . . . I don't. She had other
friends in York; probably she slept on someone's couch for a
couple of nights.'

'If that's the case someone did not come forward,' Ventnor
growled. 'Doubt if they'll come forward now, but we can hope
the publicity has jogged a memory or pricked a conscience.'

'If you dig a hole you'll fall into it', the woman said absent-
mindedly as she folded the teacloth.

'What's that about holes?' Her husband spoke angrily.

'Nothing . . . nothing,' the woman replied, 'just mumbling
to myself. It was something that was said to me a long time
ago, a very long time ago.'

'Well, just you remember who you are,' the man snarled.
'A woman has to be loyal to her husband. Loyal.'

Edward Evans turned the pages of the photograph book, slowly,
and he carefully glanced at each of the black-and-white photographs. Eventually he stopped and he tapped a particular print.
'It could be,' he said, 'it could very well have been him.' He
turned to Carmen Pharoah. 'It could . . . thirty years now . . .
but it could very well have been him.'

George Hennessey screwed on his fedora and grappled his
way into his raincoat, signed out at the front desk of Micklegate

Bar Police Station and drove home. It was for him an early finish, very early. He was taking deserved time off in lieu of overtime worked the month previously.

He drove to Easingwold, enjoying the traffic-free journey in a light September rainfall, and once through the town and on to the Thirsk Road he slowed and turned his car into the gravel-covered drive of a detached house. He smiled as he heard a dog's excited bark coming from within the house. He left his car and let himself into the house to be met by an excited, tail-wagging, black mongrel. In the kitchen he made himself a large pot of tea and, having poured the tea into a mug, carried the mug outside and sat on a wooden chair on the patio at the rear of his house as the sun was evaporating the moisture following the rainfall. 'Strange old case,' he said, addressing the garden upon which, at that moment, Oscar was criss-crossing the lawn having found an interesting scent. 'Remains of a family and one other dug up in a field, all because a man and his mate realized the significance of an area of disturbed soil in a recently harvested field. Took them over thirty years but they were right . . . five skeletons . . . they were more right than they realized.'

He sipped his tea and as he did so, he felt again the great sadness, the great unfairness of it all. That his new, young wife, just three months after the birth of their son, should be walking in Easingwold and then, as she was walking, just collapse. No warning. It was, as a witness said, as if her legs just gave way. People had rushed to her aid assuming nothing more serious than that she had fainted. When no pulse or sign of breathing could be found an ambulance was called and she was taken to York District Hospital only to be pronounced 'dead on arrival', or 'condition purple' in ambulance crew speak. No cause of death could be found. The best the pathologist could manage was 'Sudden Death Syndrome', a symptom of a condition, which was, and remains, inexplicable by medical science, that causes healthy young men and women to have their life-force suddenly taken from them, as indeed Louise D'Acre had said earlier that week.

George Hennessey had been obliged to cremate his wife, as was her wish, and then he scattered her ashes on the garden at the rear of their house and knew again the sadness, the incongruity of a summer funeral. It seemed so wrong that death had come in the midst of so much life. Just as some twenty years previously he had watched his elder brother's coffin being lowered into the ground as butterflies fluttered by and the distant chime of an ice-cream van playing *Greensleeves* echoed over the cemetery. His father, by contrast, had died during the winter months and his coffin was lowered in a scene of silence and stillness, in the midst of which occurred a brief flurry of snow. It was, he recalled, very, very poignant.

Following his wife's death, he had thrown himself into rearranging and rebuilding the back garden according to a design she had drawn whilst heavily pregnant with Charles. When he was working he felt her presence and had then taken to telling her of his day upon his return home, no matter what the weather. Just as that day he sat in the warmth of a mid-September afternoon, equally he had stood in pouring rain at two a.m., but it did not matter. Jennifer, beautiful, beautiful Jennifer, his wife of just two summers had to know of his day. One summer's afternoon he had told her of a new love in his life, not a replacement, he had assured her, there could never be a replacement, but more of an adjunct, and he had then sensed a feeling of warmth about him that could not be explained by the sun's rays alone.

It was, he thought, as he sipped at the tea, still too warm to take Oscar, a dark dog, for a walk, despite the cooling brought by the rain, he would do that later in the evening, prior to his own walk to the Dove Inn in the village for a pint of brown and mild before last orders were called. Hennessey turned and walked back into the house . . . jobs, jobs, jobs to be done.

It was Wednesday, 12.30 hours.

FIVE

Wednesday, 14.40 hours – Thursday, 01.35 hours

*in which Webster and Yellich are obliged to extend their
visit to London and are later both at home to the too
kindly disposed reader, and Thomson Ventnor pays a call
on a long-serving prison inmate.*

Yellich and Webster strolled slowly and casually through
the streets of Camden to the chambers of Oldfield and
Fairly, Solicitors and Notaries Public, having ascer-
tained the address by consulting the *Yellow Pages* telephone
book supplied by an accommodating publican. The streets
were, both officers noted, of early Victorian, perhaps even late
Georgian terraces, set back a little from the narrow streets, of
four storeys with square, sash windows and flat roofs. Anyone
who believes that flat roofs do not work, thought Webster as
he walked beside and half a step behind Yellich, should come
and visit London NW1 where the flat roofs seem to still be
going strong after nearly two hundred years. At the street level
there were small cafés, pubs, delicatessens, a Jewish museum
and many interesting-looking restaurants. It was, thought
Webster, a very pleasant pocket of the capital, with greenery
in the form of Regent's Park on its doorstep. Had he the funds,
Webster believed that, despite what he had felt about London
as a whole, he could settle in Camden. Had he the funds.

The two officers located the chambers of Oldfield and Fairly
and walked up the short flight of steps to the front door and
turned the highly polished brass doorknob. The large, gloss-
black painted door swung open silently at Yellich's push and
they entered a narrow corridor, carpeted with a dark brown
carpet and with prints of sailing vessels decorating the walls.
A door to the right-hand side was labelled 'Reception'. Yellich
tapped gently on the door and entered, followed by Webster.

Three young women occupied the room, each sitting at a desk and working with evident concentration upon a computer. The young woman nearest the door looked up at Yellich and, smiling warmly, asked if she could help him.

'Police.' Yellich showed his ID. 'DS Yellich of the Vale of York Police.'

'York!' The woman gasped. 'You're a long way south, sir.'

'Yes, I know.' Yellich returned the smile. 'This is DC Webster. We would like to see someone about the Parr family estate.'

'The partners don't see anyone without an appointment, I am sorry, gentlemen.' The woman wore her hair short; she was dressed in a blue business suit. She was, it seemed, more of a personal assistant than she was a secretary.

'Please will you ask them to make an exception.' Yellich continued to smile. 'As you have just observed, we've come a long way and this is in connection with a murder investigation.'

'Multiple murder in fact,' Webster added.

'Oh . . . I see.' The woman reached for the phone on her desk and dialled a two-figure internal number. The other two women continued typing and did not even glance at Yellich and Webster, though both officers sensed that they were listening carefully and that they were missing nothing.

'Mrs McNair will see you, gentlemen,' the first woman said after having spoken to someone and informed them of the arrival of the two police officers from Yorkshire. 'If you would go up the stairs to the first floor, Mrs McNair's office is on the right, more or less above this room.'

'Thank you.' Yellich and Webster turned and left the reception area and climbed the deeply carpeted stairs, and both did so sensing that Mrs McNair was agreeing to see them without an appointment because of a personal curiosity rather than a desire to be public spirited.

Moments later Yellich and Webster were seated in richly polished Chesterfield-style armchairs in front of Mrs McNair's desk. Yellich commented on the calmness of the office.

'Yes, I am familiar with the sort of solicitors' office of which you speak, Mr Yellich.' Mrs McNair revealed herself to be a middle-aged woman whose facial features, Yellich thought, might best be described as 'handsome', in a feminine way, having, it seemed, a certain strength of bone structure that the word 'beauty' would not convey. Mrs McNair was dressed in a black, pinstripe suit with a white blouse beneath. She wore a gold watch, a heavy-looking gold necklace, gold and silver bracelets on each wrist, and wedding and engagement rings. Her office was lined with wood panelling, all highly polished, save for the wall behind where she sat, which was shelved from floor to ceiling with said shelves containing thick and expensive-looking law textbooks. Yellich noticed that none of them had creased spines, which indicated that they had not been much consulted, and were there mainly for purposes of show and impression. 'Offices of frenetic activity,' Mrs McNair suggested, 'where every ten minutes has to be accounted for.'

'Yes.' Yellich smiled. 'That describes them well.'

'Small firms struggling with poorly paid crime work, all done for Legal Aid.' She paused. 'Well, thankfully that is not the manner of Oldfield and Fairly, as you have observed. Our clients are prestige clients, minor aristocracy, major entrepreneurs, and large, established companies. We represent airlines, shipping companies, stockbrokers. We do a little conveyancing work and no crime . . . unless, unless it is white collar crime . . . infringement of patents, that sort of thing, and that can be very lucrative indeed. So we can appear a little "laid back", as my son might say, but the firm's turnover is never less than nine figures per annum. And the partners or salaried solicitors still have to account for every ten minutes of their day.'

'Impressive.' Yellich inclined his head.

'We are not unhappy,' Mrs McNair replied with what seemed to the officers to be very evident smugness. 'Our reputation is excellent and the engagements and instructions keep coming. So, how can I help you, gentlemen from the North?'

Yellich shuffled in his leather-covered chair thus causing the fabric to squeak. 'Well, it is in respect of a client of this firm, or an ex-client, one Mr Parr who, along with his wife and daughters, disappeared. They vanished when visiting York some thirty years ago.'

'Thirty years! And York!'

'Yes.'

'Time and distance,' Mrs McNair replied sniffily. 'I must tell you that I have never been north of London in my life and I never want to. Thirty years . . . I was still at school then, so well before my time.'

'It would be,' Yellich replied. 'Before our time also.'

'I read *Wuthering Heights* once so I know all about Yorkshire . . . such a desolate, windswept landscape. But the client's name Parr; it means nothing to me, except as being the name of one of the wives of Henry Tudor. Catherine Parr. She was the one who outlived him. Doubt it is the same family.'

'Whether or not, they vanished thirty years ago . . . caused quite a splash in the media, as we have said . . . the firm Oldfield and Fairly must have records?'

'Oh yes, of course, going back a few hundred years would you believe. We are a very old firm and our archives are kept in a vault in our cellars . . . down in the dungeon.'

'The dungeon?' Yellich smiled.

Mrs McNair also smiled showing teeth of such whiteness and such perfection that Webster was certain they were dentures. 'That's what the girls in the front office call the cellar and they never like having to go down there. In fact, they are convinced it's haunted. They often report a sense of a presence in the cellars and so usually they go down in pairs, one to retrieve the bundle and the other to lend moral support.'

'So, a case file, or bundle, of just thirty years old could be easily accessed?' Yellich pressed.

'Accessed?' McNair queried. 'What do you mean by accessed?'

'Accessed by the police,' Yellich explained, 'if it was relevant to a murder investigation.'

'A court order would be required of course, but with a court order, then, yes, yes, access can be arranged.' Mrs McNair nodded gently. 'It wouldn't be a problem, but only with a court order compelling us to release the documents in question.'

'I see.' Yellich took a deep breath. 'I wonder . . . would there be a solicitor in the firm who might have a personal recollection of the case to whom we could speak. We might be able to pick his brains?'

'I don't see why you should not talk generally.' Mrs McNair paused. 'But not in detail. Anything said would be off the record of course.'

'Of course,' Yellich agreed.

'Accessing documents would be a different matter, but talking about the case . . .' Mrs McNair picked up the phone on her desk and dialled a two-figure number. When her call was answered she asked, 'Sandra . . . is Mr Tipton within chambers . . .? He is? Good. Can you ask him to come to my office, please? Thank you.' Mrs McNair replaced the receiver. 'Mr Tipton is a long-serving employee of the chambers . . . a clerk, not a fully qualified solicitor, but if you want to pick brains, then his are the brains to pick.' She fell silent and then asked, 'Are you gentlemen planning to remain in town overnight?'

'No . . . no . . .' Yellich replied. 'We plan to return to the desolate landscape upon picking Mr Tipton's brains. Even calling here was unexpected.'

'Good.' Mrs McNair smiled a cold smile. Her response was said in such a manner that both Yellich and Webster tried hard not to read too much into her reply, though both had before met the charming way of insulting which had been polished by the English middle-classes; their practised way of wrapping an insult within what first appears to be a compliment. Mrs McNair and Yellich and Webster continued to sit in a stony silence until there came a reverential tap on the door of Mrs McNair's office. Mrs McNair pointedly waited for a few moments before calling out, 'Come.' Not, Yellich and Webster noted, 'Come in', or 'Please come in' or even 'Enter'. Needlessly haughty they both thought.

The office door opened and a short but broad-chested man, who seemed to Yellich and Webster to be over retirement age, and who was dressed in a black three-piece suit and wearing highly polished black shoes, entered the room. A black tie over a white shirt completed the image he presented, suggesting an undertaker rather than a clerk to a firm of solicitors. 'Yes, ma'am?' He addressed Mrs McNair. 'You sent for me?'

Both Yellich and Webster stood in deference to the elderly gentleman.

'Ah, Mr Tipton, thank you.' Mrs McNair did not look at Tipton; rather she kept her eyes focussed on the surface of her desk. 'These gentlemen are from the police in York.'

'York!' Tipton smiled at Yellich and then at Webster. 'A most delightful city.' He shook hands with the officers as he spoke, pronouncing 'delightful' as 'day-layt-ful', and then he said, 'Delighted to make your acquaintance, gentlemen, I am sure.' Pronouncing the sentence as 'Day-layt-ed to make your haquaintance, hi ham sure.'

'Thank you, sir,' Yellich replied, equally delighted. He was very pleased to find Mr Tipton's handshake very appropriate, a gentleman's handshake, not challengingly firm nor yet offensively loose. It was in fact, he thought, just right.

'Do please take a seat, Mr Tipton,' Mrs McNair invited as Tipton and Webster also shook hands. Tipton then sat in one of the two vacant chairs in front of McNair's desk. The officers similarly resumed their seats.

'Mr Tipton,' Mrs McNair began, 'is the clerk of this firm and I must say that he is utterly invaluable to us . . . utterly, utterly invaluable.'

'So kind, ma'am.' Tipton bowed his head slightly. 'So very kind.'

'No . . . no . . . you really are, Mr Tipton, invaluable. Perfectly filed documents are all very well but only the human brain can keep the overview and recall details that are otherwise difficult to see. We are indeed fortunate Mr Tipton has elected to stay on after his retirement age.'

'Again, so kind, ma'am.' Tipton replied in his sibilistic speaking voice, 'but it is the work that keeps me going, it's the work that keeps me alive. Mrs Tipton went before, you see, and I would doubtless have soon followed were it not for Oldfield and Fairly, who allowed me to continue in my position. It is as my dear father was oft wont to say, "Life can be a dog at times, but you'll be in the clay soon enough, my good boy, so you may as well keep walking the dog as long as you are able".'

'Fair enough.' Yellich noted how the outside noise didn't

penetrate Mrs McNair's office as it had at Nigel Parr's home even though the two buildings were only a few hundred yards distant from each other, yet the double glazing was not evident from the window frames. 'I can understand the attitude, Mr Tipton,' Yellich explained. 'My father had a similar attitude; he'd say, "Carry on . . . just carry on regardless, while there's breath in your body . . . carry on". He was an old soldier, you see.'

'Indeed.' Tipton smiled.

'Well, Mr Tipton,' Mrs McNair interrupted, 'the officers are inquiring about a brief handled by this firm some thirty years ago.'

'The Parr family,' Yellich added. 'Mr and Mrs Parr and their daughters.'

'Oh yes, the family who disappeared while in York and hence, I assume, the interest of the York police?'

'Yes, that family,' Webster confirmed. 'Parents, two daughters and another female believed to have been living with them at the time and who was of the same age group as the daughters.'

'Yes, I do recall those clients. I remember it very well, but the fifth person, the family friend, that is news to me. I really have no recollection of a fifth person in the situation. Have they been found?'

'Yes,' Yellich replied.

'Alive? Alive after thirty years?' A note of optimism was in Tipton's voice.

'Sadly, no,' Webster replied solemnly. 'All five are deceased. They were found in a hole in the ground, quite a deep hole, so not the conventional shallow grave, but very deep. They were clearly not intended to be found. Ever.'

'Oh,' Tipton sighed. 'So sorry. Were they dug up by some form of building work?'

'No, in fact two schoolboys came across the grave when it was freshly filled in,' Webster explained. 'It took them thirty years to realize the significance of what they had found and to come forward and give information.'

'Well I never.' Tipton heaved a deep breath. 'Thirty years . . . And it took them that long to realize what they had seen?'

'Yes,' Webster replied, 'but at least they came forward, which is the main thing.'

'There is that in their favour.' Tipton opened his palm.

'And in fairness it was a freshly harvested field, so not so obviously a grave,' Webster explained.

'I see,' Tipton replied softly.

'Do you know who was the interested partner?' Mrs McNair asked.

'Yes, ma'am.' Tipton addressed Mrs McNair. 'That was Mr Hillyard.'

'Retired,' Mrs McNair explained, 'just in the last year or two.'

'So we might still be able to speak to him?' Yellich asked.

'You might, if he agrees to speak to you,' Mrs McNair replied icily. 'If not, you'll have to subpoena him.'

'Yes,' Yellich answered drily, 'we know the procedure.'

'Do you know anything of the Parr case, Mr Tipton?' Mrs McNair asked.

'I can recall only the gist.' Tipton glanced at Yellich.

'And the gist, even the gist will have to remain confidential, Mr Tipton. The gist is too close to the details.'

'As you say, ma'am' Tipton stood. 'I would like to leave early today, ma'am; I have a dental appointment. I did put it in the book, ma'am.'

'Of course, Mr Tipton.' Mrs McNair smiled a thin smile as if to say, 'Thank you for towing the party line,' and then added, 'Thank you for your time.'

Mrs McNair waited until Mr Tipton had left her office before speaking. 'Not much of a useful visit for you, gentlemen. I am sorry that we could not have been more helpful.' She stood and extended her hand, then held Yellich's hand for an instant, very loosely, before pushing it away from her, as if handing it back to him. She did not extend her hand to Webster.

'Well, we only called here on the off chance anyway.' Yellich turned to go. 'We really travelled south to interview the Parrs' surviving son and that proved to be very useful indeed.'

'Very useful,' Webster echoed, with a smile.

'Oh . . .' Mrs McNair looked crestfallen. 'I assumed . . .'

'And we will be able to obtain a subpoena to oblige

Mr Hillyard to provide a statement and for Oldfield and Fairly to allow the police to access all the relevant documents held in your vault,' Webster added. 'So, quite a useful trip south. Good day.'

'It's the breathtaking wonder of the microchip.' Thomson Ventnor sat opposite Robert McKenzie in the agent's room in Full Sutton prison.

'Really?'

'Yes, really, and it shows the value of methodical recording, and keeping hold of all records and all photographs no matter how dated. We put your father's details into our search engine: Scottish, approximate age, description, ginger hair, married . . . at least one child.'

'You can do that?' Mr McKenzie sounded genuinely surprised.

'Oh yes, and it threw up one name . . . Robert McKenzie . . . but Robert McKenzie senior and also Robert McKenzie junior. The man in our dated files, identified by a member of the public, had a son whom he called after himself. We are interested to know all about the man who hired a mechanical digger thirty years ago.'

'Well I never.' McKenzie reclined in the metal chair and looked across the table at Ventnor. 'My old man reaches out from the grave and gets me visited by the police . . . that is so very nice of him.' He paused, and then added, 'Mind you, I am very pleased that my dad isn't here to see this.'

'Oh?' Ventnor looked round the room, crimson-painted walls up to waist height, cream thereafter, white ceiling, a block of opaque glass set high in the wall to permit a little natural light to enter. Metal chairs, metal desk, a large metal, blue polished door with a heavy brass lock. 'He tried to keep you out of trouble?'

'He tried.' McKenzie nodded gently. 'It was a difficult thing to do when he was a petty crook himself, but he did try; always going on about keeping on the right path, saying, "Look what crookin's done for me", and that old baloney. I suppose it's true but it's also true that the apple never falls far from the tree.'

'I see,' Ventnor replied, 'but, as you say, at least he tried.'

'So, I still followed him, didn't I, became a career criminal?'
McKenzie raised his eyebrows in a gesture of despair.

'Do you think you'll turn yourself around?' Ventnor asked.

'If I can, but it's not easy. Hardly any job opportunities for
someone with a record like mine.' Robert McKenzie sighed.
'You try to keep out of trouble but the dole money goes
nowhere . . . I mean, nowhere. You have contacts, they offer
you a job – I mean a criminal job – if a crew needs a driver
or a bit of muscle. The offer is made. You think you'll get
away with it, but sooner or later you're back inside; it's the
old revolving door. So, will I turn myself around? Dunno . . .
it's not easy, but, tell you the honest truth, I sometimes wonder
if I want to. I sometimes wonder if I am not better off in here.
I get the opportunity to exercise, I get three meals a day, I get
an education . . . I am doing an Open University course, it
could lead to a degree . . .'

'Good for you.' Ventnor smiled approvingly.

'Possibly. The course is useful because it keeps my mind
focussed on healthy things but what can I do with a degree?'

'It's a positive thing to do as an end in itself,' Ventnor
encouraged. 'It'll make you feel good about yourself. It's a
healthy use of time.'

'Well, I've got plenty of that, but I'm still on the wrong
side of the fence. It's OK for you, sir; you'll retire at fifty-five
with an index-linked pension.'

'I wish I could say something to help you, but I can't.'
Ventnor felt at a loss.

'That's honest of you anyway.' McKenzie nodded. 'I am
old for a lag; turned forty some years ago. I'm overdue for
the grey house; I'll be sent there soon. It's for old lags, anyone
over fifty. They say it's calm and quiet, like the reading room
in a public library, they say.' McKenzie had hard and cold
eyes, thought Ventnor, set in a scarred face.

'Yes.' Ventnor sat forward. 'I hear the same.'

'It'll be good to finish off there. My dad keeled over when
he was in his early sixties; he had a massive heart attack. It
runs in the family, weak hearts, so I am also probably two-
thirds through my race. Nothing good behind me and I bet
there's nothing good ahead of me.'

'So, tell me about your father,' Ventnor pressed.

'That's why you're here?'

'Yes, I am not soft-soaping you to get your spill on unsolved crimes or to grass anyone up.'

'Good job.' McKenzie spoke with a sudden menacing edge to his voice. 'I wouldn't do that anyway.'

'Understood,' Ventnor replied. 'I hear what you say, but I am here because I am interested in anything you can tell me about a bit of work your father probably did once. You'd be a mid to late teenager. It was probably legitimate work, a bit of labouring for hard cash. It could also have been iffy . . . it could have been very iffy in fact. There is just the possibility that you know a little about it.'

'Fair play.' Robert McKenzie leaned forward and rested two muscular arms on the tabletop. 'That sounds fair. I can't say that I dislike the police. You have a job to do and you've always been fair with me. You have never planted evidence on me, never lied on oath to get a conviction, not like some in here who claim to have that happened to them, and I have long decided that I want to have something to think about when I am dying, something that I can feel good about myself for. So, how can I help you?'

'Thank you.' Ventnor held eye contact with McKenzie. 'Thank you very much. Well, your father fits the description and has been identified from this photograph of the man . . . as the man who once hired a small mechanical digger from a plant hire company. He collected it using a trailer pulled by a Land Rover and he returned it the following day. He is reported to have paid for the hire with a large wedge of hard cash. I can tell you he was entrusted with a large amount of money . . . a suitcase full of the stuff, by all accounts.'

'Entrusted.' McKenzie took a breath. 'Or someone had something to hold over him, something that made the old man scared of stealing it, because the old man was a tea leaf. He was just so light-fingered, it wasn't true. I don't know about a suitcase full of money, but it does make sense of what he once said when he was on the way out . . . and a mechanical digger . . . a small one. I did go and dig a hole with him one night in a field.'

'You did?' Ventnor's interest rose sharply.

'Yes, it was out in the sticks one night. It was a freshly harvested field; I can remember the stubble underfoot.'

'That sounds like the incident we are interested in. Go on . . . please go on.'

'So, it was the people who were found, that missing family? It was that hole?' McKenzie asked.

'Yes.' Ventnor sat back in his chair. 'Yes, it was that family. It was that hole.'

'Well, well, I never figured the old man for the big "M". I thought he was nothing more than a small-fry tea leaf. He's just gone up in my estimation.' McKenzie grinned. 'So, like father like son, only I got caught.'

'Possibly, but he was also possibly no more than a gofer.' Ventnor glanced round the room again, finding it hard and functional. 'He was probably not a murderer.'

'Probably you're right, but even if he dug a hole and helped to put bodies away, that makes him a conspirator, doesn't it?' McKenzie spoke eagerly. 'He was an accessory after the fact?'

'Yes,' Ventnor agreed. 'Yes, it does.'

'So he was bigger than I thought.' McKenzie seemed to Ventnor to be glowing with sudden pride. 'Good for the old boy.'

'Do you know who paid him to collect the digger and excavate the hole?'

'The landowner,' McKenzie replied quietly. 'My old man told me it was the landowner who wanted the hole dug on his land but it had to be done at night. I was the lookout . . . I kept the edge. Then, when the hole was dug, the old man told me to take a hike, so I went, not too far away really, just into a nearby wood, took cover and looked back. Then I saw headlights approaching, driving across the field . . . but it was a four-by-four, I could tell by the way it bounced across the field. It stopped hard by where the hole was, then a few minutes later it drove away and I heard the digger start up. When I got back the old man was filling the hole in. So, he was more than a gofer.' McKenzie's chest swelled. 'He put those bodies away, my old man did, conspiracy to murder . . . not bad.'

Ventnor paused. He felt he should be used to the misplaced sense of pride exhibited by criminals but it still came as a shock to him whenever it was met. 'What was it he said when he was dying? You mentioned it just now.'

'Oh . . . yes . . . that he was given a large bag of cash once and he was tempted to run away with it, but he didn't because it would mean running out on his family. He had a sense of honour, my old man.' McKenzie smiled. 'He did have a sense of duty to his family. He also said the people he was working for were a heavy duty team. They were, he told me, not the sort of people you'd want to mess with. He said the wedge he got for the job was a good size so he settled for that. You know he probably saved his life by taking that decision, putting his family first.'

'He probably did.' Ventnor nodded in agreement. 'But your father definitely told you that he was paid to dig the hole by the landowner?'

'Yes. A guy called Farrent, I think. The old man often did work for Farrent, so they knew each other and he knew Farrent wasn't to be messed with,' McKenzie added. 'Not to be messed with . . . not at all was he a man to mess with.'

'Heavy duty.' Ventnor stood.

'Very heavy. You don't want to take a statement?'

'No point.' Ventnor tapped on the door of the agent's room. 'It would be hearsay but, nonetheless, it has been very useful hearsay. Best of luck in the grey house when they do decide to move you.'

Yellich and Webster stepped out of the dim interior of the chambers of Oldfield and Fairly into Camden Street, which was bathed in the brilliant sunshine of a late afternoon in mid September. The white-painted buildings reflected the glare of the sun and caused the two officers to half close their eyes.

'So you survived the Great Camden Ice Maiden?' Mr Tipton stood by the railings close to the steps leading up to the premises of Oldfield and Fairly.

'Mr Tipton.' Yellich beamed at the elderly gentleman. 'Sorry, I didn't recognize you . . . the sun . . .'

'Yes, it glares angrily at times,' Tipton replied.

'I thought you had a dental appointment?' Yellich enquired. 'I hope you didn't miss it on our account, sir.'

'Tom . . .' Tipton smiled. 'Please call me Tom. No, no dental appointment, but I doubt ye Ice Maiden will check the book, and if she does, well, do I care? I am allegedly totally invaluable and I am beyond retirement age anyway. There are things in life which no longer concern me, such as becoming HIV positive or losing my job. They and other issues are for younger persons. Come; let us go to The Eagle. I can tell you a few things that might interest you, gentlemen.'

'The Eagle?' Yellich queried.

'The nearest pub and a very nice one too. This way, gentlemen.'

At The Eagle they were served by an alert and polite young barmaid. Tom Tipton ordered a whisky while Yellich and Webster both requested tonic water.

'You don't drink, gentlemen?' Tipton indicated a vacant table in the corner of the pub. 'Let's sit here.'

'Duty.' Yellich followed Tipton to the table. 'Also, it's a trifle early and we have a journey home ahead of us. We are Somerled and Reginald.'

'Strange name . . . Somerled, how is it spelled?'

'It's Gaelic,' Yellich explained and told Tipton how his name was spelled as he sat at the table.

'Somerled and Reginald. Here's health.' Tipton raised his glass. 'Tell you the truth, the honest truth, it's this stuff that keeps me going, not working for Oldfield and Fairly.' Tipton spoke in a different, quite normal voice, without a trace of the hissing speech of before.

'So why carry on working, Tom?' Yellich sipped his tonic and glanced round the pub. He saw polished wood, solid furniture, rural scenes in frames on the wall. No music, he noted. The Eagle was blessedly free of music.

'Because it gets me up in the morning and because it gets me out of the house. It's a big house to be alone in after forty-five years of happy marriage. Now, being at home is like bouncing round inside the Albert Hall . . . just me and my shadow and my echo . . . all three of us.'

'I see,' Yellich replied. 'And your voice, Tom, it's changed.'

'Hasn't it just.' Tipton grinned. 'It's a game I have kept up throughout my time at the firm, just my little joke. I am an actor . . . drama school . . . just couldn't get a part, hardly at all, and took a job as a clerk in a firm of solicitors to see me by. Always dreamed of going back to acting but it never happened. Clerking continued, but my voice at work, that's the only real acting I have done.'

Yellich and Webster smiled warmly at Tom Tipton.

'So,' Tipton continued, 'I usually stay here until seven p.m. and go home after the rush hour. I get home at about eight p.m., with just two hours to kill before I retire at ten p.m. So, you gentlemen want to know about the Parr case?'

'Yes,' Yellich replied. 'Yes, we do, anything and everything you can tell us.'

'I remember the case. The clients were comfortably off . . . this being Camden.'

'I can bet.' Webster grinned. 'From what we have seen, they must indeed have been comfortably off.'

'Well, you'll need a million plus to buy a modest two bedroomed flat in a conversion. Minimum.' Tipton savoured the aroma of his whisky.

'Again, I can bet,' Webster replied.

'Their solicitor,' Tipton continued, 'Mr Hillyard, the one who you really must speak to, he has retired to Barnet.'

'Where is that?' Yellich asked.

'North London . . . still on the tube network . . . just. In fact the northern line stops there, or starts there, depending on the direction you are travelling in. I mean the northern terminus of the Northern Line is High Barnet.'

'I see.' Yellich sipped his tonic water.

'The useful thing is,' Tipton continued, 'is that Mr Hillyard and Mr and Mrs Parr seemed to "click" as personalities. They just seemed to get on with each other very well, so on that basis I think Mr Hillyard will be very keen to help. While Mr Hillyard never did any pro bono work in those days, he did not feel Mr Parr's pockets as deeply as he otherwise might have done.'

'Interesting,' Webster growled as he turned his mind to the size of his own recently levelled conveyancing fee, which had seemed and still seemed to him to be unreasonably large. His pocket had evidently been quite deeply plundered.

'But the case in question,' Tipton continued, 'it became known as the "Altered Case". It was a land dispute: ownership of.'

'The "Altered Case"?' Yellich sat forward intrigued.

'Yes.' Tipton nodded. 'The case reaches back in time quite a long way. I believe the land in question was up in your neck of the woods and was a large amount of land, hundreds of square miles, a very substantial amount of land indeed . . . about half of Yorkshire.' Tipton paused. 'I understood that Mr Parr is the . . . was the direct descendent of the family who lost the dispute.'

'I am beginning to understand,' Yellich replied. Beside him he felt Webster was also listening intently.

'It was Parr's claim that the title deeds had been unlawfully altered,' Tipton explained.

'Hence the "Altered Case"?' Yellich offered.

'Yes, Somerled, it was a form of theft.' Tipton sat forward. 'It was, I believe, the case that during the confusion and turmoil that followed the Civil War, one family somehow acquired the deeds of the land in question, but did so unlawfully. The details are known only to Mr Hillyard, but what I can tell you is that the family who are now the apparent owners of the land are also direct lineal descendants of the family who allegedly acquired the land unlawfully.'

'So the issue of land ownership is just as immediate as if the land had changed ownership last week?' Yellich clarified.

'More or less,' Tipton confirmed, 'but you'll have to talk to Mr Hillyard for the details and legal position to be made clear.' Tipton shrugged. 'I, being a humble clerk with a decayed ambition to be an actor, have friends who lament that they never played the Dane. You're lucky, I say; me . . . I never played anything.'

'So we really need to speak to Mr Hillyard in Barnet?'

'Yes. I made a phone call before I left chambers. He's expecting you. This is his address.' Tipton handed Yellich a piece of paper. 'It'll mean a late return for you two gentlemen tonight.'

'For this we don't mind.' Yellich took the piece of paper.

'Take the Northern Line,' Tipton suggested. 'The nearest

tube station is at the bottom of the hill, a few hundred yards away. If you go now you'll easily miss the rush hour.'

'You're staying here, Tom?' Yellich stood.

'Yes.' Tipton drained his glass and smiled. 'Many whiskies to drink between now and seven of the clock. Many whiskies.'

'So I want to know what you've done with her,' Farrent snarled. 'You've done something with her, haven't you?'

Standing on the other side of the enquiry desk and beside the uniformed officer who had asked for his presence, Hennessey remained silent.

'What have you done with her?' Farrent repeated.

'Nothing.' Hennessey remained calm and softly spoken. 'We have done nothing, nothing at all.'

'Well, she's not at home. Not home. She's either at home or at the shops . . . nowhere else. So where is she?' Farrent raised his voice. 'Where is Mrs Farrent?'

'I'm afraid I don't know, sir.' Hennessey continued to remain calm.

'You were talking to her . . . not you . . . the other one, the other officer, talking in the middle of York, in the street, talking to my wife. She wouldn't tell me what was said. She said nothing was said but who stands next to a policeman and says nothing? Who? *Who?*' Farrent paused and held angry eye contact with Hennessey. 'Then this morning she was gone . . . gone. You took her in the night . . . You took her! She wouldn't leave me, she knows better than to do that. You've taken her . . .!'

'Please take a missing person report in respect of Mrs Farrent of Catton Hill,' Hennessey said to the officer. Then he turned to Thomas Farrent. 'It's all we can do.'

Sara Yellich sat on the settee in the living room of her house in Huntingdon. Jeremy, aged twelve, had just been returned by the escort from the school he attended and was sitting cross-legged in front of the television. 'Hope he stays calm,' Sara Yellich hissed with a smile to her neighbour who was sitting in the armchair sipping a cup of coffee. 'Somerled has just phoned me on his mobile telling me he's going to be late

tonight and Jeremy can be difficult if he's upset. The psychologist says he is frustrated because he can't express himself. It
must be difficult for him, body of a twelve-year-old, with the
mind of a five-year-old.'

'Yes.' Mrs St John, the neighbour, nodded her head sympa-
thetically. 'I must say you are doing a magnificent job. I
doubt—'

'We just found it makes us love him all the more,' Sara
Yellich explained. 'We knew disappointment at first, but he's
been such a source of joy.' She reached forward and closed
the dictionary which lay open on the coffee table. 'Don't want
to get coffee on this; it's Victorian . . . quite valuable.'

'Looking up an obscure word?' Mrs St John asked.

'"Mendicant",' Sara Yellich replied. 'Not so obscure.'

'It means a beggar, doesn't it?'

'Yes, it's leaving the language now, few people know of the
word but originally, so I found out, it had a high moral value,'
Sara Yellich explained, 'and meant a holy man, a priest or a
monk who had taken a vow of poverty and wandered the land
existing on whatever folk put in their begging bowls, be it
food or coin. Then, in Victorian times, it suffered semantic
spread and became a word used in a derogatory sense to mean
beggar, and now it's leaving the language altogether, as some
words tend to do.'

'As you say. Why look it up?'

'Somerled asked me what it meant. Apparently someone
described someone else as a "mendicant" and neither he nor
his boss knew what that meant. I said I thought that it meant
"beggar", but when he gets home I can let him have a fuller
answer.' Sara Yellich stretched her arms. 'I am so pleased my
degree isn't being totally wasted.'

Yellich and Webster both thought Harold Hillyard Esquire to
be every inch what they imagined a recently retired solicitor
from a successful London firm of the manner of Oldfield and
Fairly should look like. The two officers and Harold Hillyard
sat in the drawing room of Hillyard's house just as the sun
was setting over the north London suburbs. The house itself
had, the officers found, been a little further from the tube

terminus at High Barnet than they had anticipated, but the walk through the well-set and leafy suburbs to Hadley Green Road was no mean compensation. Hillyard's house proved to be a late Victorian detached property with a U-shaped 'in and out' driveway leading up to a porticoed front door. The building was painted a pleasant shade of off-white under a red-tiled roof and blended, it seemed, very sensitively with the surrounding area. The front of the house looked out across a narrow road to a small area of grassland, which had evidently been allowed to remain as a wilderness.

'So, quite a turn up for the books.' Hillyard was a portly man who, Yellich and Webster thought, looked much younger than his sixty-seven years, and who was casually dressed in denim jeans and a blue-and-white rugby shirt. The athletic dress, Webster saw, contributed much to his youthful appearance. Put the selfsame man in a tweed jacket and brogues, Webster pondered, and then he would look much nearer his actual age.

'Seems so, sir.' Yellich glanced round the room. He saw solid but tasteful furniture, sober decor, with a hint of wealth provided by clearly original oil paintings hanging on the wall.

'I understand that you have the outline of the story from our clerk, Mr Tipton?' Hillyard clarified.

'Yes, sir.' Yellich felt himself settling into the great comfort of the armchair. 'Just the barest outline . . . a land dispute we believe, but one which goes back a few hundred years.'

'Yes, that is the essence of it. Mr Tipton is a good man, a very good man, very discreet.'

'How well did you know the case, sir?'

'Very well indeed. I also got to know the family, the Parrs, prior to the land dispute issue emerging and we just seemed to click. I was a family friend not just their solicitor. We exchanged Christmas cards, that sort of thing, and one day I bumped into Gerald Parr in Camden High Street late one morning as I was looking for a place to partake of luncheon, my usual dining place having closed quite unexpectedly, and, good man that he was, he invited me to his home for lunch and I accepted. I had met his lady wife before but not his children; never been to his house.'

'I see.'

'Well, what can I say?' Hillyard continued. 'Hardly know how to describe what I met . . . the house . . . the family, sort of eccentric, jumbly, mumbly, happy-go-lucky crew. So much so, and, I kid you not, that as myself and Gerald were sitting at the breakfast bar in their kitchen and were both tucking into our Spanish omelettes when in trooped their daughters . . . Isabella and . . . What was the name of the second daughter, the younger one? Her name escapes me . . .'

'Alexandra,' Webster prompted, his eyes drawn to the vast crimson sunset. 'Her name was Alexandra.'

'Ah, yes.' Hillyard smiled. 'Of course, Sandy for short. Anyway, in they came, then they were in their late teens, and they were both totally naked.'

'Really!' Yellich smiled and gasped at the same time.

'Yes, really.' Hillyard also smiled. 'I confess it was quite an eye-fest for me . . . being my age at the time . . . and a lifetime since I had seen a nubile woman, naked, and just inches from me. They were a little on the short side. The family was very short in terms of stature.'

'Yes,' Yellich commented, 'we discovered that.'

'But heavens, they were in the right proportion . . . The two girls just breezed in without saying a word. They knew I was there and calmly made themselves a mug of tea each and calmly walked out again. It was a most pleasing sight . . . it brightened my lunch no end.' Hillyard chuckled.

'I imagine it would.' Yellich smiled.

'Gerald looked a bit sheepish and said, "It's their form of self-expression" or something of that sort and added "Why should they be ashamed of their bodies?"'

'A liberal-minded family,' Yellich observed.

'Very . . . liberal-minded in the extreme. It was just that sort of family; very bohemian. Gerald was an artist after all. Their lifestyle would not have suited me or my wife; we both have more conservative tastes, as do most members of the legal profession.'

'Yes.' Yellich continued to read the room. 'Yes, I would also be of the same persuasion, as most police officers, similar to lawyers, are conservative in terms of taste.'

'Well . . . to continue.' Hillyard relaxed back in his chair.

'I visited the family a few times after that and came to know them quite well. Their easy-going lifestyle was like a ray of sunshine in the closed world of Oldfield and Fairly and then . . . then arose the issue of the "Altered Case".'

'Of which we know very little,' Yellich appealed.

Hillyard took a deep breath. 'I will tell you the story as succinctly as I can. It turned on the issue of ownership of land, that is to say the disputed ownership of a substantial amount of land. I mean about half of Yorkshire, an area measured in hundreds of square miles; that sort of area of land.'

'I see,' Yellich replied. 'So big money was involved?'

'Huge money.' Hillyard raised his eyebrows and nodded gently. 'An awful lot of pennies. Gerald Parr is a direct descendent of the family who had lost the land in the seventeenth century.'

'Ah . . .' Yellich replied.

'It was Gerald Parr's claim that the deeds of the land, that is to say the title deeds of same, had been unlawfully altered.'

'Hence the "Altered Case",' Yellich offered.

'Exactly. It was the claim that the deeds had been unlawfully . . . fraudulently altered so as to confer the ownership of the land on to another family.'

'Understood.'

'It was a fraud which was made possible it seems for a number of reasons, the first being that the Parrs were absentee landlords. They lived in a property in the London area but owned the land in Yorkshire, which was largely an unsettled area . . . one or two small farming communities . . . but it was in fact a forest in the true meaning of the word.'

'Which is,' Yellich asked, 'not a large wood?'

'No . . . no . . . the word "forest" has come to mean that, but originally it was an area of land subject to forest law, that is to say it was a large area of land reserved for the King and his retinue to hunt royal game; deer, boar, that sort of thing.'

'I see.' Yellich smiled. 'I do like a good history lesson.'

'Good . . . so the second reason why the fraud, if it was a fraud – it never went to trial – the second reason why it was possible was that it took place in the years of turmoil following the English Civil War when one family, it is alleged, obtained the deeds of the land in question and scratched out the name "Parr" and substituted their own name, being that of "Farrent".'

'Ah.' Yellich glanced at Webster who nodded his head slightly. 'Yes, we have met Mr Farrent.'

'It was the case,' Hillyard continued, 'that the Parrs were Royalists and the Farrents were Parliamentarians; consequently the Farrents enjoyed favour of what passed for justice in the land in the immediate aftermath of the Civil War, also sometimes known as the War of the Three Kingdoms.'

'Friends in high places,' Yellich commented, 'always useful.'

'Indeed,' Hillyard replied, 'as you say, always useful. So the Parrs were dispossessed of the forest in Yorkshire, and they probably did not put up a fight because they doubtless thought that being highly placed Royalists, which they apparently were, they were lucky to keep their heads.'

'I see,' Yellich commented.

'It was the case,' Hillyard explained, 'that many Royalist families lost their lands following the victory of the Parliamentarians. It seemed to be that the attitude was "you're alive – don't complain", and it's crucial, utterly crucial to the argument that both the families when the case came to light were direct descendants of the Parrs and the Farrents when the deeds were allegedly altered in the 1640s.'

'So,' Yellich asked, 'that means that the Parrs had a legal claim to the land which was, in the eyes of the law, equally as strong as it would be if the deeds were altered within the lifetime of the present Parr and Farrent families, Mr Farrent also being a linear descendant of the Farrent who acquired the land in 1640. How interesting,' Yellich added softly.

'Isn't it?' Hillyard replied. 'If the Parr line had dissolved and there was no direct lineal descendant of the Percy Parr who had owned the land before the Civil War, then there would be no legal challenge to the validity of the Farrents' ownership of the land.' He paused. 'So the years went by, the Parrs could not raise an action to dispute the ownership of the land, all they could do was to pass the story of the "Altered Case" down the family from one generation to the next until . . .' Hillyard raised a finger.

'Duplicate documents?' Yellich gasped.

Hillyard nodded his head. 'Yes, exactly. It was the story that Gerald Parr was sifting through bundles of documents and family heirlooms, which had been stored in the basement of his property, when he stumbled across a deed which showed one Percy Parr to be the rightful owner of the land in question.'

'Being a large part of Yorkshire?' Yellich sighed. 'What a find! Confess I could do with making a find like that in my house.'

'Couldn't we all?' Hillyard gave a soft laugh. 'But it seems that it must have been the case that the original Parr, Percy Parr, either did not know of the document, or did know of it but sensibly kept quiet about its existence given that particular political climate. The policy being that he handed it to his son or sons saying, "Keep this safe and when there is some semblance of law in England and fair justice, then that is the time to dispute ownership". But it also seems that at some point in the family history, while the story of the "Altered Case" was kept alive, the existence of the duplicate deed seems to have been forgotten.'

'Did Mr Parr have a good case?' Yellich asked.

'Very good,' Hillyard replied. 'If – and only if – the duplicate document was accepted as being authentic. The document analyst engaged by Oldfield and Fairly reported that they believed the document to be authentic. We had not yet begun proceedings but there was some phoning between ourselves and the Farrents' solicitors in York, a firm called Fyrst, Tend and Byrd. They wanted their own experts to look at the document.'

'Seems fair enough,' Yellich said.

'Oh, it was most fair,' Hillyard agreed, 'most fair and a wholly correct reaction from Farrent's solicitors. We would have done the same.'

'Where is the document now?'

'In the vaults of Oldfield and Fairly,' Hillyard replied, 'and who, it may be said, were smelling large amounts of money . . . It was about this time that I may have done the firm out of a fortune.'

'Oh?' Yellich queried.

'Yes . . .' Hillyard paused. 'Yes, you see, by this time I had grown quite fond of the Parr family and the lawyers . . . the legal teams on both sides were circling like hyenas round a stricken calf . . . and one day after work I called at their house, sat in their lounge and gave them a bit of sound Scottish advice.'

'Scottish advice?' Yellich queried.

'I have come up in the world from humble stock and am proud of it. My grandmother, God rest her, was the wife of an Aberdeen trawlerman and she lived with the constant fear of losing "her man" – as she was wont to refer to her husband, my grandfather – "losing her man to the sea", and she contributed to the reputation that the Scots have of being penny pinching; she was just so very tight-fisted. You know, I have a framed print of the *Punch* cartoon from the nineteenth century which depicts a Scotsman upon his return from London saying to another Scot, "Mon, it's a ruinous place, I had not been there above two hours when bang went sixpence!"'

Yellich and Webster grinned.

'Well, my granny, lovely woman, she had that sort of attitude, "Come in, you'll have had your tea", but . . . and here it gets less humorous, she was fond of the old Scottish saying, "The law's expensive, take a pint and settle".'

'Meaning,' Yellich asked, 'have a drink and sit round a table and reach an agreement, there being no need to line the pockets of lawyers?'

'Yes . . . it's probably what prompted my father to enter the legal profession, canny old soul; he must have worked out that if the law's expensive it was clearly the game to enter if he wanted to be wealthy. He came south and worked in Kent as a solicitor. My son is now a solicitor, so we are three generations and possibly a fourth and fifth.'

'Well done, sir.' Yellich inclined his head.

'I am not displeased,' Hillyard replied, 'not displeased at all. But that evening I went to see Gerald and Elizabeth and I said, "Look, I am probably talking myself out of a job here but the solicitors on both sides are scenting big money". I also pointed out that the dispute was not going to be settled in a brief hearing in the magistrates court, but was a case that could drag on for years, and the barristers will drag it out for as long as they can because barristers get paid for court time, so they will slow up the case all they can, and they really know how to charge . . . They all have children in private schools so they charge . . . don't they just.'

'Yes,' Yellich growled, 'I am aware of that tactic. No wonder they are all so wealthy.'

'I won't comment.' Hillyard managed a brief smile. 'Even though the land in question is not as large as the original parcel, it's been broken up over the years; compulsory purchases to build roads and new rail links, and they lost a lot to the government during the Second World War. The Farrents also sold some of the land to raise money, but nevertheless a substantial amount still remains and since the Farrents have been there for nearly four hundred years it might be agreed that they have some moral claim to the property, especially since they believe that it is theirs; they most probably are entitled to something.'

'Yes, I can understand that.' Yellich nodded his head. 'It seems fair.'

'The Farrents would not be thrown off the land,' Hillyard continued, 'they would not be cast into homelessness and poverty, and when chatting to another senior partner about the case, Charles Bentley, he said that he could foresee the judgement as being to divide the estate equally. If the second document analysis proved the Parr family's deed to be authentic, both families would have a claim. Owning the land for four hundred years counts for something.'

'Would squatters' rights apply?' Webster asked.

'No.' Hillyard shook his head. 'Squatters' rights only apply to houses occupied by people who know they are not the legal owner, not the disputed ownership of hundreds of square miles of land.'

'I see.'

'Another partner, Adrian Wenlock, also thought that an equal division would be a likely outcome, and he added, "But not for a few years, and what lovely deep pockets"; the other partners chuckled at that, as I also did, but only to go along with them. In my mind I knew what I was going to do.'

Hillyard paused. 'We do have a conscience, Mr Yellich, despite popular opinion.'

'You were going to tip the Parrs off,' Yellich replied. 'A nod and a wink?'

'Yes. That very day, after work, I called on them, with their naked daughters and stray animals and youngsters taken off the street, and said, "Look, Gerald, look, Elizabeth, the received wisdom is that after a lengthy and costly court case you will probably be given half the land in question".'

'So take a pint and settle?' Yellich asked.

'I said contact these people, they are not your enemies, you are strangers, talk to them, tell them both families are going to lose a fortune in legal fees only for each family to end up owning half the land at the end of it all. So sit round a table, with or without your solicitors, agree an equal divide, then get the county court to ratify the decision.' Hillyard stood and walked to the window of the room. 'It was about then they disappeared, only to be exhumed a few days ago. I may . . . I probably sent them to their deaths, and all the while I thought that I had retired with a clear conscience. Oh, heavens . . . what did I do? The Parr family and the girl they took in . . .'

'You gave good advice, sir,' Yellich replied. 'You could not have foreseen what we believe might have happened. No one could.'

'Possibly.' Hillyard looked into the sunset.

'So the Parrs drove north, leaving the foster son, Nigel, behind?'

'It seems so. Confess I never did take to Nigel. He towered over the family, lowering his head to enter rooms – to get through the doorway, I mean, not bowing out of respect. Found in a phone box I believe. I dare say he could have been rescued if he had been fostered at that age but after ten or so years in an institution he was too far gone. The Parrs tried to make a silk purse out of a sow's ear. Can't be done.' Hillyard turned round. 'I am not a child psychologist but I do believe that there is much truth in the saying that you can take the child out of the ghetto but you can't take the ghetto out of the child. It seems that once that ruthless, survival-at-all-costs attitude has been put into the child then it never, ever, leaves . . . I recall

Nigel as being an intense, brooding youth; him and his girl-friend. She was an equally cold fish; one Florence Nightingale.'

'You are joking.' Webster grinned.

'Nope, it was her name and that's why I remember it. She was not happy with the name. I commented on it and she just snarled as though she had heard the jokes and comments often enough. She said she wished her parents had gone the whole hog and called her "Boadicea"; pronouncing it "Bo-di-see-a" rather than "Boo-dikka", being the correct rendering.'

'Really?' Yellich replied. 'That's the correct pronunciation?'

'Yes, the Romans would have called her by the first pronun-ciation. She and the Iceni would have used the second.' Hillyard smiled. 'Another history lesson for you, Mr Yellich.'

'Indeed, sir.' Yellich returned the smile.

'But,' Hillyard continued, 'Nigel Parr and Florence Nightingale gelled well. They found each other all right.'

'And he avoided the trip north?' Yellich asked.

'So it seemed. He went somewhere with Florence Nightingale.'

'Probably saved his life,' Webster commented.

'Probably,' Hillyard replied, 'dare say we'll never know.' He drummed his fingers on the window sill. 'You know, I never did take to him at all, as I said, and Gerald became worried about him.'

'Oh?' Yellich queried.

'Yes, over a beer one evening Gerald confessed to me that he thought that they had made a terrible mistake in fostering him. He grew to feel that they had brought something poisonous into their home. He really was quite depressed about it.'

Yellich glanced at Webster. 'That is interesting, because his brother-in-law clearly thought otherwise.'

'Whose brother-in-law?'

'Gerald Parr's brother-in-law, chap yclept Verity. He collected Parr's possessions from the police station in York when they had been reported as missing persons. Anyway, he settled money on Nigel following the sale of Parr's property and it was sufficient for Nigel to buy a modest two bedroomed conversion, also in Camden.'

Yellich and Webster watched the colour drain from Hillyard's face.

'We visited him this afternoon,' Yellich explained slowly, 'tracked him down. It wasn't difficult because he'd kept the Parr surname rather than reverting to his own.'

'He was in the phone book,' Webster added.

'Yes, we visited him prior to calling on Oldfield and Fairly, meeting Mr Tipton and then your good self,' Yellich continued. 'One contact led to another for us today.'

Hillyard's head sank forward. He glanced up at Yellich and then at Webster. 'I did wonder what had become of young Nigel Parr, but I can tell you that he didn't receive any money from Gerald Parr's brother-in-law following the sale of the Parrs' property.'

'No?' Yellich and Webster both sat forward, their interest raised.

'No, Elizabeth Parr didn't have a brother. Both Gerald and Elizabeth were only children, neither of them had any siblings, their children grew up without anyone to call aunt or uncle.'

Again Yellich and Webster glanced at each other. 'But the house sale,' Yellich asked, 'that must have happened?'

'Yes, it did. Gerald and Elizabeth made wills and asked Oldfield and Fairly to accept power of attorney and act as executors in the event of a common calamity; that is, if, for example, both Gerald and Elizabeth were to lose their lives at the same time . . . a car crash, for example.'

'Yes . . . yes,' Yellich replied.

'So after two years they were officially deemed deceased, along with the beneficiaries of their will . . . or wills . . . being their two daughters . . . then Oldfield and Fairly liquidated everything, cleared the house and sold the contents, then sold the property . . . and the money in question is still gathering interest in a trust fund administered by Oldfield and Fairly, where it will remain until a lawful claimant presents themselves.' Hillyard paused. 'So wherever Nigel Parr got the money to buy his little pad in Camden it did not come from the estate of Gerald and Elizabeth Parr.'

Yellich reclined in his chair. 'Now that is very interesting.'

'Very interesting, indeed,' Webster added. 'When did you last see Nigel Parr?'

'When Gerald and Elizabeth were still alive. By the time

we accessed the property – we had to use bailiffs, then change the locks – Nigel had flown the coop. I assumed that he had been told he wasn't going to inherit anything and had left to make his own way in life. I only ever gave him a passing thought after that.'

Walking back to High Barnet tube station in the warm dusk, Webster said, 'So, now what? Back to Camden and arrest Nigel Parr? He's got some explaining to do methinks.'

'Methinks likewise,' Yellich replied. 'But he's not going anywhere. No, we return to York, and tomorrow we talk this over with the boss. Softly, softly, catchee monkey, that's the trick, we must not go blundering into things.'

'Softly, softly,' Webster echoed, 'suits me.'

Later, much later that evening, Reginald Webster crept into his bedroom in his house on the outskirts of Selby. As he entered the room his wife levered herself up and groped for her watch.

'Sorry, Joyce,' he whispered, 'didn't mean to wake you.'

'I was getting worried. I know you phoned and said you'd be late but I can't help worrying.' Joyce Webster lifted the glass cover from her watch and read the time with her fingertips. 'So late.'

'Yes.' Webster let his clothes lay where they fell and slid into the bed beside her, folding his arms about her. 'Rather later than I had anticipated but it was a very productive day . . . very useful.'

It was Thursday, 01.35 hours.

SIX

Thursday, 09.45 hours – 16.45 hours

in which Webster, accompanied by Ventnor, returns to the south of England, Carmen Pharoah silences a pub and the most courteous reader is introduced to George Hennessey's pride and issue.

Webster held his mug of tea in both hands. 'Met a solicitor yesterday, worked for a firm, one of whom was called Fairly . . . A solicitor called "Fairly"!'

'I can top that,' Ventnor said above the laughter. 'I met the wife of a solicitor called "Fleece".'

George Hennessey joined in the laughter. 'A lawyer called "Fleece", that I do like. But let's get down to business; it seems to have been a very productive day yesterday, going by what I have heard.' He glanced to his left out of the window of his office, his eye being caught by movement on the wall, and saw a group of brightly dressed tourists ambling along the battlements. He turned back to the group of CID officers. 'So, who wants to kick off? Thomson, why don't you start the ball rolling.'

'Very good, boss.' Thomson Ventnor leaned forwards. 'Well, the Mrs Fleece I mentioned was a mate of Michelle Lemmon. It seems she was hitching a ride home with the Parr family, who were travelling to York to talk business with someone. She was returning home to patch things up with her parents. She appeared to have stayed with some other friend between the time of arriving in York and guiding the Parrs to their destination. Thus far that person has not come forward, but the Parrs were in York for two days before they went missing, so she was probably sleeping on someone's couch plucking up the courage to go home. In the afternoon I went to Full Sutton, interviewed the son of the man identified as having hired the mechanical digger. He's a lifer in for murder but he was very cooperative. He confirmed that his father did hire the digger and he went out with him to dig the hole, but was sent away as a lookout before the bodies arrived and returned once the hole had been filled in, but he made the clear statement that his father told him that he was employed by the landowner to dig the hole.'

'Farrent?' Hennessey confirmed.

'Yes, sir. I didn't get it down in writing because it was hearsay, but if the Crown Prosecution Service would like a statement – a signed and written statement – I can easily return.'

'Yes, but as you say, it was hearsay, so I don't think you'll have to do that. All right, Somerled and Reginald, what did you turn up?'

'Quite a lot, sir.' Yellich leaned forwards as Thomson Ventnor sat back in his chair. 'The dispute between the Parrs and the Farrents is over the ownership of a huge area of land which was probably acquired fraudulently by the Farrents in the aftermath of the Civil War.'

'Strewth . . . that's four hundred years ago.'

'Yes, sir, but it was explained to us that because both families were direct descendants of the original Parr and Farrent families, then the land ownership could be contested.'

'How interesting.' Hennessey sipped his tea. 'So that's why the Parrs came to York. Why didn't they let their lawyers handle the situation?'

'They were advised by a family friend to sort something out with the Farrents, come to some agreement then ask the courts to ratify it. The gentleman to whom we spoke used a Scottish expression to explain the advice: "The law's expensive, take a pint and settle".'

'That sounds to be good advice,' Hennessey growled.

'It was probably the suggestion that the families divide the land equally and call that the end of the matter,' Yellich explained. 'We are talking of vast acreage, I should explain.'

'The Parrs had a strong case, it seems?'

'Yes, sir, so it seems,' Yellich explained. 'The document was apparently examined by an expert who reported the signature to be genuine. He did not look at the deed showing the

Farrents to be the legal owners. It is the story that the name
on the deed was scratched out and replaced by Farrent.'

'As easy as that?'

'Well, yes, sir, this was four hundred years ago and the
Farrents were Parliamentarians, and it did not help the Parrs
that they were high-level Royalists. They didn't kick up a fuss
and appear to have kept their heads thereby, but they also kept
a duplicate of the original deed showing them, the Parrs, to
be the rightful owners of the land.'

'But who lived on the land?' Hennessey queried.

'Neither family, sir, both lived in the south. That also helped
the Farrents because the Parrs didn't have to be evicted.'

'Neat for the Farrents, difficult for the Parrs,' Hennessey
said quietly.

'Indeed, sir, but the story of the "Altered Case" lived on in
the Parr family by word of mouth from generation to generation, and then, apparently, Gerald Parr came across the duplicate
deed and a document expert pronounced it to be genuine . . .
so jubilation in the Parr camp . . . but a bolt out of the blue in
the Farrent family. If the deeds held by the Farrents proved to
have been adulterated then the Parrs had a solid case, but the
Farrents, having held the land in good faith for four hundred
years also had a claim.'

Hennessey ran his fingers through his hair. 'So the Parrs
wanted their land back and the Farrents were not going to give
it up without a fight? That I can understand.'

'The Farrents hired a firm of solicitors in York, Fyrst, Tend
and Byrd . . . very posh . . . don't do criminal work. The two
firms of solicitors made initial contact with each other, but it
didn't proceed much beyond that because it was just about
that time that the Parr family, plus Michelle Lemmon, vanished.
It may have been that the Parrs were travelling to York to meet
the Farrents for unofficial talks about the issue.'

'"Take a pint and settle".' Hennessey drained his mug of
tea. 'The Parrs were on a sticky wicket there. Didn't they
realize they might be putting themselves in danger by walking
into the Farrents' backyard?'

'We'll never know, sir,' Yellich replied. 'No danger at all
if they were meeting at the premises of a solicitor's, but the

Parrs were a bit of an odd crew by all accounts, a bit eccentric. They might not have seen the danger in going to the
Farrents' home to open any discussion, if indeed that's what
happened.'

Hennessey folded his hands and leaned forward, resting them
on the desktop. 'So, the motivation for the crime is coming
clear and the finger of suspicion points to the Farrents. Anything
else before I feed back a significant development?'

'Yes, sir,' Yellich said. 'We were misled.'

'Interesting.' Hennessey smiled. 'I do so like it when people
try to mislead the police. It always means they have something
to hide.'

'Indeed.' Yellich also grinned. 'Doesn't it make a nice
smell? In a nutshell, Nigel Parr, who was fostered by the Parr
family and who kept their name, told us that the house in
which he lives was bought by money provided for him by
Mrs Parr's brother, one Mr Verity, when he, Mr Verity,
wrapped up the estate of Gerald and Elizabeth Parr, because
Gerald "would want him to have something". But the solicitor
told us that no such relative existed and that the firm of
Oldfield and Fairly wrapped up the estate. They liquidated it
and all the money generated is still in an account administered
by the solicitors.'

Carmen Pharoah gasped. 'So, who was the man who travelled north to collect the possessions of the Parr family – the
possessions they left in the hotel – and drove away in their
Mercedes Benz?'

'Dunno.' Yellich turned to her. 'But whoever he was, he
wasn't Mr Parr's brother-in-law. No such person exists.'

'That's a very nice weakness to exploit,' Hennessey said
with an air of satisfaction. 'It smells most malodorously. So,
what do we know about Nigel Parr?'

Yellich glanced at Webster. 'He presented well to us,
wouldn't you say, Reg?'

'Yes, he seemed very cooperative, affable, welcomed us into
his house. We haven't done a criminal record check on him
though . . .' Webster added as an afterthought.

'Do that,' Hennessey said.

'Yes, sir,' Webster replied.

'Dare say I should have thought of that as soon as suspicions arose,' Yellich added.

'No damage,' Hennessey reassured Yellich. 'You must have been exhausted, but do it a.s.a.p.'

'Yes, sir. But Mr Hillyard, the retired solicitor, described him as a cold, calculating, unpleasant youth who was badly damaged by childhood experiences. Left in a phone box as a newborn infant and brought up in an institution until he was ten, when he was fostered by the Parrs. Mr Hillyard reported that Gerald Parr expressed a fear of him. He was away on the south coast with his girlfriend, one Florence Nightingale, when the Parrs vanished,' Yellich reported flatly.

'Who?' Hennessey gasped.

'I kid you not, sir, that was her name, probably still is. We'll do a CR check on her as well. She was a cold fish by all accounts, with a chip on her shoulder about her name . . . but she and Nigel Parr teamed up.'

'OK . . . OK, well, my news is that Thomas Farrent has reported his wife as a missing person,' Hennessey announced flatly, and remained silent as a stillness settled in the room. 'Then,' he added, 'he said she was last seen talking to DS Yellich and accuses us of abducting her.'

'I met her in York,' Yellich said. 'She just planted herself in front of me. I didn't recognize her at first but no conversation took place, there was no time. Her husband appeared out of the crowd, grabbed her by the arm and pulled her away, but I do remember a look of fear in her eyes. She was a very frightened woman.'

'That is also interesting.' Hennessey leaned back in his chair. 'So, what's for action?'

'We have to go to Fyrst, Tend and Byrd,' Webster suggested. 'See what they can tell us about the land ownership issue.'

'Yes, I'll do that.' Hennessey scribbled a note on his pad. 'We need to find Florence Nightingale . . . do a CR check on her. If she's known, go and visit her. Ventnor and Webster, that's for you two . . . Another trip to the south for you, Reg. Bad luck,' he added with a grin.

'Yellich and DI Pharoah.'

'Sir?'

'Follow up on the mis per report. It'll be a chance to look round the Farrents' bungalow. I want us inside that home.'

'Yes, sir.'

The woman walked slowly along the promenade from the North Bay towards the South Bay, savouring the sea air which added to her sense of new-found freedom. She was reminded of the day she truanted from school and discovered a strange mix of emotions: exhilaration in freedom and a sense of comfort in flight. Now it was the same. It was just her and a single room in a cheap hotel, but it was her room and only hers. The table to herself at breakfast; a small table tucked away in the corner of the dining room, but it was hers and hers alone. She cared not one jot, not one iota that the other guests glanced at her with pity, because she, in her solitude, knew only joy: the joy of the bird released from its cage, or the wild animal released from captivity.

'Heavens, that's a long time ago. I was a junior then, serving articles. It seems only yesterday, though, and I recall the case very well indeed.' Elizabeth Nosser was a small, finely built woman in her fifties. She had short, black hair and alert brown eyes. She wore a black, pinstripe suit over a cream blouse. Rings, bracelets and necklaces and a gold watch spoke of wealth and her marital status. 'The case made quite a stir with us; that is it made quite a stir with Fyrst, Tend and Byrd.'

'Really?' Hennessey adjusted his position in the armchair.

'Yes, in our deliberations we felt the Parrs had a winnable case. We were permitted to see a photocopy of the original document, which had not been altered, plus a signed statement from a respected and indeed eminent document analyst who declared his opinion that the deed was genuine. They would not allow us to look at the original, which was quite fair enough, but they indicated their willingness to allow our own document analyst to access the document at their chambers and, I confess, the partners got very excited.' She smiled briefly. 'I mean, what with a substantial remnant of a forest estate, which once covered a large area of land stretching from here to the coast, up for grabs, the media interest would be intense.

The fees we could charge would be astronomical; both firms smelled money.'

'And your advice?'

'To settle out of court,' Elizabeth Nosser replied in a calm, matter-of-fact manner. 'We and the London firm hoped for instructions to dispute the claim, in which case much coinage would pour into the coffers of both our firms, but we were ethically obliged to offer our clients the best possible advice. In this case, it was for both families to reach an agreement between themselves.'

'I see.'

'We do have a code of conduct that we have to honour. I don't know what advice the Parrs were given, but we said that if the deeds the Farrents hold can be shown to have been fraudulently altered and the deed the Parrs hold is genuine and unaltered, then the case would be settled in the Parrs' favour, with the Farrents getting something in recognition of the fact they had "owned" the land for four hundred years and that they believed their ownership to have been lawful, but the Parrs would be the major beneficiaries. In that light we felt that if the Parrs made a reasonable offer, the Farrents should accept it.'

'That accords with the advice given to the Parrs.' Hennessey's eye was caught by a pheasant which landed in the landscaped gardens he could see behind Elizabeth Nosser. The office smelled richly of furniture polish. The walls were lined with shelves on which sat row upon row of legal textbooks. 'In fact,' Hennessey continued, 'we have information from the Parrs' solicitor, no less, that the Parrs were advised to offer to share the land equally with the Farrents.'

'That would indeed have been a very fair offer.' Elizabeth Nosser nodded. 'To draw up new title deeds, confirming the ownership of one half of the lands to the Farrents and the other half to the Parrs would have been fair and reasonable.'

'Do you know if the Parrs' offer was put to the Farrents?'

'If it was, it was done privately. It was not made to the Farrents through this firm. We did talk to the Farrents and suggested they agree to relinquish a proportion of the land as a settlement of the claim.' Elizabeth Nosser scratched her left palm with her right thumb.

'How often did you meet the Farrents?'

'Once or twice, here in our chambers, and also once at their home . . . a bungalow, very newly built then . . . out at Catton Hill,' Nosser explained.

'Yes, I have been there.'

'Modest bungalow, for the owners of such a vast amount of land,' Nosser commented. 'I was disappointed when I saw it; I expected something grander. Hostile family, I thought. Their friends were there, young Thomas' friends . . . the son . . . he is the owner now; inherited the whole estate. His friends were there, southerners by their accents. I took a dislike to Thomas and his friends. No reason, just feminine intuition. You learn to listen to it; it has never let me down. Thomas was married by then but it was clear that, even at the early stages of their marriage, his wife was already frightened of him.'

'And the case itself?' Hennessey asked.

'Still open. We received no word from the Parrs' solicitors, largely, I assume, because it was about then that the family vanished.' Elizabeth Nosser paused. 'There is a story there.'

'Did you think it suspicious?'

'Only in hindsight,' Elizabeth Nosser replied. 'Life moved on, other work came in . . . had to be addressed, but in hindsight, yes, I think it suspicious. You know you could try . . . what's his name . . . William . . . William . . .' Elizabeth Nosser bowed her head and held it with both hands. 'What was his name . . .? Pargeter.' She looked up smiling. 'William Pargeter.'

'Who is he?' Hennessey took his notepad from his pocket.

'Don't know his designation. He just seemed to be in with the bricks of the Farrent household, as though he was an old family retainer. Again, so I assumed, with nothing more than feminine intuition. I felt he was not at all happy with whatever was going on in the Farrent family.'

'Where might we find him? Do you know?'

'I'd try the pub if I were you. If he is still with us; he was middle-aged then, thirty years ago.'

The two men sat at the same table, facing each other in the restaurant. They had both enjoyed the first course of soup and had settled most enjoyably into the second course of haddock and chips. The two men had also settled into each other's company, as they had always done and as they always did. After a brief lull in the conversation, George Hennessey, the elder of the two men, said, 'So, you're in Newcastle next week? Lovely city; it has a certain vibrancy, I have always found. What's the story?'

'Yes, I do like Newcastle as well.' Charles Hennessey sipped his tea and glanced round the restaurant. Quiet. Just two other tables occupied despite the excellence of the meal, but, he pondered, it was a little late for lunch and he and his father must represent the tail end of the midday trade for the restaurateur. 'It's the old story. I am representing an old lag who should know better. He is insisting on going NG . . . He really did not commit the offence despite a pub full of witnesses.'

'One of those.' Hennessey senior sighed. 'We meet them all the time.'

'Deny everything and it will go away, such a juvenile attitude. He is certain the CPS will drop the case if he pleads not guilty.'

'That's a new one.' George Hennessey grinned. 'Where on earth did he obtain that notion? I mean, the Crown Prosecution Service is under pressure to get convictions. The public do not like to see felons walk.'

'Don't I know that, and do you think I haven't done my best to explain that to him? He is a simple-minded heavyweight thug, but apparently he is adamant he'll be released from custody because that is what happened to a couple of lads who live on the same housing estate as he does and they have been bragging in the pub about it.'

'Have they now?' George Hennessey's brow furrowed.

'So he says, Father.' Charles Hennessey paused to eat another mouthful of fish. 'This really is excellent. How did you find this restaurant?'

'By chance, I was visiting Knaresborough and felt peckish . . .'

'Serendipity?' Charles Hennessey replied.

'Yes.' Hennessey senior cut another mouthful of fish. 'Pure serendipity, but do go on.'

'Oh, yes . . . well, apparently what happened is that the two lads in question were caught red-handed stealing Yorkshire stone paving slabs at four o'clock one morning. The police caught them in the act and also found them to be in possession of a stolen vehicle.'

'Straightforward.' George Hennessey looked up as a slender young waitress with neat black hair, white blouse and black skirt and a pleasant manner approached their table to ask if everything was all right. Hennessey smiled his thanks and said, 'Perfect, thank you.'

'So you might think,' Charles Hennessey continued. 'But it is the case that they must have been given advice to go NG by a solicitor who knows the game and the dodges. It is true that the CPS is under pressure to obtain convictions, but it is also the case that, like all government departments, it has to work within a budget.'

'Ah . . .' George Hennessey held eye contact with his son. 'I think I can see where you are going with this.'

'Yes, so the gamble their solicitor probably suggested,' Charles Hennessey continued, 'is that if you plead guilty you'll get an immediate one-third reduction in your sentence, but if you plead not guilty the CPS might decide not to run the case because it will not be cost-effective; court time being as hugely expensive as it is. So they took the gamble and it paid off. But the theft was frustrated and the two felons were remanded for a few weeks before being released on bail, meaning they had a taste of prison life. They were also exposed to their families as being criminals and they became known to the police.'

'So what you're saying is that the CPS accepted that as a won game and dropped the charges to avoid a costly trial for what, in the overall scheme of things, was a minor offence?' George Hennessey clarified.

'Precisely. So, my man, having heard that story, is now convinced that if he pleads not guilty he'll walk free.'

'Not so simple.' George Hennessey ate a piece of buttered bread.

'But will he be dissuaded?' Charles Hennessey gave a slight shrug of his shoulders. 'Both myself and his solicitor have pointed out to him that he glassed someone in a pub for no reason at all, and that the only reason he is not looking at a murder charge is that his victim was taken to hospital just in time to save his life. That is quite different from being caught for lifting paving slabs . . . but will he listen?'

'We arrest them and charge them, and then you fight their corner.' Hennessey smiled. 'But it doesn't sound like you'll be getting this one off the hook.'

Charles Hennessey shook his head. 'Heavens, Father, I don't want to see him walk. If you ask me, prison is indeed the best place for him. It is apparently the case that he is the bully-boy of the housing estate. People who live there are in fear of him. His wife walks into the shop on the estate, a small supermarket, and when she has got her purchases she always walks to the head of the queue; it's that sort of situation. Now she's worried because if her husband gets gaol—'

'Which he will.'

'Without a doubt,' Hennessey junior continued. 'Then she fears she'll be hounded off the estate; bricks through her window, the lot. Her husband has made a lot of enemies on the estate.'

'It's the way of it.'

'Yes, I told her to begin to pack her bags.' Charles Hennessey placed his knife and fork on the plate, having finished his lunch. 'Because her husband is going down for a long time.'

'So it seems.' George Hennessey also finished his lunch. 'So how are the children?'

'Thriving, just thriving, thanks.' Charles Hennessey smiled. 'As always they want to know when granddad Hennessey is coming to see them again. Granddad Hennessey's visits always excite them.'

'As soon as I can.' George Hennessey chuckled. 'I like spoiling them.'

'And we are anxious to meet your lady friend. I am sure she's a lovely lady; she clearly makes you very happy. You look so fulfilled these days.' Charles Hennessey leaned back in his chair. 'You deserve it, Father. It's only when I became a parent that I realized how hard it was for you to bring me up by yourself.'

'I didn't do it by myself.'

'A housekeeper and a nursery place isn't the same as a partner; it's not the same at all. You deserve a medal for what you did.'

'Whatever.' George Hennessey beckoned the young waitress. 'Can we have our bill, please?' he asked as she approached the table.

Somerled Yellich and Carmen Pharoah stood calmly side by side in front of the front door of Thomas Farrent's bungalow, having rung the doorbell, twice, to announce their presence. After a brief period of waiting Thomas Farrent pulled the door open and, standing firmly and squarely on the threshold, he glared angrily at the two officers. 'What do you want!' he demanded.

'Police.' Yellich showed Farrent his ID.

'I know,' Farrent snarled. 'I recognize you. You were here before and I saw you talking to my wife the day she disappeared. So where is she? What are you putting into her head?' He turned to Carmen Pharoah. 'Don't recognize you, never seen you before.'

'She's a police officer also,' Yellich said calmly. 'We don't know where your wife is. We are here in response to the missing person report you made.'

'We always make a house call upon such reports being filed,' Carmen Pharoah added. 'It's routine.'

'Why?' Farrent gripped the door with his right hand, causing his knuckles to whiten.

'To confirm the report; to check that she is not here.'

'Well, she isn't.' Thomas Farrent made to close the door. Somerled Yellich extended his hand and held the door open. 'It's not a question of myself and my partner disbelieving you, sir, it is just that we have to check inside the house.'

'Search it?' Farrent gasped.

'And the outbuildings.' Carmen Pharoah smiled. 'Just to make sure. Anywhere she might be hiding.'

'Or anywhere I might have stashed her body, isn't that what you really mean?' Farrent's anger showed no sign of abating. He was, thought Yellich, a man who, when threatened, responds with fight not flight, and Farrent's fight was the fight of a man who felt frightened, very frightened indeed.

'If you like, sir.' Yellich retained his calm attitude. 'But we still have to check the house, room by room, even cupboard by cupboard.'

'Cupboards!' Farrent wailed.

'Yes, sir. Rooms, cupboards, anywhere that is large enough to conceal an adult human being,' Carmen Pharoah explained.

'And the outbuildings?' Farrent growled.

'Yes, sir,' Carmen Pharoah replied. 'The outbuildings as well.'

'Everything. . . everywhere,' Yellich said calmly. 'Everything.'

Somerled Yellich and Carmen Pharoah stepped over the threshold and entered Farrent's bungalow. A musty smell greeted them. From the hallway they walked into a living room which was noticeably untidy; not particularly unclean or unhygienic, thought Carmen Pharoah, but untidy, with many items just lying about and not put away. There was also an atmosphere about the room which she sensed, and she began to feel unnerved and very appreciative of the presence of Somerled Yellich. The lounge led on to a corridor from which bedrooms were accessed, and also a wide and spacious bathroom, which, like the living room, was in an untidy state, as was the master bedroom. The two officers made a detailed search of the house, opening cupboards, checking under beds, and Yellich accumulated dust when investigating the loft space. There was no sign of Mrs Farrent.

'Satisfied?' Farrent asked with a certain undisguised smugness.

'Yes,' Somerled Yellich replied, 'yes, we are.'

'Your cooperation is appreciated. Thank you.' Carmen Pharoah spoke softly. 'Just the outbuildings now.'

'When did you last see your wife?' Yellich asked.

'The day before I reported her as missing.' Farrent paused. 'That was the day I saw you talking to her in the middle of York.'

'Actually,' Yellich replied, 'we didn't talk.'

'I saw you!' Farrent raised his voice.

'We did not talk. Hardly one word was exchanged, I assure you. You pulled her away before either of us could really say anything.'

'Why don't I believe you?' Farrent growled.

'I can only repeat what I have told you.' Yellich fought to remain calm. 'We did not say anything to each other.'

'Well, she'd gone the next day. She brought me tea in bed then ran my morning bath, but when I had got dressed and went to the kitchen for her to serve me my breakfast, she wasn't there. Her car was still in the garage but she had gone. She took the housekeeping money with her and she has a credit card to buy petrol, but she can also use it to obtain cash from a cash machine. She's not really allowed to do that,' Farrent added, 'but I'm not there to stop her and the card is in her name.'

'Has she made any contact with you?' Yellich asked.

'None.'

'Was there any trouble between you at around the time she left the house?'

'None,' Farrent replied adamantly. 'No trouble at all. There never has been, she's a good woman. She does as she's told so we never have any trouble.'

Carmen Pharoah felt her scalp crawl.

When Yellich and Pharoah were driving away, having made a thorough search of the outbuildings, Carmen Pharoah said, 'That house is a crime scene.'

'Thirty years ago, you mean,' Yellich replied, 'when the Parrs were murdered there by the Farrents?'

'No . . . well, that as well, that as well.' Pharoah glanced to her left as Yellich halted the car at the end of the driveway before joining the public highway. 'But also recently. The disarray, as if things had been more or less put back in place after a fight, but only more or less in place, with other things left lying about; and the atmosphere, a very strange sense of something's happened. Didn't you pick it up?'

'No.' Yellich drove away, joining the public highway which at that moment was free of traffic. 'Confess I didn't sense anything like that.'

'I did,' Carmen Pharoah said flatly. 'I did, very strongly. I tell you a woman was battered in that living room, and out there somewhere Mrs Farrent is walking about with extensive bruising and a lumpy skull, but no marks are showing on her face or arms or legs; he's too clever and too self-controlled to allow that.'

'You've come a long way to see me, my old darlings, a long old way.' Florence Nightingale scrutinized Webster's ID card but declined to see Ventnor's. 'No, pet, if his nibs here is real, then so are you.' She turned. 'You'd better come in. York . . . that's Yorkshire, right? Me, I've never been north of London and I don't ever want to, darlings. I don't ever want to.' Florence Nightingale led the two officers into her cramped bedsit in a large, converted house. The view from her window showed a terrace of similar houses, all painted white and all of which gleamed in the strong sunlight. 'Take you long to get here?' Florence Nightingale sank on to an unmade single bed and crossed her legs in what the officers thought was a childlike posture. 'There's only the one, old gents.' She pointed to an elderly armchair which occupied floor space by the door. 'You can fight for it.'

'We'll stand, thanks.' Ventnor glanced round the cluttered, seemingly uncared for room.

'We'd prefer to stand,' Webster added diplomatically. 'We've been sitting all day. And to answer your question, about five hours from door to door; two hours from York to King's Cross, half an hour by tube to Waterloo—'

'Less,' Ventnor said.

'Yes . . . less,' Webster agreed. 'One hour to Bournemouth . . . taxi here. There is in fact a direct service between York and Bournemouth but it takes a geological age, and that sort of time we do not have. So about five hours from our door to yours.'

'Fair enough. You're not lucky to find me in; I never go out, not these days. So, how can I help the Yorkshire plod?' Florence Nightingale glanced up at Ventnor, then at Webster. 'Not much is it?'

'What isn't?'

'This.' Florence Nightingale shrugged. 'Not much of a home

for a woman in her middle-age; not much to show for fifty plus years of life, have I?' She reached for a tobacco tin, opened it and began to roll a cigarette, creating a thin roll-up. Tobacco was evidently in short supply for Florence Nightingale.

'Well, Miss Nightingale,' Webster began.

'Why did they do that? Why? I mean, love us and save us, why not go the whole road and call me Hiawatha or Pocahontas?'

Ventnor held up his hand. 'If it makes you feel better, I once met a girl called Marilyn Monroe.'

'Really? Oh . . .' Florence Nightingale sighed. 'The poor cow.'

'And I,' Webster offered, 'once escorted two runaway girls back to their children's home, their names being Tina Turner and Diana Ross.'

'Is that true?'

'Yes, in fact they were picked up by the York Railway Police getting on to a London train and the officers wouldn't believe them when they gave their names.'

Florence Nightingale giggled.

'They put them in separate rooms,' Webster continued, 'until they gave the police their real names.'

Florence Nightingale laughed. 'I feel better already. So, how can I help you, gentlemen? I am so pleased I am not alone with my name, alone in every other way but not with a silly name.' She lit her cigarette. 'Mind you, we girls can always be rescued by marriage, but that didn't happen to me.'

'You could have changed your name by deed poll,' Ventnor suggested.

'Don't you think I thought of that? But it seemed like cheating somehow.' She took a deep drag on the cigarette. 'So I clung to the hope of marriage . . . some hope.' Florence Nightingale patted her stomach. 'Fat little me, with two short, fat, little legs.'

After a pause, Webster said, 'Florence, we hope you can help us.'

'If I can.' Florence Nightingale exhaled through her nostrils. 'If I can, darlin'.' She shrugged. 'I've got nothing to hide from the old plod.' She took another deep drag on the cigarette. 'I

still do a little shoplifting, a little pilfering . . . I think it's
called street-level crime. I can't run any more so I don't do
bag snatching. Yes, I've been inside; it's OK, a cot and three
and some company. I'll probably get myself lifted near
Christmas. I hate Christmas Day in this room; just me by
myself, a few cans of lager, when the rest of the world is
celebrating, that's what it feels like anyway. You know, I am
going to really have something of a funeral, just me and the
priest. So go ahead, pick my brains; the vodka hasn't left much
for you to pick at but you are welcome to what the voddy has
left.'

'OK.' Webster lifted up his right foot and was not surprised
when he found that it had adhered to the carpet and he had
to tear it loose. 'So what can you tell us about Nigel Parr, of
Camden, thirty years ago.'

'Oh him . . . a name from my past? I can't remember what
happened yesterday but I can remember Nigel Parr. He was
part of my youth, when it was all before me. I was a bit of a
looker then, I don't mind admitting it; quite slim with the old
ding dong of church wedding bells echoing in my future. So,
he has surfaced. You know, I thought he might be known to
the old plod. He was dodgy, with a mega chip on both
shoulders.'

'Tell us about him,' Ventnor pressed. 'Anything you think
we might be interested in.'

'Well, where to start.' Florence Nightingale took another
deep drag on the thin roll-up and then flicked the ash on to
her denim jeans and worked the ash into the weave with a
slow, circular movement of the tip of her middle finger. 'I
remember a young guy burning up with resentment towards
the family who fostered him. I mean, what did they do to
harm him? They took him out of the children's home, where
he had been labelled "difficult", and gave him a proper home
. . . and he was resentful. I reckon he'd be resentful if he went
to live in a stately home and was given a Ferrari for his eighteenth birthday.'

'He told you he had been labelled "difficult"?' Webster tore
the sole of his right foot from the carpet and put it down in
a different location.

'Yes, after his foster parents had told him that in a sort of look-what-we-did-for-you sort of way. They were apparently pleased with themselves, pleased that they had rescued him · in time and set him on the right path. Sent him to a good school and all that, but he saw it like he'd been taken in like a stray dog so that they could feel good about themselves. Me, I would have cared less about their reasons. I grew up in a children's home, you see. I didn't get rescued.'

'I see.' Ventnor scanned the room, discreetly so, and saw nothing to raise his suspicions.

'I mean, so long as I was rescued I wouldn't care about the reasons.' Florence Nightingale screwed the butt of the cigarette into a small plastic ashtray, which had clearly been stolen from a pub going by the brewery logo on the rim. 'Anyway, Nigel didn't see it that way, like I said. He seemed to turn on Mr and Mrs Parr and find ways of doing them harm; like he'd steal things from their house and sell them, even though he didn't need the money, or sometimes he'd take items from the house and throw them away just to be spiteful, and he seemed to gloat when family members were going round the house hunting for whatever item he had thrown away. He used to laugh at Mr Parr's innocence in not realizing what was happening. How Mr Parr would sit on the sofa in the living room and say, "It's a mystery where whatever it was has gone, it's a real mystery." No mystery at all, the boy he fostered and had brought into his home had thrown it in Regent's Park Canal.'

'Thanks . . . illuminating,' Webster said softly, 'very illuminating.'

Florence Nightingale ran stubby nicotine-stained fingers through her greasy, black hair. 'Well, that's the Nigel Parr I knew. It's what he could be like. Maybe he still can. He was like my old bath taps, he ran hot and cold. One day he'd be fuming, burning up with anger or resentment, then the next he'd come over all Mr Nice Bloke, ever so helpful and friendly, but I got to learn that that was just on the surface.'

'Again . . . interesting.' Webster let his feet sink into the carpet pile; he had come to realize that picking them up and putting them down again was a futile exercise, utterly pointless.

'Then one day he really was about to explode like Mount

Etna, really blew his top. I remember it so well. I was frightened he'd turn on me, and he was a big bloke. Apparently he'd been told that he wasn't going to inherit anything. He'd been told that Mr and Mrs Parr were going to leave everything to their two daughters. All along he had let himself think that because he was fostered he was going to get a third of whatever they left behind them. As it was, he was not going to get a penny, but in the event he came into money and bought himself a nice two bedroomed flat in a conversion near Regent's Park, which was just round the corner from the Parrs' old house where he had grown up.' Florence Nightingale took a deep breath. 'And me . . . just then I got the push – "Time for you to go girl."'

'You and he were an item I assume?' Ventnor asked.

'Yes, I was his bit on the side. I was his old lady and he was my fella, until he got wealthy all at once.'

'Did he tell you where he got the money from?' Ventnor coughed slightly.

'Sorry, the smoke bother you, darlin'?' Florence Nightingale glanced up at Ventnor.

'It's all right.' Ventnor smiled. 'I'm just not used to it.'

'Wish I could say that.' Florence Nightingale sighed. 'But, no, he didn't tell me where the dosh suddenly came from, but it came like a win on the lottery. One minute he was looking at a life to be spent in rented bedsits . . . in dumps like this . . . and the next he was owning his own home outright in fancy NW1. Iffy, I always thought.'

'Do you know what happened to the Parrs?' Webster too felt the smoke from Florence Nightingale's cigarette tickling the back of his throat.

'They disappeared . . . abducted by aliens . . . the family who vanished. It was soon after they vanished that Nigel moved into his house.' Florence Nightingale reached for her tobacco tin, then, having second thoughts, retracted her hand. 'Yeah, they vanished. I read about it when I was in Holloway doing another short stretch for shoplifting.'

Webster and Ventnor glanced at each other. Then Ventnor said, 'Just repeat that.'

'What?' Florence Nightingale looked puzzled. 'Repeat what?'

'What you just said. You were in Holloway when you heard about the Parrs' disappearance.'

'Yeah . . . I mean, yes, I was doing bird. The Horseferry Road beaks sent me down for two months. I had shoplifted a woollen pullover so the magistrates sent me down for a two-and-a-half stretch; two months . . . for a cardigan. That morning, in the same court, was a youth who had caused death by dangerous driving and he walked with a fine to pay . . . that's justice, I don't think.'

'It can seem a bit unfair,' Webster offered. 'But how long after you went down did you hear about the Parrs disappearing?'

Nightingale shrugged. 'Now you're asking . . . thirty years ago. You can check, they'll keep records.'

'We will, but just for us, now, can you remember how long you had been inside when you heard about the Parrs?'

'Probably about a month, it wasn't right at the beginning and it wasn't just before the end.'

'I see,' Webster said. 'Now this is important, Florence . . . You were not with Nigel Parr on the south coast when the Parrs disappeared?'

'No, I was doing bird in Holloway, working towards an early parole.'

'Do you know if Nigel Parr had another girlfriend?'

'She'd be blind if he had 'cos I would have clawed her eyes out.' Florence Nightingale grasped the air with her right hand.

'What about after you were sent down?' Ventnor asked.

'My girlfriends in the gang visited me. If Nigel was playing away from home they would have told me, I'm certain they would.' Florence Nightingale looked smug. 'Yeah, they would have told me.'

'So you met his mates?' Webster pressed.

'Yeah, we ran in a gang, his pub mates, the girls and a geezer from up your way, posh sort of geezer.'

'Do you remember his name or anything about him, the posh geezer, I mean?' Ventnor asked.

'Name . . . Tarrant . . . Farrent, something like that. He had a big red birthmark on his right hand –' Florence Nightingale tapped the back of her right hand – 'just here. I've seen similar on people's faces but his was on his hand. You know, I can dig out a photograph of Tarrant, or Farrent. I think I can, anyway. Would you like me to find it?'

'That would be excellent.' Webster smiled. 'If you can . . . we'd love to see it.'

Florence Nightingale levered herself upright and uncrossed her legs so that her calves hung over the side of the bed. She then began to rock herself backwards and forwards, and on the third forward tilt she stood and walked across the room to a chest of drawers and pulled the top drawer open. From the drawer she extracted a large, circular tin, which had once contained biscuits by its pattern and design, and holding it in both hands, she turned and walked unsteadily back to the bed. Once again seated on the bed she pulled the lid off the tin and began to sift through the photographs which comprised the contents. 'All my little old life is in here,' she mumbled as she tossed one photograph after another on to the bed beside her. Then she triumphantly held up a small colour photograph and handed it to Ventnor. 'Here,' she said proudly. 'I knew I had one of him.'

Ventnor looked at the photograph and handed it to Webster, who, looking at it, saw that it showed a group of young people sitting on the grass in a park one summer's day. 'That was taken in Regent's Park,' Florence Nightingale advised. 'The guy in the middle is Nigel Parr. I took that about a week before I got sent down. I remember that because we talked about what sentence I could expect. If we hadn't had that conversation I couldn't have remembered so well when it was taken.'

Webster smiled. 'Useful; that's a very useful statement, helps us a lot.'

'The guy on the left is the posh geezer . . . Tarrant or Farrent . . . with the red birthmark on his hand. They didn't like me taking the photograph. They said they didn't want their photographs taken, not when they were together. They got really angry and told me not ever to take another one.'

'That's also very interesting,' Ventnor said still looking at the photograph. 'Did you?' he asked. 'Did you take another?'

'No.' Florence Nightingale shook her head. 'Parr smashed my camera later that same day, spiteful young rat that he was. Years afterwards I realized he was trying to destroy the film, not the camera, but I had changed the film by then. He didn't know that; he never knew that photograph ever existed 'cos I never showed it to him, or to the posh northern geezer either.'

'Can we keep this photograph?' Webster asked.

'I can sell it to you,' Florence Nightingale offered. 'Look, gents, I don't like asking but I'm short . . . no food . . . and I don't want to do crime, not until nearer Christmas . . .'

Webster and Ventnor both took out their wallets and each gave Florence Nightingale twenty pounds.

'Keep the photograph,' she said, holding the money tightly in her hands. 'And thanks.'

'Buy food with it,' Webster said, 'not vodka.'

'I will. Promise. I'll use it all for food. Promise. Promise. Promise.'

'OK –' Ventnor held up his hand – 'we believe you. So, do you know how Nigel Parr and Thomas Farrent met? Did one approach the other?'

Florence Nightingale smiled. 'Yes, Nigel Parr went north. You see, I don't know the full yarn but it seems that the Parrs were claiming some land in Yorkshire belonged to them and they were talking to lawyers about it, and it was right about that same time that Parr found he wasn't going to inherit anything. He was well upset about that, he was; he got well drunk one night and said that being done out of a third of the value of a house in Camden is bad enough, but being done out of a third of a big chunk of Yorkshire was "criminal". He kept putting away the whisky and muttering about them not getting away with it. It was about that time he went north and came back looking like the cat that got the cream. He took me for a drink that night and said that he'd "worked something out"; it didn't matter that he wasn't going to inherit anything from Mr and Mrs Parr because he'd "done a deal" that would see him "all right". I never knew what.'

'He was still living with the Parrs at that time?'

'Oh, yes, still at home in his early twenties and Mr and Mrs Parr were not pushing him out or anything; they were still happy for him to be there. Most foster parents would have kicked out at sixteen when the local authority stopped paying the fostering allowance, but the Parrs let him continue to live

with them, even though he was an idler . . . no job. He went
to art college but that was later. At the time he was just loafing
about; he was a complete waster but that was the Parr family,
even their daughters used to walk about with no clothes on in
the middle of the day and they'd bring in stray dogs and
homeless people. That's how Oranges arrived; the girls found
her sleeping rough in Regent's Park and brought her home
like she was another stray dog. It was that attitude that annoyed
Nigel, really got his back up. He felt insulted by it.'

'Patronized?' Webster suggested.

'If that's the word, but like I said, it wouldn't have bothered
me, wouldn't have bothered me one bit. Any reason to live
with a family was better than a children's home. But thanks
for Adam Smiths.' Florence Nightingale held the two twenty
pound notes tightly and looked up at the two officers. 'It'll all
go on food. Promise.'

'Hope so. So, have you got a coat? Do you need one?'

'Why, where am I going?'

'The police station.'

Florence Nightingale paled. 'You're arresting me? I've
helped you and I haven't done anything.'

'We are not arresting you, don't worry,' Webster replied
calmly. 'We need to get everything you've told us down in a
written statement and for you to sign it.'

'I'll be giving evidence?'

'Probably . . . possibly,' Webster said. 'But we can't take a
statement here, we need to use the interview room in the
nearest police station.'

Florence Nightingale nodded. 'I'll get a jacket.' She stood.
'The police station is a short walk, just past the mini market.
I can buy some food on the way home.'

It was to prove to be an experience that Carmen Pharoah would
recall with pleasure. Never before had she silenced a pub just
by walking into it off the street, but that was what happened
when she walked into the snug of The Black Bull in Catton
Hill, having first enquired of the postmistress where she might
find William Pargeter. 'An old boy,' she explained, and added,
'he's not in any trouble,' and she was directed to The Black

Bull. She stepped into the taproom of the pub and found it a small room, as taprooms are wont to be, no more than ten feet by ten feet with a small bar adjacent to the door. It was full of men, mostly elderly, and the hubbub of conversation halted abruptly as she entered the door and stood there. Not only did all conversation stop but all movement also, save for the heads of the men sitting with their backs to the door, or side on to the door, who turned to look at her. Even the barman, who was wiping the bar with a towel, froze in mid motion. Carmen Pharoah stood there relishing the silence, relishing the impact she had made, a woman in the snug of The Black Bull, and a black woman at that. It had to be a first in the history of Catton Hill, it just had to be. 'I was told I could find a gentleman called William Pargeter in here,' she said at length after she felt she could not hold the silence any longer.

'Who are you?' A middle-aged man in a crumpled suit asked with hostility more than with curiosity.

'Vale of York Police,' Carmen Pharoah replied calmly. 'Mr Pargeter is not in any trouble, I just need to ask him a couple of questions. Just a little local history.'

'Be it about the bodies in the field?' another man asked.

'Possibly.' Carmen Pharoah smiled and glanced around the snug; low oak beams, panelled walls, a small window looking out on to Catton Hill Main Street. Polished horse brasses and Great War artillery shell casings being the only decoration. A sign above the bar read, 'The clock ticks but we don't'.

'Nothing else it could be about.' An elderly man stood, and took his weight on his walking stick. 'I be William Pargeter, I'll tell thee what I can.' He edged out of the corner where he sat. 'Can we go across to the other pub?'

'Of course.' Carmen Pharoah smiled. 'We can go anywhere you like.'

'They're a queer lot in The Shoes, but we'll get peace.'

William Pargeter's comment was greeted with laughter by the men in the snug. Carmen Pharoah turned and stepped out of the pub, hearing the conversation pick up again as she did so.

William Pargeter walked slowly and unsteadily across the road to the other pub, which Carmen Pharoah noted was called

The Three Horseshoes, hence, she realized, The Shoes for short. She bought the old man a half pint of beer, as he requested, and a tonic water for herself. The Shoes was less crowded than the snug of The Black Bull, but nonetheless she and William Pargeter attracted stares and caused conversations to enter a lull before they picked up again.

'So, the bodies?' Pargeter lifted the glass of beer towards his bewhiskered chin.

'Yes.'

'Always thought there was something in that field.'

'Oh?'

'The disturbed soil . . . a few boys saw it.'

'You didn't call the police?'

'Why for? Someone might have buried a sick calf. No one in the village was missing so there was no reason to call the police. You're not supposed to bury dead animals, there's a law against it, but it goes on. Things happen in the country that don't happen in the town, it's the way of it.'

'So it seems.'

'Farming is a hard way of life, Miss, you can't afford to be sentimental. Sickly calves and sheepdogs that can't stand up to the sheep get a spade over the head and a hole in the ground. It's cheaper that way. Happens all the time.'

'Well, we won't go there.' Carmen Pharoah sipped her tonic water and looked across the room from the corner seat where she and William Pargeter sat; a grey carpet, wooden circular tables with wooden chairs, a long bar on the further wall. It was light, spacious and airy in comparison to the snug of The Black Bull. 'So who buried the bodies?'

'Wasn't the tenant who rents the field, he was away at the time; him and his family on holiday straight after harvesting. But the land itself is owned by Farrent. You should be more interested in him . . . in Farrent.'

'Oh?'

'Shifty old family.' Pargeter glanced to his left. 'I worked for them over the years. I was working for them when they thought they were going to lose their land to a family in London.'

'You know about that?'

William Pargeter grinned. 'You can't keep a secret in a

village, Miss. Word gets out, workers overhear things, especially when employers think their workers don't have ears. The woman talking on the phone as the maid is dusting the room . . . the maid hears it, the word is out. But the Farrents were worried about losing their land, the old man was and so was the old woman, but they're dead now, they're in Paradise. Thomas and the old man were talking one day when I was there, and I heard Thomas say to his dad that there's someone he wants him to meet, someone that could help them but that it would cost. The old man replied, "But I am prepared to settle."'

'You heard that?' Carmen Pharoah asked.

'Yes . . . it could have meant anything of course, but I was forty then, a boy from the village. They talked like that in front of me and the housekeepers, like we were not there. Anyway, it was shortly after that that the hole was dug in the field and they never talked any more about losing their land.'

'That's very interesting.' Carmen Pharoah glanced at a man who was staring at her. She raised her glass and smiled at him. 'That's very interesting indeed. Would you make a statement saying that?'

'Yes . . . yes, I will.' William Pargeter nodded briefly. 'Yes, I will.'

It was Thursday, 16.45 hours.

SEVEN

Friday, 09.15 hours – Saturday, 12.37 hours

in which our tale concludes.

Thomas Farrent smiled at George Hennessey. Hennessey in turn looked coldly at Farrent, irritated by his transparent smugness. George Hennessey glanced at Thomas Farrent's solicitor who had introduced himself for the benefit of the audio tape as John Jacobs of Ellis, Burden, Woodland and Lake of St Leonard's Place, York. Jacobs seemed to Hennessey to be anxious to avoid eye contact with both himself and Reginald Webster, who sat beside Hennessey, and kept his eyes downcast as if focussing his attention on the notepad he held in front of him, resting it at forty-five degrees on the edge of the small table which separated him and Farrent from the two police officers. Jacobs, noted Hennessey, was a middle-aged man, a little overweight perhaps, and smartly dressed in a dark blue suit with a gold hunter watch chain looped across his waistcoat. Hennessey's eye was drawn by the red glow of the tape recorder which was set in the wall of the interview room within which the twin cassettes spooled round slowly. This silence had gone on too long, he thought, far, far too long, and he said, 'All right, let's cut to the chase.'

'Suits me.' Farrent relaxed back in the chair in which he sat. He was dressed casually in a yellow tee shirt and denim jeans.

'Thirty years ago,' Hennessey began, 'your family and a family called Parr of London began a dispute, a legal dispute, over the issue of the ownership of a large amount of land near York. The issue was never resolved because the Parr family disappeared.'

'Yes, I remember reading about it, strange case, very mysterious . . . a whole family.'

'But the unofficial negotiation between your family and the Parrs had reached a state whereby your father was ready to relinquish half the land in question to the Parrs as an equitable solution if the analysis of the deeds held by your family were proven to have been altered fraudulently.'

'Were they?' Thomas Farrent replied softly. 'That is news to me.'

'We have a signed statement from Mr Pargeter to that effect.'

'A hard-of-hearing old boy who overheard one side of a small part of a larger conversation.'

'Point –' Jacobs raised his gold plated pen – 'that conversation could have been about anything.'

'And it took place thirty years ago,' Farrent added. 'That sort of time lapse can play tricks on anyone's memory.'

'Again, a valid point,' Jacobs remarked.

Hennessey bulldozed forwards, regardless. 'At that time, when you didn't want to relinquish any of the land, you were approached by Nigel Parr who had been fostered by the Parrs and who had just found out he wasn't going to inherit anything from their estate. Nigel Parr had a plan to get rid of the Parr family, but it was going to cost you. Nonetheless, you were interested enough to talk to Nigel Parr and visit him in London.'

'Was I?'

'We have a photograph of you and Nigel Parr in the same group.' Hennessey placed the snapshot on the table. 'For the benefit of the tape, Mr Farrent has been shown the photograph in question.'

'The . . . copy . . . of the photograph in question . . .' Jacobs argued slowly, 'is . . . well, it is of questionable accuracy. It seems to have been taken on cheap film within an inexpensive camera. The background in the photograph is just vegetation. There is no landmark, but the main issue is that the image is sufficiently blurred that it is not possible to say that the two men in the group of young persons are my client and Mr Nigel Parr, not with sufficient proof to satisfy legal requirements. It will be my advice to my client to contest the validity of that photograph.'

'It is sufficiently clear,' Hennessey growled. 'It links Mr Nigel Parr with your client.'

'Even if the photograph was accepted as showing my client with Mr Parr, it is a tenuous link at best.' Jacobs paused and, still refusing eye contact with Hennessey, he said, 'The alleged crime here is multiple murder; you are going to need a very solid case to achieve a conviction.'

'You and Parr hatched a plan,' Hennessey continued, ignoring Jacobs' argument. 'You lured the Parrs to Yorkshire for peace talks with the proposal to divide the land and paid a man called Verity to act as the nearest relative—'

'We did?' Farrent smiled.

'And the Parrs, being the naïve, trusting family that they were, were not only happy to meet with you, they actually agreed to meet you at your bungalow.'

'So you believe.' Farrent raised his eyebrows. 'You have proof of nothing.'

'It's what happened within your father's bungalow, now your bungalow, that we want to know about.'

'That's quite an admission of having no case against my client.' Jacobs inclined his pen towards the tape recorder.

Hennessey's head sank forward. He had wrong-footed himself by his admission of ignorance. 'It just needs one of you to turn Queen's evidence.' Hennessey clutched at the final straw. 'That act will be reflected in any sentence.'

'Nobody will turn Queen's evidence.' Farrent smiled. 'There being no evidence to turn. And I want to know where my wife is.'

'This is what happened.' Yellich leaned forward. 'You were angered that the Parrs were going to, or already had decided to leave you out of their will. You felt you deserved a share of their property in Camden, despite the fact that you were not related. So you made contact with the Farrents, particularly Thomas Farrent; he was of your age group . . . he still is, and also, like you, he stood to lose a substantial part of his inheritance . . . and the two of you hatched a plan.'

'Over numerous visits north, and him visiting you in the south,' Ventnor continued, 'you conspired to murder the Parrs . . . but only for a price. You wanted the equivalent of what one third of the value of the Parrs' house would have been upon their eventual passing, thus fully compensating you for the loss of what you believed to be your rightful inheritance. In return for your help, the Farrents held on to the vast area of land which, four hundred years earlier, their ancestors may have acquired fraudulently.'

Nigel Parr sighed and looked around the interview room, taking in the hard-wearing Hessian carpet, the plaster walls painted a dark brown up to waist height, cream above that, and the Perspex shade over the filament bulb in the ceiling directly above the table at which he was currently being interrogated. 'You brought me all the way from London, overnight, to listen to this fairy tale? What nonsense is this?'

'It is fair comment, gentlemen.' Christopher McGuire, also of the specialist criminal firm of Ellis, Burden, Woodland and Lake, spoke calmly and authoritatively. 'This is an interview, please conduct it as such. Ask questions but do not put words into my client's mouth. If you do, any confession obtained thereby would be invalid.'

'Fair enough.' Webster sat back in his chair. 'But you are not denying knowing Mr Thomas Farrent at the time the Parr family disappeared?'

'Sorry, sorry.' McGuire held up his hand. 'You are putting words into my client's mouth. Ask questions. Please.'

'Did you,' Yellich asked slowly, 'know Thomas Farrent socially at the time the Parrs disappeared?'

'No,' Parr said. 'We never met.'

'The photograph says otherwise.'

'The photograph is too blurred,' McGuire stated. 'It shows a group of young people in a park, which could be anywhere, any park anywhere.'

'We have a statement from Florence Nightingale that you and Thomas Farrent knew each other. She remembers him by the distinct birthmark on his right hand.'

'Faggie Annie, the vodka queen? Yes, I knew her, but she's hardly what you might call a creditable witness: a petty crook, one-woman vodka disposal unit.'

'We believe you—'

'No, no.' McGuire held up his hand. 'We are not going to respond to what you believe.'

'If your client was to turn Queen's evidence—' Yellich began.

'Enough!' McGuire folded his notebook. 'If you had any shred of evidence of my client's involvement you would not have even thought of asking him to turn Queen's evidence. All further responses from Mr Parr will be "no comment", and having said that I think the only thing you can do now is to furnish my client with a rail travel warrant and allow him to return home.'

'Mr Parr will be detained for the time being,' Yellich answered coldly. 'This interview is terminated at ten thirty-seven hours.' He switched off the tape recorder. Yellich and Ventnor stood. 'A constable will return Mr Parr to the cells.'

The office was filled with silence. It was the sort of silence which falls upon a room after a heated argument has ensued. Hennessey was silent, Yellich was silent, Ventnor was silent and Webster was silent. Carmen Pharoah was silent. All looked downwards. None sought eye contact with any other. Eventually, the sixth person in the room spoke. 'I don't like it any more than you.' Francis Fox of the Crown Prosecution Service was a smartly dressed man in his early thirties. 'But if this is the sum of your evidence, and it is now time to charge or release . . . then we have to release.'

Hennessey slowly reached for the telephone which stood on the desktop. He picked it up and angrily jabbed a four figure internal number. 'Custody Sergeant . . . release the suspects in the Parr family and Michelle Lemmon murder inquiry. Yes . . . thank you.'

It was Friday, 14.15 hours.

Thomas Farrent prowled about his house, angrily striking out at any object he came into contact with. It was, he thought, the one loose end, the one unknown. Even his father had said that before he had died, 'Watch her'. That's all he had said. Now she was out there, out of his grasp and not contacting him, no contact at all. Thomas Farrent strode across the room to where a table lamp stood on a small chest of drawers and powerfully knocked it on to the floor, causing it to break into

many pieces. No contact. That was the worrying thing, she
was thinking for herself. Dangerous. Very dangerous.

It was Friday, 22.10 hours.

Saturday, 09.20 hours

The woman walked out of the inexpensive boarding house and
turned her collar up against the unexpected squall, which she
thought was most likely to be heralding the arrival of autumn.
She walked away from the seafront up the narrow street which
rose out of the town to the railway station at the summit of
the hill. She bought a return ticket to York and then patiently
awaited the arrival of the train. Again she felt a most profound
sense of liberation. Never before had she felt the complete
correctness of what she intended to do. The train arrived,
slowing into the terminus. She boarded it and considered
herself fortunate to find a forward-facing seat, it being the
weekend and the train being crowded. She passed the journey
in silence and found herself only mildly irritated by the use
of mobile phones by other passengers as the train progressed
at a satisfactory speed across the flat rolling countryside that
was the Vale of York. She left the train at York, just as the
guard was announcing the details of the train's onward journey
to Leeds, Huddersfield, then 'fast to Manchester Airport'. The
woman, with head held high and a spring in her step, walked
up the curved gradient of Queen Street, waited at the junction
with Blossom Street until the traffic lights changed to permit
the pedestrians to cross the road, and then walked into
Micklegate Bar Police Station. At the enquiry desk she said
to the white-shirted constable, 'My name is Virginia Farrent.
I would like to make a statement. I believe a detective called
Hennessey and also a Mr Yellich are the interested officers in
the situation in question.'

A few moments later Virginia Farrent sat in an interview
room across a highly polished wooden table from DCI Hennessey
and DC Pharoah. She spoke under caution but had waived the
right to be represented by a solicitor. 'I am happy to tell you
what happened.' She glanced at the tape recorder, at the twin
cassettes spooling slowly round and round. Everything said was

being recorded and would, she knew, be kept for all time. 'But it won't be safe for me, my husband is a violent man, and very jealous. He is capable of extreme violence.'

'We can protect you,' Hennessey replied calmly. 'In or outside prison, we can offer protection.'

'I don't want anything for myself,' Virginia Farrent added quickly. 'I just want the truth to come out; those people need justice.'

'All right.' Hennessey smiled. 'Just tell us what happened. In your own words. In your own time.'

'Well.' Virginia Farrent paused. 'It was all over before I knew what was happening. The day before, Nigel Parr had arrived at the house and slept in the guest bedroom. Nigel had visited a few times before then and my husband had visited him in London. They just seemed to have befriended each other. I was kept well out of it. We had been married for only about a year at this time, but I had already found out that I was not ever going to be party to my husband's affairs. That day Nigel Parr and my husband kept themselves to themselves and seemed to be talking very earnestly.'

'All right,' Hennessey said, 'this is good.'

'The very next day the Parrs arrived, Mr and Mrs Parr and their daughters, and also another girl who I now know was called Michelle Lemmon. I wasn't expecting them. When they arrived Nigel Parr was nowhere to be seen and Michelle wanted to leave, but my husband persuaded her to stay with the promise of giving her a lift back to York.' Virginia Farrent took a deep breath. 'They said they were there to talk to Mr Farrent senior, my father-in-law, which I thought was odd because he was not at home; he had gone away on a pensioners' holiday.'

'That is important. You are saying that Mr Farrent senior was not involved.'

'No. By then he was a widower and left the running of the estate to my husband, his son. The whole thing was cooked up by my husband and Nigel Parr.' Virginia Farrent paused and glanced at Hennessey and Pharoah. 'This is difficult,' she said, 'this is the difficult bit.'

'In your own time,' Carmen Pharoah replied. 'Like Mr Hennessey has said . . . your own time . . . your own pace.'

'Very well.' Virginia Farrent collected herself. 'So . . . when everyone was settled with welcoming cups of tea and a tray of buttered scones, my husband excused himself and then returned a few moments later and said, "My father is ready now, Mr Parr, shall we join him? His study is down the corridor at the other end of the house."' Virginia Farrent put her hand to her mouth, then removing it, she continued, 'It was then that I knew something horrible was going to happen, but I just seemed to freeze . . . I just seemed to freeze. My father-in-law wasn't at home, he didn't have a study, but Mr and Mrs Parr just stood up and followed my husband as he led them out of the room. They . . . the Parr Family were so small, so short . . . and in less than a minute it seemed like, but not a long time at all, my husband, followed by Nigel Parr, burst back into the living room. My husband overpowered the Parrs' daughters, punching one then the other. I was screaming, the girls were screaming . . . Michelle Lemmon made a run for the door and Nigel Parr tripped her up and said, "Oh no you don't," and called her a name, which sounded a bit like "Oranges", then he punched her really hard, dazing her but not completely knocking her out. He really meant business.'

'What did you do?' Hennessey sat forward and leaned his forearms on the table.

'Nothing,' Virginia Farrent replied. 'I did nothing. I started to scream and my husband walked up to me and punched me, knocked me out. When I came to I had a numb face, which became extensively bruised over the next few days and also became very sore, so I reckon he punched me several times; he made sure I wasn't going to come round in a hurry.'

'Yes.' Hennessey nodded. 'Go on . . .'

'Well, when I did regain consciousness there were five bodies on the living-room carpet and night had fallen. I clearly had been out for a few hours. All the bodies were tied with rope, hands behind their backs and one foot trapped under the rope binding their hands. You can't escape from that.'

'We know.'

'All were soaking wet. I noticed a trail of damp leading from the corridor into the lounge. I staggered about and remember a lot of dampness on the floor of the bathroom.'

'They had been drowned,' Hennessey stated. 'It ties in with the post-mortem findings.'

'I think that must have been what happened.' Virginia Farrent shuddered. 'They must have known what was happening; probably saw parents or sister being put into the bath ahead of them and not being able to escape . . . trussed up like they were. I'll never know . . .'

'We won't either.' Hennessey sighed. 'We won't either; only if your husband or Nigel Parr tells us.'

'Where are they?'

'Both released. We couldn't hold them,' Hennessey advised.

'I didn't know you had arrested them. I had to go away for a bit. I knew what I had to do; I just had to collect myself before doing it.' Virginia Farrent sank back in her chair.

'Yes, your husband reported you as a mis per.'

'Mis per?' Virginia Farrent questioned.

'Missing person,' Carmen Pharoah explained. 'He was worried about you.'

'No . . . no, he wasn't.' Virginia Farrent shook her head. 'No, he wasn't and, no, he isn't. What he is, is worried that I will do this – make a statement – that is what he is worried about. I have had cause to fear for my own safety. My husband can make people disappear. I know enough to put him away. I could have even saved my life by leaving him when I did.' She paled. 'I'll never know how close I came.'

'So what happened then?'

'Well, then Nigel Parr and my husband carried the five bodies out of the house and put them into a trailer which they covered with a tarpaulin. Then we drove the Parrs' car into York and left it in a car park.'

'We?'

'Yes . . . we . . . my husband wasn't going to leave me in the house unsupervised. I would have phoned the police and he knew it. So we drove into York. Parr followed in his car and drove us back.' Virginia Farrent collected herself and then she continued, 'So then we drove the trailer into a field, pulled it behind a four-by-four, and in the field was a guy with a mechanical digger. I don't know who he was.'

'It's all right.' Hennessey smiled. 'We do. He is now

deceased but we know who he was. Please, carry on.'
Hennessey noticed how fetching Virginia Farrent was: balanced
face, high cheekbones, wisdom and kindness in her eyes.

'We then returned home . . . job done . . . that's what my
husband's attitude seemed to be . . . job done . . . home for
supper and bed and a good night's sleep. My husband told me
to clean up the mess but there was no mess to clean up, only
bath water everywhere, so I left it to evaporate. After that the
press and TV were full of the family who had vanished, then
the world moved on and then . . . then the strangest thing
happened.'

'Oh?' Hennessey asked.

'I forgot it all happened.' Virginia Farrent looked at
Hennessey then at Carmen Pharoah. 'I mean, can you believe
that? It evaporated like the water on the lounge carpet, for the
next thirty years. I just got on with life . . .'

'Yes, we can believe it,' Hennessey replied. 'In fact, that
aspect of human behaviour has been a bit of a hallmark of
this inquiry. It's called "blocking out", apparently it's a coping
mechanism. This whole inquiry started when two men in their
middle years came into this very police station because they
had both realized the significance of a patch of freshly turned
soil in a field which they noticed thirty years ago when they
were schoolboys walking in the woods and fields near Catton
Hill village.'

'Oh . . . so I'm not insane?' Virginia Farrent blushed with
relief.

'No.' Carmen Pharoah smiled. 'Seems to me like you were
a terrified woman.'

'So why did you come forward now?' Hennessey asked
softly.

'Simple . . . when the bodies were discovered and the press
covered it the memory returned. It all just flooded back but it
didn't come back suddenly. At first, I wondered if I was
remembering a dream, then bits came back, like an episode
here an episode there, over a few days, then I had to put the
episodes all into chronological order. It was helped by my
husband making all sorts of threats to me about what he'd do
if I went to the police,' Virginia Farrent added. 'That helped

confirm that I wasn't remembering a dream and . . .' she paused. 'If I tell you my full maiden name was Virginia Mary Theresa Bernadette O'Driscoll, you can guess the implication.'

'Roman Catholic?' Hennessey smiled.

'Yes . . . Irish at that . . . lapsed, but Roman Catholic. Girl's boarding school in County Mayo, run by nuns. It's the old Catholic guilt thing. It takes control, it emerges, it dictates . . . and here I am.'

'And here you are.' Hennessey smiled. 'You'll give and sign a statement to the effect of all you have just told us?'

'Yes, yes I will. Will I be charged with anything?' Virginia Farrent asked.

'It's too early to say.' Hennessey stood. 'But I think it highly unlikely since you have come forward as you have and you were not a part of the conspiracy. I think it's highly unlikely the CPS will frame charges. We certainly won't be arresting you. Where can we find you?'

'I'm staying at a small hotel in Scarborough. I'll give you the address.'

'Good.' Hennessey reached for the door handle. 'If you'll be good enough to give your statement to DS Pharoah? I have two arrest warrants to prepare.'

EPILOGUE

The following June, a man and a woman walked slowly arm in arm, early one evening, up the long winding incline that was the driveway of the hotel in which they were staying for a brief two-day break.

'So, justice was served . . . eventually.' The man glanced up at the rich foliage which overhung the driveway and which was at that moment sharply defined against the scarlet sunset. 'And for the living there was closure. Michelle Lemmon's brother found out what had happened to his sister and now has a grave to visit.'

'It must have been agony for her family.' The woman looked down at the gravel surface upon which she and her partner walked. 'The not knowing where your loved one is . . . the not knowing what happened to them. Oh . . . should that ever happen to me . . .'

'Yes, it isn't funny, not funny at all. As you say . . . should that ever happen. It was though, in the event, a very short trial. Parr and Farrent instructed their barrister to go NG, as my son would say, but Virginia Farrent proved a very strong witness for the prosecution. She was solid and angry, her sincerity shone through and her husband condemned himself by throwing a temper tantrum from the dock, shouting across at her that she was "no good as a wife", that she "had no loyalty", and Nigel Parr turned to him and said, "You idiot, that's an admission," and put his head in his hands. It was then that their barristers requested a brief adjournment so as to consult their clients.'

'And they changed their plea?'

'Yes.' The man's eye was caught by a swift darting about against the sunset. 'Yes, from NG to G, also as my son would say.'

'From not guilty to guilty?' the woman asked.

'Yes, guilty as charged, my Lord,' the man replied. 'They

both collected five life sentences with a minimum tariff of twenty-five years, and so they won't be much of a threat when they breathe fresh air again, if they ever do, being in their fifties now.'

'So what happened to the land?' The woman glanced at the man.

'A very good question, and the answer is that it is all still up in the air. I spoke to Virginia Farrent just after the trial. Her divorce is still to be finalized but her lawyer is requesting half the Farrent estate. She said she wanted half of the value of the bungalow because that was her home. She is entitled to it, but she said she doesn't want the land. She said she felt it was tainted with blood.'

'Noble woman,' the woman commented.

'Yes, I thought much the same. So her half of the land in dispute will be taken into public ownership and unless Thomas Farrent makes a will leaving it to a named person or organization then his half will also, in the fullness of time, be taken into public ownership,' the man explained. 'The Farrents' marriage being childless.'

'I see.'

'Nigel Parr loses his house in Camden. Thomas Farrent made a statement in which he confirmed that he took money from the Farrent estate to compensate Parr for not inheriting anything from his foster parents, as we suspected, in return for Nigel Parr's help in their murder.' The man inclined his head briefly. 'So we will seize the house under the Proceeds of Crime legislation.'

'So.' Louise D'Acre squeezed George Hennessey's arm against her. 'The Parrs lost everything . . . their lives . . . And Michelle Lemmon, who just wanted to get away from home for a while, just happened to be in the wrong place at the wrong time, lost her life as well.'

'It happens.' George Hennessey stopped walking and turned to take one last glimpse of Lake Windermere before guiding his lady onwards to their hotel, dinner, and an early night.

M

ML   6/12